Lindsay Clarke was born in Halifax and educated at King's College, Cambridge. He has worked in further education in Norfolk, and with an American college of experiential learning. He and his wife now live in Somerset. His second novel, *The Chymical Wedding*, won the 1989 Whitbread Prize for Fiction.

Lindsay Clarke

Sunday Whiteman

In association with Jonathan Cape

First published 1987 by Jonathan Cape Ltd
This Picador edition published 1991 by Pan Books Ltd
Cavaye Place, London SW10 9PG
in association with Jonathan Cape Ltd

9 8 7 6 5 4 3 2

ISBN 0 330 32067 X

Copyright © Lindsay Clarke 1987

Printed and bound in Great Britain by
Cox & Wyman Ltd, Reading, Berkshire

For Phoebe Clare
and in memory of my father

Presently he cryeth out of some poor innocent neighbour that . . . she hath bewitched him. For, saith he, such an old woman came lately to my door and desired some relief, and I denied it, and, God forgive me, my heart did rise against her . . . and presently my child, my wife, myself . . . was thus and thus handled in such a strange manner, as I dare say she is a witch, or else how should these things be?

Thomas Ady, *A Candle in the Dark*, 1656

Contents

Part One

APPAEA

Afterwards, when life in that small bush-town returned to normal, no one cared to talk about Austin Palmer. Even those Africans who did not believe that the Sunday Whiteman had been bewitched were embarrassed by events; and a residue of guilt hung over the little expatriate community.

True, Salvador Rodriguez might sometimes murmur that Austin had always been an impossible man, but Sal was rarely seen outside the Paradise Bar these days. Looking around at the dreary town with its drab backdrop of forest, you felt more inclined to put the blame on the dispiriting nature of the place.

A wiser man might have taken a job in one of the more established schools on the coast: Austin Palmer was not interested in soft options. He wanted to know the real West Africa; he wanted to work where it mattered. So he'd brought his wife 200 miles up-country to the new government secondary school at Ogun-Adoubia. Nobody had told them that the school was sited five miles outside the town in a desolate clearing at the heart of the bush.

The pink and white buildings of the compound were marooned beside a dirt-road that might reasonably have been mistaken for a dried-up river bed. It was enclosed by forest on all sides – rain-forest, a forest without seasons, perpetually green except where the coppery dust of the dry months settled on the leaves. The trees were as dense almost as a stockade, and hung with a matted web of undergrowth like mildewed tapestries that would crumble at a touch. Here and there a lightning-crippled ashen-grey trunk jutted through the canopy into the clear. Otherwise the shadowy modulations of green were so oppressive that the unexpected flash of pure white from an egret's back came like the slaking of a thirst. And upwards, where one might have expected some release, the sky was fitted across the clearing tight as a hot tin lid.

It had been already dark when Palmer and his wife Kay arrived on the compound. The flight from rainy Heathrow to the wobble of heat at Badagry International Airport had been so swift that entering Africa was like dropping into a dream.

Then there had been the long drive up-country through the forest, and the dark arrival at the school. How innocent they'd been, how unprepared! They had not even been warned that the generator would be switched off at ten-thirty when they were ambushed by a complete, impermeable blackness such as neither of them had experienced before. It dropped from nowhere, severing them at one blow from surroundings that were still unfamiliar. They were isolated by its sudden flood – barely even together.

So they'd groped their way to bed, resolved to have candles ready in future, and lay for a long time listening to the clamour that seemed to have struck up with the quenching of the light. Over the raucous chorus of frogs the crickets shrilled a high-pitched note that must soon have proved intolerable had not the ear so rapidly attuned to it. Beyond these a racket of unidentifiable noise encroached from the bush on all sides.

They were on the brink of sleep when the night was cut open by a ghastly screaming. Even as Palmer tensed he felt Kay stiffen beside him. They said nothing as one terrible shriek fled before another, each fracturing in hysterical echoes. Then suddenly it stopped, came to a dead halt at the heart of a critical silence.

When it was not resumed Kay released her breath and spoke in a whisper. 'What on earth was that?'

'God knows!'

'It was horrible.'

'Yes.'

After a moment she said, 'It was a woman, wasn't it?'

'I don't know. It could have been an animal. Or a bird.'

They had both lain rigid, trying to square that hope with the horrid memory.

Kay said, 'It sounded as though someone were being raped. Or murdered.'

And spoke his own thought.

The silence was insufferable. She asked, 'What should we do?'

'Nothing. What can we do? We don't know our way round yet, and it's black as hell out there.'

'But if it was a woman?'

'I'm sure it wasn't.'

'God alone knows what . . .'

'There's nothing we can do. Anyway we can't have been the only ones who heard it. If there's anything wrong someone will go and see.'

They had lapsed into apprehensive silence, straining to catch the worried murmur of voices, or a cry – any sound that would indicate a sequel to those hideous screams. But their anxiety met no answer in the wilderness outside, and eventually sleep took them by surprise as the darkness had done earlier.

That had been two years before, in 1960, when the country still exhilarated in its recently accomplished freedom. Much had happened since.

Alone now, Palmer sometimes found it hard to recapture even the memory of the enthusiasm that had brought him here. How many nights since had he heard that din shriek across the roof of the forest, and known it nothing more sinister than the song of the tree-bear – a creature so small and defenceless that only its terrifying cry could hold predators at bay?

Yet, after all that had happened, he was left wondering about their first uneducated suspicions. What was already built into the structure of their minds that they should have projected such dark imaginings on to the darkness around them? Was it possible that those first years had been closer to the truth for them? For there were still times when the sound reverberated in his memory as the cry of a woman at extremes.

Towards the end Kay had been so wretched that their life together in the bungalow on the school-compound had become insupportable. Palmer was numbed by it, beyond all feeling, so that when the taxi drove his wife away he was aware only of a sense of finality and relief. It was as though Kay had been suffering from an illness so unendurable that death was a release for her and all concerned. Except that Kay was not dead, and he himself was profoundly implicated in her suffering. Nevertheless, it was over. Kay was gone. For good, he must assume. He was breathing a little more freely now.

He had entertained such dreams of Africa and they had been other than this. As a child, school atlases and stamp albums with the odour of exotic places secreted in their bindings, and names like the beat of talking drums – Ouaga-dougou, Dahomey, Calabar – these had stirred something tremulous and eager in his restless spirit. Later he had been intoxicated by the literary romantic's Africa – Rimbaud at Harar, sleek negresses out of Baudelaire, Marlow's encounter with Kurtz at the heart of darkness. Finally, as a schoolteacher in London's East End, frustrated by his work with the Labour Party and CND, he had watched Africa rising – surely one of the great symbolic moments of the century – and that exuberant reach for freedom had answered an unrequited passion of his own. *Seek ye first the political kingdom*, one of its leaders had bravely, blasphemously, promised, *and all things shall be added unto you*. In Africa, it had seemed, all things were possible again, the world was demanding to be made new.

He was convinced that something vital was arrested at the heart of England, and that nothing there would ever really change. Perhaps least of all himself. So they had come to Africa in search of hope, he and Kay. Gradually they found themselves instructed in despair.

However, he would renege neither on those dreams nor on the coarser, less tractable reality that lay around him. He would not return to England, for he remembered too well the nullity of his life back there. Yet gazing out across the still-incomplete buildings of the school-compound into the hot green dream of the forest beyond, he felt his life increasingly encircled.

He reapplied himself to his work. Obsessively so. In the classroom he was voluble enough, stretching Charles Smart in his aspirations towards LSE, signalling Comfort Okelo to waken Emmanuel Cuffee when he nodded off, patiently explaining to Regina Bimpong that irregularities in English grammar, though mysterious, had not been introduced for her particular confusion. Otherwise his life was taciturn and remote.

The headmaster, Mr Quagrainie, a formal and diffident man who had suffered agonies of embarrassment at Kay's behaviour, thought it best to relieve Palmer of his duties as housemaster. So these days he was spared the dismal routine of dormitory inspections – the students standing stiffly to attention beside their iron beds, regulation gear laid out, chop-boxes open, illicit possessions stashed away in hidey-holes. Spared too the supervision of fatigues – hot afternoons out on the compound where the same delinquent faces turned up again and again to keep the wilderness at bay with cutlasses. His days now were simple and repetitive, from the sound of hymnsong raised against the disbelieving bush each morning, to the throb of drums echoing across the forest from the distant villages by night. The long empty afternoons were the worst of it, the heat insufferable, time stopped like the electric fan on his ceiling that would not turn again until the generator was switched on at dusk. But they passed and blurred.

For the most part the rest of the staff respected his preference for solitude, and he might have stayed in the remote, manageable world of the compound for ever had not his friend and colleague, Sal Rodriguez, decided it was time the Englishman got outside himself, rejoined the human race.

There was to be a dance in Adoubia that night, at the town's one hotel, The Star of Africa. 'As you can see I'm going anyway,' Sal said, and opened his arms the better to display his battered linen suit and colourful cravat. There was a raffish air about him that lent style to the Indian's gangling seediness. 'But you know how I hate to get drunk alone. Opambo has promised to sing. I think you should certainly come. When I pass out you can drive me back . . . Make yourself useful . . .'

Even when he was not drunk Salvador Rodriguez shimmered like a mirage. Though his elusive, sardonic manner had concealed the fact, he had been quietly terrified of Kay. Now that a decent interval had elapsed since her departure he had plans of his own for Austin; they included his redemption

15

from misplaced guilt and idealism. If necessary he would make a nuisance of himself, but entertainingly.

So before the Englishman could begin to refuse, he added, 'Life may be a pig, my friend, but one must not wallow in the mire.' As always his Goan accent made the English idiom sound absurd, and he was astute enough to know it. Sal's yellow vellum skin was stretched so tightly across his face it gave the impression that an attempt had been made to shrink the head with the skull still intact. His grin enlarged the teeth and nostrils out of all proportion. It intensified the glitter in his eyes.

In any case, Palmer was ready to be seduced. The day's newspaper had made depressing reading, he had no heart for a pile of third-form essays waiting to be marked, and the bungalow was appallingly empty. Also he was feeling a little pleased with himself. Late that afternoon he had written in his journal for the first time in ages:

Perhaps after all despair is not the last cruel fact, but the last illusion. Something is happening to us which we do not understand: we despair. It is no more than our ignorance in action, blind.

Of course that 'Perhaps' carried an awful lot of weight, but nevertheless the thought consoled.

So, a few drinks, a dance at The Star. Why not?

The two men drove into Adoubia together that night.

Under hot stars, to the lilt of saxophones, they sat for a long time watching the easy commerce of the dance-floor swirl about them; women with piccins nodding at their backs, men dancing with men, others flourishing their bodies solo to the moon; all in concert, gliding, drifting, twisting sinuously away.

Brassy and syncopated over its percussive rhythms, at once wistful and gay, the Highlife music never failed to stir a longing in Palmer's heart. It was like a nostalgia for what was present, but passing. It was like the name of a flower that his servant Mamadou used to place on the dinner-table for Kay's

16

pleasure – a flower that changed colour from pallid white to deep crimson during the course of a meal. *Yesterday, Today and Tomorrow* it was called. Like the flower, the sound and spectacle of the dance saddened and delighted him in equal measure. For these dancers inhabited another world, one which he envied and desired, but from which he felt himself for ever excluded. And more by the cast of his mind than the colour of his skin. Yet a world too from which he would never now be able to drag himself away.

So he clapped and cheered with the crowd as Samuel Opambo slid his stout frame up to the microphone and whispered to the band.

When he was not rejoicing in the irrelevant business of teaching the students Latin, Opambo was more typically to be seen stepping out into the bush by night in khaki battlejacket and mosquito-boots with a lamp fastened to his hat and a gun slung at his padded shoulder. The nights on the compound were loud with his reports, and morning would show the carcass of a deer in his yard, or the heads of hornbills hanging over his wall in a bloody row like glove puppets. But here at The Star he was suave in a white dinner-jacket and dicky-bow, his face a ripe black moon, as he crooned into his favourite song, 'You Are the Girl of my Dreams'. His hands addressed the air in neat, Oliver Hardy gestures, as though each phrase of the melody were an orchid to be arranged in some invisible vase. He was in love with the microphone, and received the applause with extravagant diffidence. Then the band swung from the slow foxtrot into a popular Highlife tune, and Opambo was all African again, his manner, rhythm, language riotously changed.

It was then that an extraordinary thing happened. A girl detached herself from the crowd, approached the table where Palmer was still tipsily applauding Opambo and, with an odd mixture of shyness and aggression, demanded that he come dance with her.

Startled, Palmer looked across at Sal's bleary grin, then back at the girl. She was wearing a bright green dress cut short above the knees. Her hair was braided in hundreds of small tight plaits. A tribal mark like a thin crescent moon was etched into her cheek. She was scented in lavender. 'I'm afraid I don't dance very well.'

'I will show.' She was breathing quickly as though her courage had been fixed for this moment. Her eyes darted to the side.

'I really don't.'

'Surely, Austin,' Sal grinned, 'after you've been asked so sweetly . . .?'

'Come,' the girl insisted. 'Is easy.' She reached for Palmer's hand and pulled him towards the swaying circle on the dance-floor. 'You watch me how.'

He stood hapless for a moment until the girl shook her head, smiled – a vivid taunt of white teeth – and sailed off, beckoning him to follow. Awkwardly he shuffled his feet in stiff imitation of the Highlife rhythm. His eyes were fixed on the smooth black shoulders of the girl, who revolved to face him and smiled once more, saying, 'Is good. Like so. Come.' Arms twisting, her lithe hips weaved and swayed ahead of him, pleasure made flesh. There was no physical contact between them. He bobbed in her wake – the butt of someone's joke, perhaps; or maybe she really had wanted to draw him into the dance? Who cared? Several beers answered to the music inside him. Immersed in a crowd which seemed to float through the air, he could feel himself loosening. He tried a flourish which met with her amused approval. The rhythm entered him, informed his limbs. His head was afloat. Nothing much mattered after all. Kay was gone. Life went on. The music played.

Then these thoughts too were gone. There came a moment where dance merged into trance. His eyes were closed as he listened with his limbs and moved. And when they opened again he saw two African men beside him, crouched and snapping their thumbs, drawn along in his orbit, smiling, tipsy, and murmuring over and over again, 'Too good! Too good!'

Yesterday, Today, Tomorrow: the music stopped. The girl turned to him, laughing, a rich African laugh, and before he could thank her even, she was gone, laughing still, among her friends. Bemused by the crowd's congratulations, he left the floor, running with sweat.

'They'll make an African of you yet,' Sal said. 'Now come on, drink up. I promised Henry I'd take you out to his place.'

Palmer felt the old impulse of recoil. 'No way, Sal. Not tonight.'

'He's terribly hurt that you haven't been out to see him since . . .'

'Oh God, do we have to? I was just beginning to enjoy myself.'

'Mario will be there,' Sal insisted. 'We can make up a four. You might win some of the old Phoenician's money.'

But Palmer was shaking his head over his beer.

'I see,' Sal said. 'Perhaps you have other ideas now? The girl, I mean. She seems to have taken a fancy.' He nodded across to where she stood giggling with her friends, their eyes glancing away as they saw themselves observed. 'I understand of course. I can always take a taxi . . .'

Why don't you do that? Palmer might have answered. *I want to stay here, to get drunk, to dance some more.* Instead he scowled and emptied his glass. 'All right,' he said. 'But I'm not staying long. You either leave when I do or sleep it off there. Okay?'

Palmer sank back among the cushions of a large chair and gazed in resignation at the fiendish green walls. Even as he had been regaled with an effusive Arabic welcome he knew he should not have come. He had always found the atmosphere of this house as sticky as the sweetmeats Henry Jalbout served with cups of bitter coffee. Kay had hated being there.

The old Lebanese must have known as much but chose to believe otherwise. 'A great pity that Kay was not happier in Africa,' he was saying. 'We shall all miss her. There is little enough beauty in these parts. Isn't that so, Mario?'

Mario Baldinucci smiled amiably up from the plush depths of the couch, baring his gold tooth. The Italian had been site-foreman at the school in the days when there was still money for building – a familiar figure in dusty bonnet and white shorts, stalking among the breeze-blocks, shouting polyglot abuse at his labourers. Palmer had not seen him since work ground to a halt months before.

'I think mebbe you get sense and go for UK yourself same soon, eh?' Baldinucci suggested. He spoke a corrupt pidgin-English further disfigured by his native accent.

'I don't think so.' Palmer would have preferred some other topic of conversation. 'I'm okay as I am.'

'Nobody okay in this bush country. I think mebbe I get bush in the head I don't stay in Milano myself. One time I come back. Two time I come back. Never I come back one time again.' The Italian shook his head. 'I tell you what – for why a man get money when he don't see his wife? Sometime I think these bush farmers get more sense – plenty wife, plenty piccin. No money but no problem, eh?'

Henry Jalbout smiled wanly at the remark. This mansion, standing beside his sawmill half-way between the town and the school where the iron railway bridge spanned the river's narrow gorge, had been designed as a home for the wife he had married on the strength of a photograph. But as soon as her eldest child was of school age she had returned to the Lebanon and now visited her husband only intermittently. He consoled himself by lavishly entertaining his friends from the profits of his vast timber concession. What else was to be done with so much money locked into the country by the exchange control regulations?

He must have been a good-looking man once, and was still distinguished, but his waist had run to fat. Now in his late fifties, there was an air of acquiescence about him. It was, above all, acquiescence in his own loneliness, and in its way austere. He gave the impression of having penetrated one of the bleaker secrets of life – that it is always in the end a disappointment. Palmer had sensed this in him at first meeting. Nor did he trust Jalbout's condescending irony towards those younger and less prosperous than himself. Yet one could not entirely dislike a man who took such generous interest in the welfare of his friends; whose glasses, the attentive host noted, were almost empty now.

'Fuseini,' Jalbout shouted over his shoulder.

A white-jacketed servant appeared from the kitchen-quarters and stood to attention. His face was etched with tribal markings as though a comb with needle-sharp teeth had been drawn down its full span. Jalbout ordered more wine and, despite Palmer's demurral, food. After all, the caviare had been brought from Badagry that day and was to be enjoyed. Then he turned to his guest again. 'So, Austin, how are you feeling now? It's good to have friends at a time like this I think?'

'It's certainly a singular feeling being single again.'

Jalbout laughed, an amusement out of all proportion to the joke. 'That's good. I see you have not lost your wicked tongue. I think you are in good shape. What do you say, Sal?'

But Sal had sensed his friend's discomfiture. 'He'll do,' he said drily. 'In any case life goes on, and of course it gets worse all the time. I suppose you saw this morning's paper? *Watchdog* is on the prowl again.' He picked up a copy of *The Party Banner* from the coffee table and read from the front page. '*Everyone within our socialist society must either accept the spirit and aims of our glorious revolution or expose themselves as the double-dyed deceivers and betrayers of the people. Let the Tshombe-faced running-dogs of neo-colonialism beware.* WATCHDOG DOES NOT SLEEP.' He tossed the paper aside. '*Watchdog!* Running-dogs! What is this place – a country or a kennel? I mean, one can forgive most things – corruption, ballot-rigging, the suspension of habeas corpus, even – God help me – the taste of nationalized gin, but' – the expression on his face was truly pained – 'such prose?'

Palmer listened as the conversation drifted into discussion of the recent arrests under the Preventive Detention Act. There was little sympathy with the government's dilemmas here, and no real interest in exploring their complexity. Having heard such talk in this house many times, Palmer knew it pointless to demur, yet it still left him heated and angry. He could feel his heart beating as though he were under personal attack – as, obliquely, he was, for Jalbout's sidelong glances baited him to rise. On his first visit to the house at the sawmill Palmer had innocently expressed his admiration for the President, and ever since the old Lebanese had been at pains to educate him into maturer judgment. This was not the

21

least of the reasons why the Englishman had steered clear of the place.

Long before Palmer had come to Africa he had seen the President as a credible example of achieved manhood – a visionary and a pragmatist, a man of the people who had freed his people, and spoke now with impassioned authority for all the wretched of the earth. It was his voice that had called Palmer to Africa, his vision that had kept him there throughout such difficult times. If there was justice in some of Jalbout's remarks, some measure of accuracy in Sal's laconic wit, it still agitated Palmer to hear the President demeaned by men who leeched on his achievement. Out of these small mouths the criticism came as no more than peevish gossip. And if Palmer had reservations of his own, this was no place to air them. He struggled to hold his peace.

'I will make you a small wager,' Jalbout was saying. 'Before the year is out the opposition parties will have been abolished. Though, God knows, there will hardly be need when all the sensible men are already behind bars. Then the Party will turn on its own. I have seen it coming for some time. Freedom has always been a divisible commodity in Africa.' Again his eyes strayed towards the silent Englishman. 'You are very quiet, Austin. Dare one hope that you no longer carry the flag for African socialism?'

Palmer stared at his glass. 'There's more hope that way than the other,' he said quietly.

'Hope?' Jalbout smiled. 'When you have been here as long as I you will see that Africa is an enterprise that finally lacks all hope. The NLP's ambitious charade is merely an overture to disaster. One can see the signs everywhere.'

Palmer was shaking his head, but Jalbout insisted. 'I think you blind yourself, my friend. Our esteemed President and Redeemer is a megalomaniac. His socialism is that of the fish pond – eat or be eaten.'

'We've been here before, Henry. We'll never agree.'

'Despite the evidence?'

'You should come out to the school. I could show you other evidence there.'

Again Jalbout smiled. 'I think you are still too much the

idealist, Austin. It will cause you more grief. One must not let the heart rule the head.'

Unwilling to be patronized, Palmer looked away. 'Africa is the shape of the heart,' he murmured, though he might have been talking to himself for lack of companionship. He was remembering the remark once made to him by Christian Odansey, the local MP and Deputy-Minister of Finance, who was also Chairman of the school's Board of Governors.

'I see you have been listening too much to Mr Christian,' Jalbout laughed. 'I agree – that man is entertaining. No doubt he'll delight us all with a vanishing act one day.'

'You're a cynic, Henry. That causes grief too.'

'A realist, my friend. I have been here a long time.'

'Perhaps too long?'

Immediately Palmer regretted the reproachful frown that crossed his host's face.

'Perhaps so.' The old Lebanese opened his tobacco pouch and pressed some of the tawny flakes into his pipe. 'No doubt the government would agree with you. We expatriates are vulnerable now. Sooner or later they will try to dispossess us.'

'I really didn't mean . . .' Palmer began. But he had meant. And they both knew it.

'No matter, Austin my friend. Each of us has his dream of Africa. If you wish to keep yours simple who can blame you? Education, development, progress . . . a united continent of free peoples . . . the old dark Africa safely illuminated with street-lighting. Not a bad dream.'

'It's possible, Henry. The resources are there. And the will.'

Jalbout shrugged. 'As you wish. It's simply that whenever I listen to the President on the radio, or talk to Mr Christian and the DC – yes, particularly the DC – I think of this fellow.' He turned in his chair and gestured with his pipe to the wall where hung an enormous ritual mask carved from ebony. Horned, curved like a disastrous black moon, it peered with unmitigated malice through slots like the eyes of a goat. A shaggy ruff of raffia and clay beads dangled from its oval jawline. Across its brow and cheeks cowrie-shells glinted like

23

bone in the harsh fluorescent light. 'I find,' Jalbout said, 'that it restores perspective.'

Palmer had often admired the mask but he studied it thoughtfully now. 'That's a vanishing world,' he said at last.

'You think so? Fuseini would not agree.' Jalbout looked up at the servant who had re-entered while they were talking and was unloading a silver tray on to the coffee table, impervious to the conversation. 'Fuseini, dat man who be number one forestry officer in dis town one time – what happen wit him?'

The servant straightened, holding the now empty tray before him like a shield, and stood uncertainly, eyes averted among the needlecord corrugations of his frown. 'Sah?'

'Tell Mr Palmer what happen wit him,' Jalbout demanded.

Fuseini's eyes flickered momentarily towards Palmer, clearly resenting the interrogation. His nostrils flared. The man's shoulders were stiff and quivering slightly. 'Dat man go bush and die, sah.'

'For why he die, Fuseini?'

Again the servant hesitated. The answer when it came was addressed to no one – a low, barely audible imposition on the silence, uttered only because there was no choice. 'He die for juju, sah.'

'Thank you, Fuseini. You may go.' Jalbout gestured towards the food. 'Please, gentlemen, help yourselves.'

Of course Jalbout wanted Palmer to ask what had happened to the forestry officer, but he resisted the temptation. 'That was meant to prove something?' he asked lightly, allowing a dismissive smile to say the rest.

'You are free to make of it what you like. The fact remains – Fuseini believes it even if you do not.' The old Lebanese sighed as though losing interest. 'Perhaps in one thing I was wrong. I said "the fish pond" . . . of course I should have said "the forest".'

'It's bound to take time,' Palmer insisted, impatiently now. 'There will be problems, mistakes . . . but history is on my side, Henry. Nothing changes overnight.'

'Exactly,' Jalbout returned. 'Do you think the forest cares about history? But sorcery – ah yes, that is quite another matter. Juju it understands. Like it or not, sorcery is alive in

Africa, my friend.' He raised a finger to silence the Englishman's protest. 'I know what you will say. But permit me to suggest one thing: when you teach your students at the school about the Queen's English and William Shakespeare, try to remember that yours is only one, very recent voice in their education. Do you imagine it is as powerful as this?' Once more he flourished his pipe towards the devil-mask, and turned again to take in the shake of Palmer's head. 'Believe me, I have seen many strange things in these thirty years. I know – you think maybe that all this long time in Africa has made me racist, eh? That I despise the African? You are very wrong. Who else has given us such powerful images of what goes on inside us all?'

'You said it yourself – there's more than one dream in Africa . . . for the Africans too. We should distinguish between our bad dreams and theirs, don't you think?'

Jalbout smiled, unconvinced. Sal Rodriguez, who had listened uneasily to this exchange, intervened once more. Spreading caviare on a biscuit, he said, 'That monstrosity certainly gives me bad dreams. I don't know why you keep it there, Henry.'

'Politics! Juju!' Mario Baldinucci exclaimed. 'All be same here. I get rich small, make fit go home for Italy, and let these animal eat each other. Is all right for me.'

'Speaking of getting rich,' Sal said before Palmer could explode, 'I'd thought I might relieve you of some of your vast wealth tonight, Henry. How about a hand or two of Brag?'

'If you wish,' Jalbout said, smiling, his eyes on the Englishman still. 'Fuseini,' he shouted, 'bring the cards. And more wine.'

Bottle after bottle had been emptied. Palmer was irritable and depressed by his waste of breath, aware of Jalbout's ironical regard, ill at ease. After several desultory hands of Brag – a game that had never been much to his taste – he declared himself skint, hoping to hasten the evening to an end. Jalbout merely smiled and pushed more cash his way. 'Please,' he said, 'I've never thought of this as real money anyway. We

25

lonely men must amuse ourselves as best we can.'

Baldinucci had also been losing, and here was a cue to regret his own wife back in Milan. Woozily, he brought out a wrinkled snapshot of an Etruscan-eyed woman with a small girl in the spread of her lap. 'My wife, Teresa, see, and my . . . *mia figlia*, Sophia.' They had all seen the picture before but it was not to be spurned. The cards were laid down and soon Jalbout and Baldinucci were consoling one another for their common amputation from their wives. They tried to draw Palmer into their sympathy but he was having none of that. His head cloudy with a mix of beer and wine, his speech slurring a little, he puzzled the others by insisting that his present circumstances were the result of his own choice.

'You don't understand me,' he repeated. 'I've chosen this. The decision and the action were Kay's, but the choice was mine. It's the left hand, you see. What the left hand does. Behind the back. That's where the real choices are made.'

They humoured him, agreed, condoled. They were all philosophers by now. But Jalbout continued to eye the Englishman dubiously. It pained him that his many gestures of friendship had failed to win anything warmer than a wary extension of Austin's good nature. Jalbout had hoped things might improve now Kay was gone. She had been a termagant, that one, rarely willing to make the smallest moral adjustment to those around her. It was clear that Austin was still in awe of her memory.

Perhaps something might be done about that?

'Austin, my friend,' he said at last, 'I don't care to think of you alone in that god-forsaken spot where they have built your school. You should move house. Start afresh. It's not good for you to stay in that same place.'

'I'm all right, I tell you. You needn't worry about me.'

'I don't think so. I think maybe your wings still burn?'

Momentarily arrested by the image, Palmer considered the possibility. 'In any case, where would I go? I'm needed at the school.'

'Of course you are.' It was characteristic of schoolteachers, Jalbout had noted, to be convinced of their indispensability. 'But listen – I have a house standing empty in Adoubia. It's not a palace, you understand, but it's comfortable enough. I think you should have it. Make a new life for yourself.'

Palmer's head was reeling now. He smiled vaguely. His hand moved as though to push the thought away. 'I couldn't possibly.'

'Why not? You could drive easily to work each day. You could enjoy more time outside the school. Meet people. Open up your life.'

'No, really. It's out of the question.'

'Do not misunderstand me. It's not the money that interests me. No, you can have the place rent-free. I should be glad to see it occupied. But I think the change would do you good. You need more of the real world around you. What do you say, Sal? Is this not a good idea?'

Rodriguez arched his eyebrows over a bleary smile. 'I'm not sure,' he said. 'You weren't with us at The Star, Henry. Some dark-skinned lovely asked him to dance and I practically had to drag him away. Who knows what he might get up to on his own in Adoubia?'

'Is plenty woman in town,' Baldinucci enthused. 'I think, Austin, you get more good time there.'

'On the other hand,' Rodriguez continued, 'a *pied-à-terre* in Adoubia might have its advantages. When I got too drunk to drive back to school you could put me up . . . Yes, on second thoughts it seems far too good a chance to pass up.'

The Indian knew enough about Palmer's reduced duties at the school to counter all his objections. He joined forces with the Lebanese and the Italian. Suddenly, the upright, aloof, and now rather drunk English teacher had become their client.

Palmer struggled to hold his ground. He had never cared to stand in Jalbout's debt – even his Levantine prodigality as a host was almost suffocating. Yet secretly the idea appealed. The bungalow at the school might have been unbearable in those last weeks with Kay, but there were times now when its cataleptic silences were even worse. The garden with which Kay had struggled so valiantly was rampant with wilderness already, a constant accusation. And there were all those eyes, day in and day out, on the compound. Even such a recluse as he'd tried to become could find little privacy there.

Eventually, if only to put a stop to this ordeal of kindness, he agreed to give the matter thought.

It was very late and the two teachers were the worse for wear when they got back to the school-compound. Staggering towards his door, Rodriguez dropped his key, so for a time they grovelled about on hands and knees, chuckling at their own incompetence. At last it was found. Sal opened the door, lit a tilley-lamp. 'A nightcap,' he offered, ' – to celebrate your return from the dead?' He seemed a little hurt by his friend's refusal. 'Ah well. But we shall have more good times together, don't you think? Now that you're free . . .?'

Swaying slightly, Palmer held up his torch. 'We prefer the dangers of Freedom,' he declaimed, 'to the tranquillity of Servitude.' It was a slogan of the National Liberation Party. He knew Sal would be amused to hear him ape it so. The Indian chuckled as his friend walked off into the night, but the answer, he saw, had been less than a promise.

Palmer stood for a time on his own veranda, hoping the night air might clear his head. The crickets whirred. A symposium of frogs belched together. All the school buildings were in darkness. In a swing of his torch-beam he saw the tall trees of the forest loom. But the light attracted a swarm of moths and flies. He extinguished it, and the night around him was black as hot tar. Somewhere far away a tree-bear cried. It might have been insisting that, after all, Jalbout was in the right.

On such a moonless night he and Kay had once been woken by an unholy wailing from the girls' dormitory. Beatrice Osu, the girl's housemistress, had come running across the compound, summoning Kay and Efwa Opambo to help. They had found one of the girls stark naked on her bed, her face powdered in white chalk, rocking and chanting. The entire dormitory was in hysterics around her, some believing that they had been visited by the Holy Ghost, others that they were possessed by evil spirits. It had taken two hours to settle them again.

Afterwards Palmer had remarked on the improbability of the whole affair, but Kay had said quietly, 'Oh no . . . not at all . . . I know exactly how they felt.'

Disturbed by the memory, he closed his eyes against the night and felt his head sway. It was obvious; the school-compound could only ever be provisional. Against all effort it must remain the long-term quarry of the forest.

Perhaps, after all, he would take a look at Jalbout's house in Adoubia.

With a long-unaccustomed sense of exhilaration he drove into Adoubia that next afternoon. He had spoken to Jalbout on the phone, made arrangements to view the property. Perhaps a fresh start was possible.

Adoubia was two towns really, perched on twin hills with a marshy valley simmering in the haze between. To the east stood New Town, the asphalted commercial centre of the region. Built under the old colonial regime, it had recently seen much development along Independence Avenue – petrol stations, a new bank, the local headquarters of the National Liberation Party where Krobo Mansa, the District Commissioner, kept court. Old Town drowsed across the valley to the west, dry green and umber, its galvanized iron roofs shining among the palms. This was the tribal capital of the Ogun-Dogambey Traditional Area, and the seat of its Paramount Chief. The two towns lay uneasily adjacent, disputatious of the character of Africa.

The site of the house promised to be interesting. It stood in a square off the road linking New Town to Old. 'Just beyond the lorry park,' Jalbout had said, 'where the electricity stops.' It offered, Palmer anticipated, the best of both worlds.

Instead of taking his usual route he turned by the new Texaco petrol-station up the hill towards Old Town. The lorry park was busy with Benz buses and crowded mammy-wagons, each a wayside pulpit with a motto blazoned on its side or over the cab. EXCEPT GOD WE SHALL FAIL, said one. KILL ME AND FLY, another. He looked for, but could not see, his favourite – the blue lorry that plied the route between Adoubia and

Badagry with the legend THEY HAVE JESUS FACES BUT STAN-
DARD INTENTION large along its length.

He made the right turn where Jalbout had indicated, then a
left into a square of baked earth. Slowly he circled a tamarind
tree and braked. If things went, unusually, to plan, he should
shortly be joined by Jamil, Henry's Lebanese friend, who
owned the Cold Store and the General Trading Company in
New Town.

He stepped out into the stench of open drains and a tinge of
smoke and spices on the air. The sky was low and drab.
Beyond the scent of flowering trees he caught the damp,
vaguely narcotic odour breathed across the town from the
surrounding forest. Within moments he was surrounded by a
gaggle of children shouting the familiar refrain, 'White man,
Sunday Whiteman' in their own guttural tongue. Since the first
missionaries had appeared in the forest 'Sunday' had been the
common day-name of all Europeans. Palmer had no idea on
what day of the week he had been born, but it would have
made no difference. He was white, and so – though he was
certainly no Christian – his name was 'Sunday'. Drying his
neck with a handkerchief, he shooed the children to a distance
and looked around the square.

In one corner stood the DONT MIND YOUR WIFE Chop Bar
where a group of young men were drinking palm-wine. One of
them called out something and the group laughed together at
the white man's uncomprehending smile. A woman came to a
window hitching her cloth over her breasts and grinned down
at him. Already he was a celebrity.

His attention was drawn across the way by the sound of
weaver-birds wrangling in a mango-tree. Then he noticed
someone working in its shade – a man at a loom, whistling his
shuttle through a warp of shining thread, who grinned at the
white man then paused in his work to spit kola-juice. Palmer
walked over and offered him a cigarette. Looking up at the
nests in the boughs then down at the loom, he said, 'I see this
is the weaving tree.' The African liked that.

Did he know which of these buildings belonged to Mr
Jalbout?

By all means he did. The weaver brandished his cigarette

towards the largest, most strongly built of the houses. It had two storeys, jalousied windows, a balcony overlooking the square, and an asbestos roof. 'Also electric,' the weaver pointed out, 'and water come from the tap inside. Very fine house, eh?'

It certainly was, Palmer agreed, and would have questioned him further, but at that moment a procession of dusty tribesmen shambled across the square behind a man who pushed a rickety handcart. The men wore long smocks of faded grey and blue, and the women's heads were tied in elaborately knotted scarves. They walked through the square in silence, as though out for a stroll, and Palmer was shocked suddenly to realize that the box balanced precariously on the cart was a coffin.

As they passed, one of the men stopped and bowed slightly towards Palmer, lifting his skull-cap in greeting. Palmer nodded uncomfortably. Then a young man at the Chop Bar raised his calabash of palm-wine, jeering noisily at the mourners, and turned back to his friends with a coarse laugh. The children, who had watched the procession in solemn silence, took up his shout.

'That man is drunk,' the weaver said. 'He is scorning these people because they don't get money to bury the man in the box.'

Palmer looked at him, puzzled. There was more laughter from the group at the bar as the young man shouted further abuse at the departing handcart-hearse and its followers.

'They will take the body from the box before putting him in the earth,' the weaver explained. 'They are poor people from the zongo. By all means, the box will be used again. But that,' he nodded in disapproval at the drunkard, 'is not a cultured man.'

A white VW Beetle swerved around the cortège as it turned into the square and Palmer recognized Jamil's simian grin through the windscreen. Again the children clamoured as Jamil stepped out, bronze-skinned and curly-haired, dapper in white shirt, white shorts, white socks and shoes.

'Mr Palmer, Mr Palmer, I promise myself I not be late, but here you are before me. Welcome. Welcome. Come, I have the key.' Palmer raised his hand to the weaver and followed Jamil who stopped at the door, turned and tapped him on the chest with the key. 'Mr Palmer, I promise you one thing. You like this house too much. Is very good building. Very cool. Very dry. I tell you, I like to live in this house myself. But I must live by my store, you understand? Also you, when you live here, you must keep it locked tight when you go to your college. These people . . .' He indicated the square in general and shook his head in despair. 'But come inside. Welcome. Welcome.'

Palmer was ushered through into a gloomy reception area where a door stood open on to the kitchen quarters. There were cobwebs in the ceiling corner and an immaculate coat of dust on the table, electric cooker and an enormous refrigerator. 'Has been empty long time,' Jamil explained, 'but I get man to fix up proper before you come. Okay? Everything here work fine.' He pressed a switch and the ceiling-fan began to turn, wafting the cobwebs in its draught. He turned a tap. The pipes knocked but a stream of water appeared. 'Is best you filter all water, understand? I bring you one very good filter here. Come. Come. Upstairs.' He stopped on the landing. 'Very nice lavatory. Made in England. Very clean.' He went in and flushed it. 'Bathroom – excellent. Shower very fine.' He made a gesture of kissing his finger-tips. 'I think you be very comfortable here. Henry himself live here one time.' He led the way into an upstairs sitting-room furnished to expatriate Lebanese taste in the style Kay had once called 'Louis-Farouk'. The walls were an even more virulent green than those of Jalbout's mansion, unrelieved by pictures or any other décor save a large ormolu mirror. Palmer saw his own kestrel-sharp, lean features frowning at him from the glass, pushed back the shock of hair from his brow, looked away. He saw a telephone by the door. 'Is connect,' Jamil assured him, 'but you know what telephone is like here . . . the rain come, you hear nothing but buzz-buzz.' He threw open the shutters and mosquito-door. 'I think is very nice here,' he said, made uncertain now by the Englishman's silence.

'It looks very comfortable,' Palmer conceded, and stepped out on to the balcony. He looked down into the square with the twisted tamarind at the centre, the young men at the bar, the children playing round the two parked cars. The old weaver grinned up at him and waved. Palmer lifted his hand in acknowledgment. Like royalty, he thought, and stepped back inside.

Jamil was standing by a door, one finger raised in promise of surprise. Evidently the house had a further wonder. 'Is bedroom here,' he said slyly, opened the door, flicked two switches, then crooked his finger to beckon the Englishman. Palmer heard another fan turn and a fluorescent tube hum into action. Through the bedroom door a blue light blinked and held. He peered in.

Occupying two-thirds of the room, gleaming in the lurid light – it might have been an enormous specimen of some exotic plant that could prosper only in such blue shade – stood a huge silver-plated bedstead, bridally draped in a gauze mosquito-net. Unaccountably, at its foot, a pair of black plimsolls lay on the floor like two creatures that had expired in the attempt to reach each other.

For a moment Palmer was sure that his gasp of instant laughter must have offended the little Lebanese, but no, Jamil had taken the outburst for admiration and was beaming contentedly. 'I have know that you will love this bed too much,' he said. He crossed the room to stroke the silver pilasters of the bedhead. 'Is beautiful, eh? I tell you, many people ax Henry to sell this bed but always he say no. I think maybe he been keeping it for you, Mr Palmer. Come. Come. You must try.' Daintily he lifted and threw back the net.

Palmer sat down on the mattress and bounced the springs. He chortled again. 'Things could certainly happen on a bed like this.'

Jamil chuckled with glee. 'I think so.' Enthralled, he too sat down on the bed. 'Such a bed, Mr Palmer, such a bed.' Laughing like tipsy sailors in a Levantine whorehouse, they bounced the springs together.

What a meal Kay would have made of that outrageous bed, Palmer thought. But she was not here now to pour her scorn. It was entirely up to him to take the house, bed and all, or

33

decline it. For the first time in a long time things were entirely up to him.

Pleased by the thought he walked back into the sitting-room, surveyed the desolate furniture, found himself undismayed. He listened to the sounds – the slow beat of the electric fan, a woman shouting across the square, the distant drift of Highlife from a radio. He took in the unfamiliar musty smell.

What had he expected? A luxury bungalow in the Residential Area? – the bank-managers and the Party had commandeered those. This was probably the best he could hope for.

After all, he could always hang on to the house at the school and use this place when he felt like it. A bolt-hole. A penitential cell.

Even as he winced again at those bilious green walls he knew that something was waiting for him there.

Not long after Palmer moved into the house in the square the local touts began to pester him. His celibate life was incomprehensible to them. They were puzzled, even amused by his refusals.

One afternoon he stopped at the Texaco station for petrol, and the pump-attendant, a good-humoured man with whom he had struck up a jocular acquaintance, asked him whether he would like a woman. He might have been asking how many gallons of petrol he wanted – as forthright as that; the simple assumption that Palmer had a need which he, as a friend, could supply. He nodded across the forecourt to indicate the girl he had in mind.

She was tall, sturdily built, walking away from the water-tap with a pitcher balanced precisely on her head. Eighteen or nineteen – no older than the girls Palmer taught at the school – statuesque under her burden, with a graceful neck.

'Is a good girl,' the pump-attendant assured him. 'She likes you too much. She has fine buttocks, eh?'

Palmer realized that he had been standing in glazed abstraction for far too long. It was no longer possible to disengage himself lightly with a joke. A mammy-wagon lurched into the forecourt and the driver squeezed the bulb of his brass horn

shouting, 'Go front, go front.' The legend FOR ME TO LOVE IS
CHRIST was painted in baroque lettering over the cab. Passen-
gers leaned out of the open sides of the lorry, grinning and
calling in their own tongue: 'White man, Sunday Whiteman.'
From adult mouths the words had always sounded derisory in
Palmer's ears. In these circumstances they became a taunt.

He climbed into the car wanting to drive away, but a cripple
was hobbling past the bonnet, one knee bent against a staff.
The pump-attendant was still counting out his change. The
good-natured black face peered in through the window. 'You
don't want?'

The tone of the question, not mocking but mildly bewildered, stung Palmer into an absurd determination. 'Send her
to my house tonight. About eight.'

By now everyone in Adoubia knew where the Sunday
Whiteman lived.

Among the few possessions he had brought with him from the
school were the journals he had written since his arrival in
Africa: a crumpled pile of exercise books in which was buried
a fragmentary account of how he and Kay had failed to make a
life together there. Given a little distance now – the passage of
time and this move away from the scene of their recurrent,
cumulative wretchedness – he thought some new perspective
might be found. He thought he might begin to write once
more. Another, more exacting journal. One that might clear
his account with the past. Truly free him from it. He had even
gone so far as to buy a new exercise book from the Presbyterian Book Depot.

On his second night in the house he had opened and pressed
the pages, and stared at their waiting blankness for a long
time. Three cigarettes had been stubbed before he wrote:

You would retrace the process of your own undoing?
Forget the high talk which brought you to Africa. Forget
the excuses and the rationale. Consider the small things
first. The moments from which, for whatever reason,
you chose to avert your feelings. They were the seeds.

35

There was a fine, if somewhat literary, resolve to that. His plan was vaguer. He thought he might work back through the old journals, reminding himself of the incidents he had in mind, re-examining them. After half an hour he was so depressed he gave up. Nothing further had been written in the new book.

Now, nervously tidying away the muddle that had already begun to gather round him, he picked up the pile of old journals intending to shove them in a cupboard. He would have done better to open the door first, for one of the books fell off the pile, and from it a folded piece of lay-out paper. He put down the pile of books, picked up the thin paper and unfolded it.

The drawing had been sketched so lightly it was barely decipherable among the wrinkles, but he recognized Kay's plan for an ideal garden back home in England. Two acres of riverside property were landscaped with lawns running down to the banks. There was a walled vegetable plot and herb-garden, an orchard of apple and cherry, an intricately orches-trated herbaceous border and a shrubbery neatly labelled with Latin names. Trees dotted about the grounds were sketched from above, an angel's eye view, in thin spidery lines. A dream of England and order.

Written across the drawing in Kay's florid, speedy hand were the words: *I'm looking for something in him that he's buried so deep I doubt now he'll ever recover it. And there's no hope for us, because he'll never be able to give it, and I'll never be able to stop asking*.

He screwed up the paper, went back to the table, cleared away his draft for an article entitled 'Some Questions Raised By The Regional Evolution Of English In West African Secondary Schools', poured himself a gin, and lay down on the ridiculous silver bed.

By the time the girl arrived he was not drunk but in that state where one slips easily into a burlesque of drunkenness, or into morbidity.

She slipped off her sandals at the door and sat down in a

chair across the room from him, thighs apart, feet crossed, hands clasped in her lap. Why was it, he wondered, that the grace that dignified these women when they walked seemed to crumple inside them as soon as they sat down? Only after a moment did it occur to him that she too was nervous.

'Do you speak English?' he asked, a little too gruffly.

She nodded, her eyes fixed on a point over his shoulder. And then he noticed the small tribal mark, like a thin crescent moon, etched into her right cheek. The girl from The Star? But many girls wore such a mark. He couldn't be sure.

'What's your name?'

Her whisper was barely audible.

'Appaea?' he repeated.

She nodded again.

'A lovely name,' he said, absurdly at a loss. 'My name is Austin Palmer. I'm a teacher at the school.'

Again no more than a nod, but one indicating to him that all this was familiar to her. Her eyes inventoried his bookshelves. They sat in silence.

His mind was filled with a story he'd once been told by a Welsh engineer from the Adiri Diamond Mine who had invited an African girl to his bungalow. She had turned up with two friends, and for more than an hour the miner had sat in a quandary, attempting to engage them in converation – a task complicated by their limited English and his total ignorance of the vernacular. His problem had been solved by the arrival of one of the African supervisors who explained that the girls expected the Welshman either to choose one of them or send them all away. They certainly didn't want to waste the night in language study. So the miner had picked one of the girls, the supervisor another, and the third waited for her friends and left with them.

However, he was no mining-engineer, and the thought of taking this girl baldly to bed filled Palmer with revulsion. He felt fraudulent. Inadequate even. He was appalled by what he had begun.

'Where is sister?' the girl said suddenly.

The question confused him. 'Who?'

'Your wife. I have seen her at market.'

He remembered Kay driving back from Adoubia, white-faced, in a filthy temper, goaded almost to hysterics by the way people stared and touched her. *They make me feel like some kind of freak*, she'd screamed at him. *I'm never going near that market again, I can't bear it, do you hear . . .?*

Was this one of the women who had sidled up against Kay, laughing, to touch the strange glamour of her long auburn hair among the dried fish and the bloody meat, the vultures and the crones?

'She has gone for her town in UK?' the girl asked.

'Yes, she's gone to UK.'

'When will she come again?'

'No,' he said, 'she won't be coming back.'

'Not ever?'

'No, not ever.'

'Oh, sorry' – the African intonation of the word was not casual – 'She don't like Africa?'

How, in God's name, to explain?

'She found it . . . hard here.'

The girl nodded. 'Yes. Is hard sometime. Is hard for woman, I think.'

Suddenly across Palmer's mind flickered the thought of unburdening himself to this young woman. In however rudimentary a way she seemed concerned for him. She would listen attentively, with interest, yet without judgment. But it was absurd. And if he had wanted to talk, or the gin had wanted it, he had left it too late. Aware of his unease, and perhaps fortified by it, she cast a proprietorial eye across the room. Her face lit up as she saw the record-player on the floor.

'Oh, you have gramophone. Please' – the familiar pause before a request – 'can we have music?'

He smiled, nodded, watched her cross the room and look at the record on the turntable. 'El-gar,' she read. 'En – ig – ma . . .' and dispensed with the rest. She looked across at him, disappointed. 'You don't get Highlife record?'

He found himself smiling again, and the girl's lips opened in response. Surely he had seen that smile before? Then she laughed and bent to search through the untidy pile of records.

38

He saw the ochre pallor of her soles as she crouched on bare feet. The pump-attendant had been right – she did have fine buttocks.

Appaea found what she was looking for and her face brightened again. 'Eh,' she exclaimed, 'is very old song. Come and show me how to play.'

It was a record that he and Kay had bought shortly after their arrival. Opambo had translated the lyrics for them – the lament of an abandoned lover pleading with his girl. He wondered now what memories it might exhume.

Appaea stood, hips swaying her dress from side to side, hands held out, beckoning. Palmer wrinkled his nose and shook his head.

'You dance too good at The Star,' she reminded him, smiling.

'So it was you.'

She looked away, immersing herself in the rhythm. Her arms twisted to the music, concealing her turned face.

'You dance if you like,' he said. 'Dance for me.'

She shrugged, closed her eyes, and gave herself to the invisible drummers, to the trumpeters and saxophonists. Her head was thrown back. He could see her breasts moving beneath the dress. She saw him watching and laughed without embarrassment, as though the human body had been intended for pleasure only, had never compromised with shame. She danced in full awareness of his attention, yet not flaunting herself, not the coquette. It was all of the moment, promising nothing but itself.

The music stopped. She laughed again and clapped her hands. 'Now other side.'

'No,' he said, 'not now.'

Sensing the tension in his voice she looked up gravely from the record-player. 'You want to do the thing now?' she said.

He nodded, undeterred, in fact relieved and heated by the crude idiom. He stood up, aware of the pull of gin at his balance. 'In here.'

She followed him through into the bedroom. He saw her eyes widen at the sight of the bed, but then immediately she began to take off her clothes. Her face was devoid of expression, eyes averted. When she was naked she lay artlessly on the bed.

From where Palmer stood the girl's sturdy body was foreshortened like the portrait of a corpse. In the lurid blue light the silver bed was funereal. In that moment he almost told her to dress and go, even considered how much to pay her in the circumstances, but she reached out to touch, as though in disbelief, the silver pilasters. He caught her damp body-reek mingled with the lavender of her powderings, and felt the locked blood rush. He stripped quickly, lay down beside her, doused the hideous blue light. In the faint illumination from the window she was no more than a bruise on the darkness. He pushed his mouth to hers, but her head moved away so that his lips fell on the small sickle scar at her cheek.

She laughed, a little nervously, and turned to face him again, wide-eyed. He could not hold her gaze. His mouth moved down to take in the berry-darkness of a nipple. His fingers tangled in the braids of her hair. Then she was beneath him, her eyes turned upwards under half-closed lids, urgent, without greed, making small noises deep in her throat.

His mind flooded with images of Kay threshing and moaning in their bed back at the bungalow on the school-compound. How she had tried, kept trying, every device she knew to draw him down into meeting . . .

He opened his eyes, refusing the images, staring at the lithe body beneath him. Yet still the white, anguished flesh of his wife returned between them, whispering, wanting, insinuating all its unaccommodated rage and pain.

And suddenly he was aware that there was no effort of participation anywhere along Appaea's limbs. Only a soft, pliant stillness, surrendered to whatever he might need to do.

He supported himself arched above her for a moment, watching the beads of sweat crawl among the wiry braids of her hair. He could hear her hoarse breath, the whirr of a beetle butting at the window, the fan beating against the silence. The room was choked with its own emptiness.

Eyes closed in a grimace of self-loathing, he pulled himself away. The girl lay still on the bed beside him.

After a long time she said, 'You don't like me?'

Head averted on the pillow he muttered, 'It's not that.'

She moved. He felt her hand, tentative at his hip. 'Why don't you look at me?' she said.

He lay in silence, willing her gone.

'I think you don't like me.'

He turned over, pulling away. 'Look, it's not that. It's me. I shouldn't have asked you to come. I'm sorry.' He reached for his trousers, took the wallet from his back pocket, fished out some bank-notes. 'Here. Take this. Please.'

Appaea looked at the notes in his fist. Hurt? Puzzled? She did not move.

'Take it, for God's sake.' He let the notes fall on the bed and turned away again.

'Is too much,' she said.

He did not respond.

After a while she got up from the bed and left the room. He heard the clatter of water on the tiled floor of the shower. He stared up at the revolving blades of the fan, oddly detached, almost looking down on himself, as though his spirit had dejectedly left his body as the girl had left the bed: Austin Palmer, English teacher, humanist, lying on a grotesque silver bed in Africa, among money. And in part he detested what he had become, in part he was amused by it – as drunkards are amused by their own incompetence.

The sound of water stopped. She would be drying herself on his towel now. He prepared for her return. What to say? *Please don't be offended. It's just that I'm in a bloody mess. And not only in my sex. If there were words, if there were words you should certainly have them . . . but take the money, please. It's not unkindly meant, and you must have far better use for it than I . . .*

In the sitting-room his radio was switched on. There was a blur of static as stations were changed. It came to rest on the wistful Highlife music that would play throughout the night. The door opened and the girl came back in, uncertainly. She was wrapped in his red bath-towel, holding it across her breasts. She stood in the light from the door, studying him.

'Even I have not seen silver bed before,' she said. The

accent was on the first word, not the second – a familiar African intonation. 'Is very nice.'

'It's not mine. It belongs to Mr Jalbout at the sawmill. The whole house is his. He's a richer man than me.'

'But not such nice man, eh?'

'I don't know about that.'

She walked slowly about the room, thinking.

'You like this music?'

He nodded.

'Is Kofi Quartery and his All-stars. I like it too much.' Clearly there was something else on her mind.

'You asked me to dance at The Star,' he said. 'And I think you asked the man at the Texaco station to . . . approach me?'

She studied him again, without denial.

'Why?'

Her lips were pursed, the ox-bow line of her nostril tilted a little. Then her dark eyes shifted away across the room. The towel rose and fell at her breast.

'Will you teach me?' she said.

He was taken aback. 'I'm sorry . . . I don't understand . . .'

'You are a teacher.'

'Yes, but . . .'

'Then you can teach me.'

And, despite himself, he was intrigued.

'What do you want to learn?'

'To read books better. And to write books.'

'You want to write books?'

'Maybe. Also to write a letter to the Queen so she will understand.'

'To the Queen?'

She nodded.

'Queen Elizabeth?'

Her nod was a little impatient now. How many queens did he think there were?

'What on earth do you want to say to the Queen?'

She was displeased by his smile. 'Is woman's thing,' she answered. 'You won't understand.'

'I see.'

'I don't think so. Will you teach me?' she asked again.

'Do you mean you want to become a student at the school?'

She shook her head. 'I don't get money to go there.'

'I see. So you want me to take you on as a private pupil?'

'I want you to teach me.'

He was at a loss now. Had she come here, then, intending to use him – only more subtly than he had thought to use her? She must have seen his frown across the room.

'You don't think I'm smart,' she said, and looked away out of the window where the moon had risen high above the town.

'It's not that' – he seemed capable only of stupid repetition with this girl – 'It's just a bit . . . unexpected.'

'You want to think about it?'

'I'm not sure . . .' He looked up at her, trying to be fair.

She shrugged, prouder now. He was informed of the presence of a free spirit.

This was very awkward. He had already injured her once and would not willingly do so again. Why was nothing ever simple?

The girl drew in her breath. 'Is no matter,' she said. 'I am now going.' She let the towel drop and bent to pick up her clothes from the floor. The moment was vanishing.

'Wait a minute.'

She looked across at him, arms bent behind her back to fasten her bra.

'Let me think it over.'

She nodded impassively.

'How can I get in touch with you?' He saw her puzzled expression. 'I mean, where do you live?'

'You can tell my friend, the man at the Texaco station, when you want me again.'

She began to pull on her clothes. When she was dressed she looked down on him where he lay on the bed, a sheet over his nakedness.

'I think you are not happy fellow,' she said.

And what could one say to that?

'I am now going.'

'Yes' – did she think she needed his permission?

She stood her ground uncertainly. He saw her eyes shift.

'Look, take this, please.' He gathered the money and held it out to her. From the clutch of notes she took only two. 'And, thank you,' he added awkwardly as she tucked the notes down the front of her bra.

'Don't mention' – she was not in the least aware of the incongruity of the conventional response. She nodded, apparently content. 'Bye-bye.' As always, the African intonation set the English phrase to music.

Deliberately he did not go into town for the next few days, though he felt like a squatter in the bungalow now. The rooms were dead around him. Already he missed the sounds of the town – the laughter in the bars, the women singing as they pounded cassava, the old men arguing over their dominoes under the tamarind tree, the drone of lorries up the hill, and always, somewhere, music drifting across the iron roofs. He was bad-tempered with Mamadou. By Thursday he'd had enough of Sal Rodriguez's droll company and the otherwise dreary nights. Late on Friday afternoon he drove back into Adoubia. To his amazement the girl was waiting in the square.

She got to her feet as he stepped out of the car. 'I have brought you some fruit,' she said, 'from my farm in the bush. There is pineapple and pawpaw and plantain. Also yam. I think maybe you like to eat.'

'But how did you know I was coming back today?'

'I not know. I have wait every day but you don't come.'

'I'm sorry. I'd no idea. I thought . . .' He looked at her offering where it lay wrapped in a bright cloth. 'It's very sweet of you. Look, do come in.' He bent to pick up the bundle: it was large. There was more in there than she had mentioned. Awkwardly he held open the door. She slipped off her sandals as she stepped through.

Inside they stood looking at one another, hesitant.

'You've come about your lessons?'

'I have come to see you,' she corrected. 'Last time I think, this white man is too thin. He don't eat too good. You want that I cook you some good meal? Is very fine kitchen here I think.'

44

'Just a minute.' He stopped her *en route* to the kitchen, tried to slow her down. 'Appaea, I have a servant at the school. He looks after me very well.'

She glanced back at him dubiously. 'He Christian man or Muslim?'

'He's a Muslim. What's that got to do with it?'

'No good at all,' she declared. 'I cook you proper Dogambey food. You like it too much.'

Palmer shook his head helplessly.

'You not hungry?'

'Well, yes, as a matter of fact, I am.'

'You see.' She grinned then, all points proved. 'You go take shower now. Go. Go. I get work to do.'

Shaking his head Palmer did as he was bidden. From the moment he'd stepped out of the car he'd seen he had a problem. It was trickier than he'd thought. A shower would give him a chance to think.

He had just turned on the water when he heard her calling up the stairs. He switched off the tap and shouted back, 'What did you say?'

'I say. I think maybe I teach you something this time.'

'Oh yes. What's that?'

'I teach you how to do the thing proper. Not hard like a railway train – push, push. But soft. Like music, eh? Like dancing at The Star?'

The meal was good, spicier than he was used to, a hot mélange of tastes. Appaea chattered happily, unstoppably, throughout. He listened, fascinated.

She was a little older than he had guessed, but still the youngest member of a large family. Her mother sold earthenware cooking-pots from a market stall. Her father occupied a traditional position at the court of the Paramount Chief in the palace at Old Town. She was a little awed to discover that Palmer regarded 'the King' as a personal friend.

Proudly she explained that her father was field-commander of the left flank of the King's army. As Koranteng had no army these days – indeed, he had few powers left at all – Palmer assumed the office was a sinecure.

The family's substance had largely been spent on educating her male cousins, for under the matrilineal kinship system they were her father's responsibility as Uncle. One was a minor civil servant in Badagry, another worked as a wages clerk in the Adiri mine, a third – on whom the family's hopes were pinned – was still at the University. He was to be a lawyer, then they would all be rich. Appaea's own brothers had been cared for in turn by their own maternal uncle, and her two surviving sisters were married and had four children between them, one born only recently, a Monday child, strong as an ox. No one had considered Appaea's education a priority and so she had been to Middle School and no further.

In a way Palmer was glad of that. Her native intelligence had prospered unsullied. It was candid – alert to what felt real and what rang false – without pretension. Her poise was graver, more centred than that of the girls at school, and not for the first time he wondered what real good could come of the school's uncritical adoption of the English public school tradition.

Her frequent laughter startled and delighted him. Rough as a homespun blanket, coarse as the cry of a jay, it came often and loud. He found himself oddly pleased by its nimble mockery, and the way her whole body was thrown into the business.

Nor was she precisely beautiful. There was something recessive about the face, particularly the obeisant lines of her nose and chin. Her eyes though were bright with the mettle of a quick spirit, and the sickle scar at her cheek was a grace-note rather than a blemish to her lively features.

Later, beneath him, he saw more at which to wonder. And under his hands her skin was taut as a talking-drum; yet soft, responsive; all the colours of the night.

Patiently, with gently mocking reproofs, with small subtle insistences, her body educated his until at last he lay back, glowing, as though the pallor of his skin had taken some benison of fire at her touch. His arrested heart was abrim with gratitude.

When he agreed to give her language lessons he found himself basking in the brilliance of her smile. It was as candid, as denuded of any qualification, as her manner of speaking. It was a little like the moment on one of his first evenings in Africa when he stepped out on to the veranda at dusk and was astounded by the brave white trumpets of moonflowers; petals that had been tightly closed all day now spending their fragrance on the night, heady and somnambulant.

Flustered, apprehensive at what he had begun, he made arrangements for her return, told her that he would bring books from the school, that, no, he did not expect to be paid, and fended off an excitement that would have effused more girlishly had he allowed it room.

'There is a dance tomorrow night at The Star,' she said. 'You will come?'

Yes, he said, he would see her there. Only after she had left did he have second thoughts.

He turned up at the hotel rather late. Appaea was chattering with friends between dances on the edge of the floor and her face lit up when she saw him. Reluctant to join that gaggle of young women who beamed widely at him for a moment then resumed their excited chatter, he smiled awkwardly and went through into the bar.

In a few moment she joined him there, though a little shyly now.

'Can I get you a drink?' he said.

'I would like Fanta, please.'

It took a long time to get served. They stood uncertainly together in the press at the bar until at last he caught the barman's eye.

'What have you been doing with yourself today?' he asked.

She shrugged and made a little moue. Nothing important. The distance between them widened.

'Is too hot in here,' she said, and took her drink to the door.

He turned to follow her and saw Mario Baldinucci, lonely as a landed fish, sitting at a corner table, regarding him with a querulous eye. Palmer raised his glass then turned quickly away before the Italian could call him over.

Appaea waved back to her friends who stood in attentive conclave across the floor. She was wearing traditional dress, a tight bodice matching the long skirt that emphasized her figure. She had taken pains with the touches of make-up and powder, but he preferred her skin clean and black as it had been the night before. He saw that she was disappointed by his reserve. Her nose tilted away from him.

He was about to essay something more friendly when Sal Rodriguez came out of the Gents lavatory still tugging at his zip. He must pass through the door where they stood and there was no avoiding him.

For a moment the Indian thought that Palmer was alone. He clapped a hand on his shoulder, breathing a reek of gin.

'Austin, dear fellow. Just in time to fuel my tanks.' Then he saw Palmer's glance flicker to the girl and away again.

Steeped as they were in alcoholic fecklessness, Sal's eyes missed nothing. Palmer knew that he had seen.

'Sal, let me introduce Appaea . . .' He realized that he did not know her surname. 'I'm sorry,' he said, '. . . your last name . . .'

'Appaea Odum,' she muttered brusquely, bobbed, and turned her face away.

'This is Salvador Rodriguez. My friend. A teacher at the school.'

'Delighted,' said Rodriguez to her turned shoulder. He looked back at Palmer and shrugged. 'Mario is inside. Have you seen him already?'

Palmer nodded. 'What are you drinking, Sal?'

'Gin, dear man. I find it accelerates the liquefaction of the cells.'

Again Palmer waited a long time at the bar, and when he got back Appaea had gone.

'She said she had to join her friends,' Rodriguez remarked. 'I do hope I didn't drive her away. Cheers!' As he sipped from his glass he watched his friend's eyes survey the dance-floor. 'So that's what we're up to in town? Isn't she the one who . . .?'

'She's a friend,' Palmer said. 'I'm going to coach her in English.'

Rodriguez nodded, conspiratorial.

'Her family didn't have enough money to send her to school.'

'Please. Such charity need not explain itself. No bed in town for poor drunken Sal tonight, I see.'

'Listen, Sal, I don't want you getting . . .'

'The wrong idea? Heaven forbid. Look, I think Opambo is going to sing.' Rodriguez put two fingers to his mouth and whistled approval.

Palmer searched the floor in vain as Rodriguez swayed unsteadily beside him, singing along with Opambo out of key: 'You are – my des – tinee – lah lah – lah lah – lahdee . . .' The Indian took another swig, sniffed. 'You seem very anxious about your pupil. *In loco parentis* tonight, are we?'

Palmer could not quite resist his grin.

'It's really quite fascinating,' the Indian said. 'The eagerness . . . I mean, the positive zest with which human beings throw experience to the winds and sign up again for pain. It's quite inevitable, you know.' But he did not seem unduly depressed by the thought. 'She's sitting over there. Behind the palm tree. Don't feel you have to keep me company. Mario will take me home.'

'Look, Sal . . .'

The Indian gave him an invalid's smile and pressed a finger to his lips. 'Spare me,' he said. 'I will not believe you, and you will only despise yourself. I suppose you know what you're doing.'

'I'm old enough to make my own mistakes,' Palmer answered, a little too coldly, for he could feel his friend's concern.

'Indeed. You're rather good at it as I recall.' Sal's defences had stiffened. His voice was drier, more laconic. 'It's just that I've often been bothered by how easily our lives are mortgaged to mere bodily need. Still, you know me – on a sliding-scale between beasts and angels I'm inclined to think we don't rate very high. Life is a pig, my dear. I wish you luck with it.' He eased Palmer aside and passed through the door, singing again.

49

Palmer found Appaea where Rodriguez had indicated, alone, behind the palm. 'Why did you run away?' he said.

'I did not run away.'

'Then why didn't you wait for me?'

She stared at him a moment, then shifted her gaze morosely to the wall.

'Sal's all right,' he hazarded. 'He's my friend.'

Her silence strummed like the surface of a pond.

'Have I upset you?' he asked.

'You make me too sad.'

'I'm sorry. I didn't mean . . .'

'For you I'm just foolish African woman. Not smart. Not beautiful. Just foolish black woman.'

'Appaea, that's not true.'

'You are ashamed your friends will scorn you because you take African girl, not so?'

'No, not so. I don't give a damn what they think.'

'You say that now, but what you go say to them, eh?'

'I haven't said anything to them,' he protested.

'So you don't like to talk about me?'

'Jesus Christ . . .'

'Is bad to swear.'

'I'm sorry, but . . .'

'Sorry. Sorry. Always you are sorry.'

'Appaea.' His voice was fiercer than he had intended.

Silent, far from meek, she waited.

'I think,' he said hesitantly, 'I think where it matters you're smarter than I am.'

A grunt, unconvinced.

He tried a smile. 'And you're certainly more beautiful.'

'But you don't want me.'

'I didn't say that.'

'You don't have to say.'

He stood biting his lip, wondering how he had got here. The door stood open – out. He need only say nothing, do nothing. And yet . . .

'Now I am shamed,' she said. 'It is my friends who will scorn me.' She stared at the wall, disconsolate, fingering her necklace of bright beads.

50

A scene repeated thousands of times at dances the world over every Saturday night – the spurner and the spurned, caught up in a tangle of heart-strings, muddling in hurt. Yet here, under this hot night sky, she was all Africa, and he – what was he now? – white hunter with an eye to the gunroom wall, a taker of quick profit, rifler of mines. In short – he saw it clearly enough – the Great White Shit, of which, in his more pious moments, he so eloquently disapproved.

'Come on,' he said, 'I'm taking you home.'

'I don't want to go home.'

'I mean to my house.'

She looked up at him for the first time, then quickly away.

'Will you come?' And then, more gently, 'Appaea?'

'You want?'

'Yes,' he said, uncertain of his own certainty, 'I want.'

No, she did not think it proper that lovemaking be given in exchange for language teaching. If he would accept no payment it must be a deal of another kind. Besides, she was disgusted that after two years in this country he had troubled to learn so little of her language. Yes, in return for his efforts to improve her English she would teach him that. The lovemaking was another matter, pleasurable to both.

A barter then – though very different from the silent trade with which tribesmen sharing no common language once made their mute exchanges northwards where savannah and Sahara met. Night after night she came, and the lessons were a noisy business, laughter frolicking often across the room. Their formal structure did not last for long. Appaea seemed more interested in criticizing the way Mamadou ironed his shirts, or worrying that he didn't feed his master well. From whom did he buy meat, and at what time of day? How much did he pay for it? And why didn't the servant make a small farm so that Austin did not have to spend money on vegetables and fruit? The answers were never satisfactory.

Also the exercises in the textbook were far from her enthusiasms. Who was this Booker T. Washington with his palaver about the dignity of labour? Did he ever do woman's work? Discussions drifted uncontrollably off the point, and Palmer's attention was drawn – not at all unwillingly – to gossip of the palace-compounds and the market place. Or she would tell him stories and proverbs her mother had taught her as a child, as though all male complexities of thought were no more than dust kicked up by idle schoolboys. And then suddenly she would reapply herself to the task in hand, berating him for frittering away her precious time.

On the whole she made better progress than he, though neither would have won prizes for scholarship. 'No, not so,' she would protest in derision at his poor way with the abrasive vowels of her language, or the impenetrable clutch of consonants at the start of a word. 'So . . .' And once more his tongue would struggle to mimic a tonal variation that his ears could barely discern. It was the elusive music of the language, the cadences on which all meaning depended, that had beggared his confidence when he'd first tried to learn it long before. That, and the way the Africans had collapsed with laughter at his every effort.

His renewed efforts came to a dismal end when, one day, keen to demonstrate his command, he called to a small boy in the square outside the house. He had some chocolate to give him and was, he thought, simply inviting the boy to come and get it. His call met only with a look of startled dismay. Perhaps the boy was bashful? He called again and realized suddenly that, after a moment of stunned silence, Appaea beside him was falling about with mirth. So was everyone else in the square who had heard him.

'What is it?' he asked her. 'What are you laughing at?'

She would say nothing, could hardly speak. She stood with one hand clapped to her mouth, tears streaming down her face, helplessly out of control. It was impossible not to share the laughter; impossible also to get a sensible word out of her. The next day, in the staffroom at the school, he drew Opambo aside and asked for an explanation.

'Oh dear, Mr Palmer,' Opambo said, and began to chuckle. He called out something in the vernacular to everyone else in the room, and once more Palmer found himself the centre of an inexplicable ring of mirth. Finally Opambo enlightened

52

him. Palmer had not, as he believed, been calling out, 'Come here, little boy, come here.' A minimal error of intonation had substantially altered the meaning of his call. He had been demanding that the small boy menstruate.

After that Palmer gave up.

Gradually, almost by stealth, she claimed his thoughts. He watched Appaea as she pounded cassava, flexing her arms to lift and plunge the long pestle into the mortar. Or as she craned, tongue between her teeth, to free the ravelled thread from her sewing-machine. Or again, swaying away from the market place where she had haggled half-abusively with fat mammies – tall, perpendicular, a bundle of purchases balanced on her head. What mattered now was the daily play of affection between them, and the way it gladdened his nights. Soon his old manner of coping seemed as remote as the gossip of some distant, disastrous city.

Out at the school-compound his colleagues remarked on the change. Hearing the Englishman whistle as he passed the administration block, the headmaster puzzled for a moment over what was wrong, then realized: Mr Palmer was cheerful again. Apparently good sense had at last prevailed. Samuel Opambo was closer to the gossip of the town. '*Omnia vincit amor*,' he suggested to Miss Osu, who had been pleasantly startled that the senior English master should flirt with her again. Even Elijah Darko, the skinflint bursar whom Palmer had privately nicknamed 'Snowdunda', for that was how the man always described himself when someone needed to make an imprest on school funds – even he was greeted with a sunny grin.

In the classroom too he was an altered man. For weeks he'd done no more than go through the motions, teaching without heart, mechanically. He was in difficulties with the senior class, a sometimes truculent bunch who felt short-changed by the knowledge that the first years of the school had been disorganized and incompetent. Their grievances still rankled as they approached the Ordinary Level examinations, and the situation was further complicated by one of their set texts.

Julius Caesar might have been innocuous enough in England; here, where the destiny of the nation was inseparable from that of a President with ambitions for the entire African continent, it was a provocative choice. The members of the Party Youth Brigade regarded the play as a subversive document; other seized on the conspirators' arguments with discreetly controlled glee. Palmer's brightest students were dispersed on either side, and he uneasily between.

Tensions in the classroom were heightened by the approach of the fifth anniversary of Independence Day. For some time *The Party Banner* had been hinting that this was to be the occasion of an important new political development, though its nature remained obscure. One morning a copy of the paper was found pinned to the blackboard with the words *It is the bright day that brings forth the adder (Act II, Sc.i, 1.14)* scrawled around it. A fierce row was in progress when Palmer entered the room.

Not long before he would merely have put a stop to it. Skilfully now, he refined the shouting-match to debate, shifting its terms back and forth from modern Africa to Shakespeare's Rome. All sides of the question must be examined, he insisted; savour the ambiguities; listen to the verse. For two hours the room was alight with energy. When the bell rang and the class dispersed still arguing, he sat back in silence for a space, knowing himself a teacher again. This was why he had come to Africa.

After that first question about Kay, Appaea had not mentioned his wife again. Palmer wondered at this, for delicacy and tact were no part of her candid way. Yet if his vanity was a little wounded by such scant interest in his past, he was also relieved. He attributed Appaea's lack of curiosity to a faculty for living, as she danced, entirely in the present. Kay was not of the moment therefore she did not exist. There was much to be learned from such sublime indifference. It made life altogether possible. So both his old journals and the new lay forgotten in their cupboard. Not blindly, though with a dreamer's recklessness, he consigned himself to the present.

In those days he felt the sun's light more compelling than its heat. Each day seemed to draw to a close with an astounding sunset – vast estuaries of cloud, burnished and pacific, in which swallows celebrated the last light before quickly folding dusk in their wings. And if, in the night, listening to the distant cries of the forest beyond the silent town, he felt a tremor at the thought of death, it came as a sharpening of the moment between him and this suave African body at his side, an indispensable portion of their sensuality. As he looked into Appaea's face he felt an unfamiliar tingling between the eyes, and was sure that she must feel it too, like twin stars answering across the deeps between. He was immersed in the actuality of their being together, and aware of its tremendous pathos.

Wide-eyed she looked up at him – perplexed almost at the wonder and the sadness of his gaze; as though this man's astonished heart must be consoled for having dared to brave a woman's love once more.

Part Two

THE KING

As with the beginning of the death of love, the first waning of a once ardent political affiliation is not always immediately obvious, for more is involved than a mere shift of opinion. One's sense of the world is strangely altering; long before the house-lights go down, somewhere backstage the scene-shifters are at work.

Perhaps it had begun before he made the move into Adoubia? Certainly, as Jalbout had anticipated, that extension of horizons from the narrow perimeter of the school-compound into the hurly-burly of the streets had unblinkered Palmer's vision. He could not avoid the greater friction with the world outside the house in the square. He overheard some of the uglier arguments in the bars, witnessed the declining morale of the lorry-drivers (whose machines careered off the road too often for lack of spare parts) and of the small traders who were last in line for import-licences; and that line was very long. He observed the swift, tumorous growth of the black market. Even at the post office parcels no longer changed hands without a dash, and someone, it seemed, was tampering with the mail. Everywhere the Party was in evidence – visibly in the flagged cars taking priority at every junction, invisibly as a vigilant, over-the-shoulder censorship of word and deed. The despondent crowd of malefactors awaiting justice in the hot compound outside the DC's courtroom were not the only critics of the regime.

With the arrests at the University, Palmer finally admitted to himself that things were very wrong. The earlier detention of politicians had been, perhaps, admissible – what Moise Tshombe had done to the agonized Congo was to be avoided at all costs here. These university lecturers were another matter – sober, scholarly men deeply troubled by the Party's crass interference with academic freedom. They deserved better than a cell in Kende Castle.

The staffroom at the school was stunned by the announcement, though even there debate was strangely muffled: Elijah Darko, the school bursar, was after all a relative of the DC.

Palmer had once suggested that the bursar's principal function was to prevent the teaching staff from rushing headlong into necessities; now Opambo hinted that the man had a more sinister role.

In a quiet moment together, the Latin master had been unusually open with the Englishman. 'What has changed, Mr Palmer? I will tell you. We are told that we are politically free and economically free – but are we yet free to be ourselves? To recover our dignity as free men rather than acting out the parts written for us by an alien regime? I think not. Sometimes I read the papers these days and I think to myself that Sulla could have done no worse. No – we are free now only to dance to the Party's drum. We have exchanged one servitude for another. On the whole I preferred the days of the British – at least there was some sort of community in our resistance then.'

Opambo was too depressed for argument, and Palmer himself no longer cared to analyse the contradictions of post-imperial development. Even to his own ears his opinions had begun to sound abstract and empty, too far removed from the disenchantment of a new nation so swiftly growing old.

On the evening before the Independence Anniversary celebrations he watched a flagged Mercedes turn off the dirt-road into the tarred drive of the school-compound. Christian Odansey and Krobo Mansa, the DC, were to attend a meeting of the Board of Governors, and the boot of the car was filled with crates of beer for an informal get-together afterwards with the staff. Palmer stayed out of the school marking essays until it was time for the gathering.

Odansey was dapper and garrulous as ever, his jollity flowing easily around the staffroom like the warm beer. Since the Deputy-Minister had first welcomed him at Badagry Airport, Palmer had liked the man. One of the select band of Prison Graduates from the Independence struggle, he exuded confidence and gusto. 'We have made a start, Mr Palmer,' he had said, entertaining the new teacher and his wife in the restaurant of the Grand Atlantic Hotel, 'but it is early days. The world needs Africa more than it knows – our warmth, energy, humour, hope. Give us time and we will teach the world to dance. A united Africa will be a force in the world, I promise you – a force for peace, for justice among men. The African Personality is older than history, but it is also the key to the future. The rest of the world is weary – we are still young. Young in the heart. Have you noticed, Mr Palmer – Africa is the shape of the human heart? The President is the beating of that heart. And I' – Odansey had grinned as if amused by his own solemnity – 'I am a little red corpuscle that scurries about the world on his business. And like all healthy bodies Africa has need of a few white corpuscles too – which is why you and your kind are welcome here – on the new footing – man to man.'

That had been a long time ago. These days Palmer was less easily persuaded, yet he found himself smiling as Christian Odansey made his way across the room towards him, open-armed. 'And how is my Sunday Whiteman bearing up? I hear you are a single man these days.' He stood for a moment, shaking his head in sympathy. 'Ah well, perhaps it's for the best. We have a saying here, my friend: *Marriage and palm-wine are two different things*. A wife should be kept laden, pregnant and six yards behind. If she will not stay there it's better she be gone.' He eyed the Englishman, shrewd, avuncular. 'I think you have done the wise thing. And I hear excellent reports from the headmaster. You are working well. He likes you a lot, you know.'

'It's mutual,' Palmer replied. 'He's a fine man.'

'Salt of the earth,' Odansey agreed. 'Quagrainie and I were at school together. Always a virtuous fellow, but short on drive . . . Still, you are in good shape. No problems? No complaints?'

'I could use more money for the library.'

'Ah yes. And our science masters need more money for the labs, and the headmaster tells me he could use more staff, and no doubt the caretaker needs more money for palm-wine. Shall I take off my Chairman of the Board hat, put on my Deputy-Minister's hat, and tell you my problems too? Do you know, for instance, what percentage of our foreign exchange is eaten up in interest payments? But no, that is not your concern. Tonight we are to enjoy ourselves, eh? Take some beer – I promise you, your needs are never far from my thoughts.'

At that moment Mario Baldinucci came in, and Odansey said, 'Now here comes another of my headaches.' Before the Italian could speak the politician began to berate him for the delay in starting work on the last phase of the school-buildings. In disfigured English Baldinucci explained that he was under instructions not to touch another breeze-block until his firm had been paid for the previous phase.

'The money is on its way,' Odansey growled. 'Your manager knows that already – I gave him my word as Deputy-Minister. These things take time. You are impeding our future. Build.' He waved the unhappy Italian away, and turned to Palmer again. 'I'll tell you something, my friend – I envy Quagrainie his quiet life. I'll be in the grave long before him.'

'Not upside-down, I trust.' It was a reference to a joke made by Odansey himself when they had first met. The politician ran a busy legal practice in Badagry and he often delighted in quoting the local prejudice that lawyers should be buried face-downwards. He laughed at Palmer's reminder now. 'Excellent – I see we'll make an African of you yet, Mr Palmer. Excellent.'

Krobo Mansa came across the room to join them, blinking out of his crumpled pugilist's face under a bush of greying hair. The DC was never comfortable among the teaching-staff. They were all better educated if less powerful than he. It was clear that he wanted to be gone.

'We have a busy day tomorrow, Minister,' he said.

Odansey put an arm round the DC's shoulder. 'Krobo was ever my conscience and my strong right arm. You know, Mr Palmer, it was he who rallied all the local unions in the Independence struggle. Actually, he was known as the Porcupine because you British found him hard to handle. Practically single-handed he made Ogun-Dogambey ungovernable. Tomorrow is like Krobo's birthday too. The anniversary of the Porcupine's finest hour.'

The DC smiled blearily and looked away.

'The press seems to think there's something important on the cards,' Palmer said.

'Ah, wait and see, Mr Palmer, wait and see. The President will broadcast at dawn. We must not spoil his surprise. Krobo, Mr Palmer has no wife these days. We must see what we can do for him.'

The DC nodded without great interest, his eyes wandering impatiently across the noisy staffroom.

'Very well,' Odansey said, 'we must be on our way. Just one word more, Mr Palmer. I hear from the headmaster that you have taken a house in town and that your bungalow stands empty most of the time. If you do not need it you should remember that others do. Mr Darko, for instance, has a large family that he would like to bring to the compound. His place in town is small. Think about it. Please.' For a moment his eyelids were lowered in an iron stare, then he released a rich laugh, squeezed Palmer's arm, and was gone.

After the politicians had left the staff relaxed and the room hummed with speculation about the next day. Mr Quagrainie returned from his last words with Odansey and sought out Palmer. 'If I might have a word . . .' he said, and drew him out on to the veranda.

The headmaster had been educated too severely out of his native gaiety. He was embarrassed by his authority and, Palmer suspected, never quite believed in it. Had he not been fortunate in his wife – a vast hill of a woman whose impeccable cloth was stuffed like a bustle with her soft bulk – he would have found his responsibilities at the school insupportable. He tapped nervously at the rail of the veranda for a long time before speaking.

'I believe the Chairman spoke with you just now,' he said.

Palmer knew what was coming, knew too that his contract entitled him to accommodation on the school-compound, but he could not bear the headmaster's discomfort.

'About the bungalow, you mean?'

'Ah yes. Indeed. The bungalow.'

'I quite understand, headmaster.'

Mr Quagrainie's eyes flickered towards him gratefully, then away again. 'The bursar does have a large family in town, you see. The cost of petrol these days . . .'

Palmer nodded, aware of bridges burning but not greatly alarmed. 'Also' – he could not resist – 'he is related to the DC.'

'Ah yes. I believe that is the case.' Mr Quagrainie cleared his throat. 'I am not pressing you to vacate, of course. But . . .'

'It would be more convenient,' Palmer supplied.

'As you have alternative accommodation already . . .'

'I was thinking of it anyway.'

'You were? Then there is no great problem? You may have the school lorry, of course, to move your belongings.'

'There isn't much,' Palmer said. 'I'll see to it. It's probably for the best.'

'DV,' the headmaster agreed.

'DV?'

'*Deo Volente*? God willing, Mr Palmer. God willing.' Tight-lipped, Mr Quagrainie nodded his head two or three times, and then – as always when his nerves appeared to have survived an ordeal – began to hum.

Independence Day: a fleet of lorries was requisitioned to take the whole school into the football field at Adoubia where the Party Rally and Celebration Durbar would be held. All the local organizations from the Youth Brigade to the Market Women's Co-operative Front (an appellation Palmer had always found singularly appealing) were to be out in force. Palmer had asked Appaea to accompany him under the palm-thatched awning reserved for local dignitaries but she insisted that she preferred to remain inconspicuous in the crowd with her family and friends.

So he sat with Sal Rodriguez, gazing into the strident light where at least three worlds paraded before him under the press of sun and cloud. The Police Band, black in black uniform behind gleaming instruments, headed the procession. Then came the gawky, stiff-legged march of the Youth Brigade, carrying their Party banners high, like so many Boy-Scouts and Girl-Guides hell-bent on some terrible mission. Behind them the Trade Unions shuffled along in uncertain compro-

mise between march-time and Highlife rhythm, while the
Market Women jiggled their ample bums upwards to the sun
of Africa. At the rear, behind the motorcaded trappings of the
Party machine, came the ancient procession of the chiefs,
umbrella-shaded on their palanquins, rich in vermilion and
gold.

All stiffened to the strains of the National Anthem, and a
great cheer unnerved the weaver-birds as Christian Odansey
took the microphone on the rostrum, a white handkerchief
waving in his hand, and bellowed, 'Comrades.'

By now everyone knew the substance of his speech. In the
dawn broadcast the President had advised the nation of the
need to advance towards a single-party state. The two-party
system was a relic of colonialism, relevant only to those
nations where class division was still rife. The Party had
abolished class distinction when it freed the country from
imperial rule. Now the Party was the people and the people
were the Party. To demonstrate that this was triumphantly the
case a referendum would be held on the issue later in the year.
He was confident that this would prove to the world that such
unification was not only the need but the wish of the entire
nation. It would serve notice of the coming union of all Africa.

'Such compelling logic,' Sal Rodriguez had commented.
'What more is there to say?'

Christian Odansey would have agreed, though without the
irony. Under a flutter of Party flags, wearing the plain blue
Chinese-style tunic that had become the politician's uniform,
he was out to enjoy himself. His white teeth flashed well-
calculated jokes. All the catch-phrases of Party jargon were
subsumed within his raffish sexual rhythms. Superbly confident, he saw no need to argue the obvious. His task was to
make people feel the unity that this move towards a single-
party state would bring. He addressed his appeal most directly
to the adoring assembly of Market Women. Brimming with
vitality, he was laying them *en masse*, and knew precisely how
and when to achieve the climax they desired. 'And so I say to
you, my friends, my comrades, my fellow Africans, that from
this hour forth, one watchword shall be sealed for ever deep in
all our hearts.' He paused, lifted a clenched fist and punched

the air thrice as he declaimed, 'One Nation. One Party. One Leader.'

There was a great roar from the crowd. Krobo Mansa was on his feet taking up and leading the chant, and the world was persuaded of the rightness of everything, carried by the revelry of music where, in a thousand years of rhetoric, words would never reach.

'Doesn't this ring a bell?' Rodriguez muttered in Palmer's ear. 'I mean, don't you think Goebbels should have fled to Africa? He would have done rather well here.'

Palmer had heart neither for Sal's sarcasm nor for Odansey's jubilation. Was it possible that there had been a time – not so very long ago – when he would have wanted to travel with the crowd's enthusiasm? Publicly to burn his passport, stand up, shout, 'I'm with you. Let me belong'? Not to the slogans and the party propaganda, but to the old dream of freedom, to the promise of the new. Perhaps even then it had never been on – he was too English, too passive, too trammelled in the ambiguities of it all. How juvenile, how purblind, his high talk of a new Utopia of the bush now seemed. After all that had happened to him here he could only sit in silence now.

He looked round and saw Mr and Mrs Quagrainie, hand in hand, bemused on the fringes of the dance. In his way the headmaster was as much a high Tory as his average English counterpart, and Palmer had despaired of that in him at times. But he felt closer now to him than to the brigaded ranks of students who marched in Party rather than in school uniform. It was all too much like observing someone else's dream.

Yet somewhere in that crowd, among the dancers, was Appaea. He should find her, take her away from here, lose himself in the soft, receptive Africa of her flesh. He got up to cross the field, to look for her, and found his way blocked by the procession of the chiefs.

There were many of them – all the headmen of the outlying villages, each with his own retinue of elders. And there, in pride of place, he saw Koranteng, Paramount Chief of the Ogun-Dogambey region, carried towards him, high on a palanquin, the huge state umbrella dancing flamboyant curtsies above his head. Against the lowering mauve sky the procession was a conflagration of scarlet and gold. Palmer was startled once more by the way this drab country could burgeon thus in unexpected bursts of splendour. The tailswitch-bearers whipped spirits from the path of the King. Beside the swaying litter walked his Spokesman and ministers with their staffs, the heralds in hats of black monkey-skin, and the helmeted sword-bearers. The court musicians blared on elephant-tusk horns and beat their gongs and drums. A line of stool-bearers bobbed under their burdens in time to the music. Swathed in a gorgeous cloth, negligent and royal, Koranteng waved to the crowd on either side of his palanquin.

A hold-up further down the line brought the King's progress to a halt almost beside Palmer. The guards were sweating and panting at his shoulder, one clutching a cutlass on which a gilded lizard gleamed, another brandishing a flintlock musket from which a veneer of gold-leaf had begun to peel. In close-up there was a tawdriness to the cavalcade, like that of theatrical properties which should be seen only from a distance in artificial light.

And Koranteng himself was an even gaunter figure than Palmer remembered, his pinched body overburdened by its golden ornaments. Up there in his litter he began to cough, violently, so that the diadem of nuggets at his brow and the lustrous golden pectoral were shaking – sunlight squinting and dazzling off them as they moved. He wiped his mouth with a bangled arm, looked about and saw Palmer's white face regarding him with concern. Then he smiled, gesturing with his fly-whisk as though in reproof.

'You have not been to see me in a long time,' he said.

'Things have been . . . difficult,' Palmer shouted above the din.

'So I hear,' Koranteng nodded, his lips tautened in a frown. 'You should have come to me. I have missed you, Austin. You must come.'

'I'd like that.'

'You must come soon,' Koranteng said. 'I will send word.' And the cavalcade swayed on its way as though drawn by an eddy of the crowd.

Lost in thought, waiting for the train to pass, Palmer saw one of the elders turn to look at him – an old man in a purple and yellow cloth, with a bald head and grizzled chin, who took a meerschaum pipe from his mouth and raised it in acknowledgment, grinning broadly. He seemed to expect Palmer to recognize him, which the Englishman did indeed pretend to do before the old man ambled on his way.

For a long time Palmer searched the crowd for Appaea but could find her nowhere.

The next afternoon he cleared the rest of his things out of the bungalow on the school-compound, and wished Snowdunda well of it.

He and his servant, Mamadou, were unloading the car into the house in the square when he was suddenly aware of Appaea watching him in silence.

He smiled across at her. 'I've been thrown out of my bungalow at the school,' he said.

'For why? What did you do?'

He smiled again at her alarm. 'Don't worry. I'm only joking. I wanted to move here anyway. So I can keep an eye on you. What happened to you yesterday? I looked everywhere for you.'

'I don't go to Durbar,' she said. 'I get sick small.'

Now it was his turn to look anxious.

'Is nothing. Is woman's thing, that's all.'

'You're all right?'

'Yes, I all right.'

Mamadou came out of the house to pick up more things. Palmer introduced the two Africans who studied one another briefly, without warmth. When the servant had gone back inside Appaea said, 'He will live with you here? In this house.'

'Downstairs, in the kitchen-quarters.'

He saw her displeasure.

'Appaea, I could hardly sack the poor man just because I've decided to move house.'

Her frown disagreed, but she would not pursue the matter. Not yet.

'You have see my father?'

He had picked up a heavy box of books and stood, supporting the cardboard base on his knee, like a laden stork, puzzling.

'At the Durbar. He have smile at you but you don't speak.'

'The man with the pipe? Good Lord, I should have realized.'

'I think you will spill that box. This is servant's work.'

'They're *my* books.' He did not greatly care for this imperious side to her nature. 'Look, come inside.'

'You should put on your head. Is better.'

'Not for me.'

He struggled through the doorway, put the box on the floor. 'I hope your father wasn't offended. If I'd known . . .'

'He not offend. He like you too much.'

'But he doesn't know me.'

'Everybody know College Whiteman. Especially now that he take house in town. You know what all the people are now calling you?' She studied him a moment then answered her own question in a guttural phrase from the vernacular.

He tried to translate. 'The Sunday Whiteman who . . . what?'

She looked away from him.

'Come on. What does it mean?'

'It means: the Sunday Whiteman who likes to taste palm-wine.'

'But I never touch the stuff.'

Her disdainful pout recommended that he be less obtuse. He remembered how figurative the language was, and what Odansey had said about the difference between marriage and palm-wine.

'I see.'

She permitted a long silence, holding his frown in a critical gaze, then relented. 'I think there is good film tonight. Is *High Society* starring Louis Armstrong and Grace Kelly. Also Bing Crosby and Frank Sinatra.'

He had intended to sort out his things but, after what had just happened between them in that silence, could not bear to disappoint her. 'Good. We'll go.'

Her smile lifted his heart. These sudden shifts of mood were quite extraordinary. It was like being surrounded by changeable weather.

'Is very nice film I think. Plenty music.'

'I could do with cheering up.'

'Why? What upset you?'

'Yesterday. The Party Rally . . .'

She frowned, looked away. 'I don't like to talk about politics.'

'Then we won't. We'll go to the film and have a good time, and come back here and do the thing. Two, maybe three times. What do you say?'

'You are disgraceful,' she replied. Then looked away again. 'My father say he would like to talk with you one time.'

He lit a cigarette. 'Fine. I'd like to meet him.'

'He don't speak English too good.'

'I see.'

'Even he don't speak it at all.'

'Then you will have to explain for me.'

'I don't think so. Maybe he will bring some friend.'

'You won't be there?'

'Is not woman's business,' she said mysteriously. 'I am now going. I will see you at The Star?'

Shortly after she had left, when he was still mulling over the undercurrents of their conversation, the telephone rang. It was Koranteng's secretary from the Palace. If it was convenient the Paramount Chief would be pleased to receive Mr Palmer at the Palace on the following afternoon. An informal visit, for drinks and a chat. After Mr Palmer had returned from the school perhaps, around five?

Palmer said he would be there. Since meeting Appaea his life, so long arrested, seemed suddenly to have accelerated. It was a little unnerving.

On weekday evenings The Star doubled as an open-air cinema, but that night the management had to announce a disappointment. *High Society* had failed to arrive. Instead they were shown an ancient western that seemed to have been stitched together from the reels of a serial made years before for children's Saturday morning film-clubs. The links between instalments involved some improbable flashbacks. Apart from that, Palmer's only entertainment lay in the way the crowd on the benched dance-floor below the balcony cheered and jeered at the events on the screen.

Then he was conscious of a movement behind him and someone leaning across the seats to speak.

'It's been a long time, Austin.'

He turned and took in the doleful smile of Henry Jalbout. He hadn't seen the old Lebanese since Henry had come in with Jamil several weeks before to check that the house was in good order and that Palmer had everything he needed. Palmer had felt guilty about him whenever he crossed his mind. 'Henry,' he said, 'how extraordinary – I was thinking of coming out to see you this weekend.' He was aware of Appaea sitting stiffly beside him in the darkness, laughing no longer. 'I don't think you know Appaea,' he said. 'This is Mr Jalbout, my landlord . . .'

'I had heard that you had taken a . . .friend,' Jalbout said. 'The nights are less lonely, eh?' He spoke as though Appaea were elsewhere, unconscious that he gave offence. Palmer could smell the liquor on his breath. 'My own wife should come again soon, if her health permits . . . She has not been well, you see.'

'I'm sorry to hear that.' Palmer's head was half-turned towards the screen where a fight was in progress, the crowd shouting with glee.

'It amuses them to see white men hit each other,' said Jalbout, 'but it's a poor film, no?'

'Terrible.'

'I had hoped to see you before this.' Jalbout's voice was reproachful.

'I've been very busy. I'm sorry . . .'

'Of course.'

There was a long pause. Palmer turned to the screen again and saw a chair shatter across a ten-gallon hat.

'Perhaps you will come this weekend after all?'

Palmer noticed that the invitation did not extend to Appaea, whose hand lay in his, taut as a knot. 'That would be nice.'

'I think so.'

Palmer thought that if the old Lebanese had made a single gesture of friendship, of true recognition even towards Appaea, he himself might have meant what he said. As it was, he felt only relief to hear Jalbout slip away a few minutes later.

When they got back to the house Appaea was in a villainous mood. It manifested itself as a morose silence interrupted by impatient sighs and an irritable toying with whatever came to hand.

'I don't like that man,' she said.

'He's been very generous to me. This is his house, you know.'

'I know. And what if he stop feeling generous? What then? Now you not got bungalow at the school no more?'

'That isn't going to happen.'

'I think maybe when he say "Come" you got to come now, eh?'

'I should go and see him anyway. I owe it to him. He's a lonely man.'

'And what you owe to me, eh? He don't ask me to come.'

'I know. I'm sorry.'

'English always sorry.'

'What else can I say? Come with me if you want. I'd rather you did.'

'I don't want. I don't like that man at all.'

'That's no reason to be sulky with me.'

She took the word as an insult, withdrew into an impermeable silence.

Disappointed with the waste of the evening, angry with Jalbout, with himself, with her, he started to remove books from a box. Nothing worked out in this bloody country. He could feel the old irritability jamming his mind. He felt like shouting, like throwing things about.

And this was not at all what he'd had in mind.

'Appaea,' he said, 'let's go to bed.'

'I don't want to do the thing in that man's bed.'

'I wish you wouldn't use that horrible expression.'

'I don't make English language.'

He shook his head in despair. 'It's making love, damn it. I think that's what you're forgetting.'

'What I forget now?'

He took a breath. 'You're forgetting that I care for you. I care for you very much.'

She snorted, unpersuaded.

He crossed the room, sat down beside her, took her hand. 'What is it? What's really the matter?'

'Is not true.'

'Of course, it's true. Why do you always make things hard for yourself?'

'Is not I who make things hard.'

'Well I didn't start this.'

'Go back to your books,' she said. She turned her head to stare at him, malicious almost. 'You understand book better than you understand love.'

'That's not fair.'

'Fair? What is fair? You don't love me.'

'Appaea, you know damn well I do.'

'Then why you don't say?'

'I thought I just did.'

'You say you care for me,' she said. 'Like I am small child.' She looked across at him, defiant, reproachful. 'I think because I don't talk smart like educated woman you think I am as small child. Not so?'

'No, not so,' he barked back, then looked up into her vulnerable eyes. Was it true? Had he allowed things to deepen so between them without ever acknowledging the change? As though, after the disaster with Kay, the very word had become a poisoned barb. And did he not know, secretly, what troubled her beyond that silence? Had his asking been anything more than an evasive shift of responsibility to her?

He experienced his confusion in silence for a time. Then he lifted her chin with his fingers, and whispered the words. Softly at first. Then again, firmly and clear, like a conjuration.

Later, in bed, he sought to prove with his body what the words avowed, but she was not wholly with him. If there was no refusal there was no complete acceptance either. She was withholding herself, almost perversely it seemed, until some

73

unspecified condition had been met. He was left feeling as though he had used her. He looked down on the closed lids of her eyes, frowning, then pulled himself away. She said nothing, did not move. He lay in his sweat, bitterly aware of the unaccomplished distances between them.

How many nights had he lain in silence so while Kay wept beside him, or assailed him with her rage and pain? He could feel an old dread gathering inside him. What did they want, these women? Why did they never accept things for what they were, cut their losses, be content with the modicum of pleasure life had to offer? English or African, somewhere they were all unappeasable. He could feel Appaea beside him now, mutely nursing her nameless expectations, wanting more of him, more than he knew how to give.

He closed his eyes against her, summoned sleep.

It was not sleep that came but the memory of Kay's voice beating in his head like a baleful angel's wings: *Can't you see what this place is doing to me? I never used to be like this, did I? And look what it's doing to you. I don't even know where you are any more. Sometimes I hardly recognize you. You sit there and say things but I can't feel you. You slide off somewhere on your own. Even now you're not really listening. Say something. Say something real to me. Please.*

Why had he never been able to say what she wanted to hear? There were reasons. He knew there had been good reasons. Yet the more urgently she demanded he speak, the less possible speech became. Again and again he had come to that barren place until finally, in the silence of his mind, he'd graced it with a name. He'd come to think of it as the Hurricane Room. For the misery between them had not only driven him away from his wife, it had prised a deep division inside himself. When Kay lashed out in her despair he'd learned to slip into a sort of padded cell within – a chamber where he was distantly aware of the violence of the elements outside, yet secure, untouched. Inside the Hurricane Room the mind drained itself of thought. One became an eavesdropper on someone else's hell; and if words did issue from him there, they had a curiously dead sound, like stones dropped down a shaft.

74

He had thought it long behind him – gone, with Kay and the need for such protection – yet he could feel its walls close round him now; still hear Kay's accusations ringing in his head: *You're not here, are you? You're somewhere safe, waiting for it to pass. You'll never come out when I need you. You won't give yourself because that's dangerous. It might make you feel something – really feel it. And then your safe little retreat might come crashing down – your common sense, your reasoning, your endless bloody rationalizations. Where are you? Where are you, for God's sake?*

He was in a silver bed, in another man's house, on the edge of Old Town; and beside him, remote as the most primitive tribeswoman, yet no more than a breath away, Appaea did not sleep. And such was the rise and fall of her breast, so great his need to feel at one again with the unexpected consolation of her presence, that he absented himself from absence, reached out a soft exploratory hand, and said – they might have been the only words he knew – 'Where are you now?'

She answered quietly, in statement rather than in reassurance, 'I am with you.'

He waited a long moment before breaching the silence again. 'And that is what you truly want?'

She sat up on the bed, her breasts falling, and leaned to press a cheek against her knees, holding her face away from him. Her hands were crossed at her ankles. Her body was entirely folded upon itself as she sighed – not in irritation or despair, though perhaps he deserved no less. 'For why you ask?'

His eyes were closed in the tight grip of his frown as he said, 'Because I don't think you know who I am.'

She turned to look down at him then. 'What is this nonsense?' Her eyes were troubled, her tone unsure.

'I mean it,' he said. 'I'm not sure who I am myself.'

'Then I will tell you. You are Sunday Whiteman – the one who like palm-wine.' She put a hand to his shoulder, shaking him, smiling, though she herself was heavy-hearted.

'That's just it. I know that name hurts you. I've already caused you pain, and I didn't know I was doing it. I don't want that. I don't want to do that.'

Even as he spoke he saw how futile the ambition was. For he had not meant to injure Kay, yet she had plumbed depths of wretchedness in their life together. And nothing – no plea of ignorance, no extenuating circumstance, no claim that there must have been some flaw in her own temperament to make her suffer so – nothing finally absolved him of responsibility for that hurt. Haggard-eyed, he looked up at Appaea. 'I warn you,' he said, 'I damage everything I touch.'

She was angry with him now. 'So what you go do?' When he gave no answer she supplied her own. 'You want me go way? You think that don't cause me pain? You want me go stay for my father's house like your wife go stay for her town, eh? Tell me, white man, what is you want?' She paused, waiting for an affirmation that did not come, and then, with the inspiration of her anger, added, 'You want to be alone like the tortoise who bears his coffin on his back and belongs to no clan, eh?'

It was too close. His breath stopped in his throat. For a moment he couldn't swallow. As he turned towards her she saw him fighting to breathe, and she held him tightly for a long time, rocking his heavy body in her embrace. How this man hurt! What harm, what foolish harm he did to himself!

'I don't think it is truly you who talk,' she said softly. 'I think is the night talk in you. When I was small girl my mother say to me that some time in the night bad spirits come. Is they who sip at the palm-wine and take all the good taste from it so is bitter to the mouth. I think maybe they come here this night because I don't be with you proper. I think they have see you are alone and come to steal the courage from your heart.' She took his chin in her hand and turned his face up towards her. 'I don't think is good to live alone, eh? I don't think is good at all.'

Astonishingly he talked and talked – a long, sometimes faltering, often painful, but surely cleansing admission of his failure in Africa with Kay. It was as though he had emerged from a dark trance at Appaea's call, only to step, tentatively at first, and then with greater daring, into another more luminous state of trance. But it was fluid now, not fixed. Had he not once dreamed of such release, long before, on Appaea's first visit to this house? Surely it must be possible now? It was necessity.

Appaea lay beside him in the darkness watching him smoke cigarette after cigarette, listening in wonder and some perplexity to this elusive, complicated man who was suddenly talking so urgently to her; and yet not to her. To himself, or to the Mother in him perhaps? Or to whatever invisible presences attend upon unhappy men. She too heard the drum, and recognized another lonely soul somewhere, rehearsing his complaint to the night. But this white man talked of troubles so far removed from her experience that she could only nod and mutter small noises of encouragement when he seemed to falter, and hold him at moments when she felt his need, and trust that the tenderness that was in her heart for him would help him through the forest of his dreams.

And somewhere also she was a little afraid, for there was so much anger in him. He was like a man who had forced an entry to the spirit realm in search of what was lost, or stolen from him, by light of day. And what a bush of ghosts he seemed to carry there inside him, what strange misapprehensions of the stuff of which a woman's world is made!

It was already far into the night when he stubbed out the last of his too-many cigarettes, looked up, and smiled at her – a dazed, oddly innocent resumption of the face he wore when it was easiest to see him and to love this man. She saw there was no further need for words, that the spirits of the night had passed and he was simply present to her now. Soon the cockerels would crow across the town. With the new day a richer life would be possible between them. She answered his smile; then slowly, gravely even, with the timidity of beginners, they moved anew into each other's arms.

Shortly before five Palmer parked his car in the square outside the King's Palace. An old man with a face as black and solemn as the Bible pulled himself up from where he had been resting in the shade, hitched the folds of his toga, and saluted like a corporal. 'You are welcome, Mr Palmer. Please.' He gestured towards a great carved door, ushered the visitor through and led him along the dusty warren of ante-chambers.

It was as well, Palmer thought, that he had been met, for he would never have found his way alone through those many passages and rooms – just as once, he supposed, others must have found it impossible to escape.

They stepped out into the light of one of the many compounds, climbed a timber staircase and passed along a sheltered gallery. Its roofposts were intricately carved with totems – apes, hornbills, an armed hunter, a fetish-priest holding a snake by the head. Palmer's guide opened a mosquito-proofed door and he was shown into a large reception chamber he had not entered before. 'You must wait here,' the African said, and left, only to return a little later with a tray of green beer bottles and three large glasses. He stood nodding in approval for a moment, then disappeared again. His gesture had invited the guest to help himself.

That third glass?

Palmer had his ideas.

There was no fan, but an open door on the outer wall kept the room reasonably aired. It led on to a balcony larger than his own, overlooking the ironstone altar in the square outside. Soft chairs were arranged around the wall as though tediously awaiting a meeting. On a long, low central table the enormous skull of a crocodile had been mounted. It grinned, monstrous and primitive. A fetish perhaps? Or a curiosity of no more account than a stuffed pike in a village pub back home?

The walls were hung with photographs – old sepia prints of Koranteng's ancestors, in full regalia, glowering out of heavy frames. In the bizarre company of those vanished tribal kings the official photograph of the President gave the clear impression of a supremely confident winner among a crowd of bad losers. Palmer studied that face for a time, as though the answers to his many questions about the state of things might lie there. It remained enigmatic as ever. In any case, the Englishman had other pressing matters on his mind.

He sat down and sipped his beer. He watched the gradual shift of shadows round the room, thinking that he should have known better than to be on time. He kept looking at that third glass, growing more uneasy about the forthcoming interview the longer it was delayed.

But he stood, smiling, when eventually the mosquito-door swung open and Koranteng came in, a well-tailored shirt flapping loose over dark blue cotton trousers, an expensive wristwatch strapped where bangles had hung before. 'Austin, dear fellow. So sorry to have kept you hanging about. Something came up and I had to deal with it – the poor devil had walked nearly twenty miles in this damned heat. Couldn't put him off. Look, do sit down. Don't stand on ceremony, please . . .'

Another much older man slipped off his sandals at the door and came in. Bald-headed, bald as a rock – but no, not, as Palmer had anticipated, Appaea's father. He picked up a bottle of beer and settled himself in a corner of the room, studying Palmer sombrely for a moment from under a ruckled brow.

'You remember Bonsu?' Koranteng said. 'My Spokesman, Chief Minister of State?'

Palmer smiled in acknowledgment and the old man held his glass up high and cracked his mouth in a wide grin. 'Bottom Zup?' he suggested, nodding his head and rasping the free hand across his chin.

'Bottoms up,' Palmer confirmed, remembering with some gratitude that the old Spokesman's English stretched little further.

Social duty done, Bonsu withdrew inwards upon himself, eyes closed, curling and uncurling his toes.

Koranteng had slumped into a leather chair. 'My God, it's good to see you again. I thought you'd buried yourself alive out there in the bush. Not that I could blame you. I've been going slightly crazy myself. Times are hard, Austin, and getting harder.'

'I was worried about you the other day. At the Durbar. That regalia must weigh a ton.'

'The cares of state weigh heavier, friend.' Koranteng hesitated. Palmer sensed the African assessing him, like a man casting the waters. 'Do you know why I was detained this afternoon? Of course you don't – you think I'm just a lazy coon with no sense of time, I know. Well, you may be right, but not today. Not today.'

'What happened?'

Koranteng's humour evaporated. He was a tired man seeking relief from burdensome pressure. 'The headman of one of the outlying villages came in to see me. Yesterday some of the DC's minions drove into his village and informed him that a new tax had been imposed. Every household had to cough up a shilling or an egg. They paid up but it sounded fishy so he came into town to check. Of course, there's no such tax.' Koranteng took in the dismay on his friend's face. 'It's not the first time this sort of thing has happened. Nor is that the half of it. I'm building up a dossier, but for the moment . . .' He sighed, gestured, empty-handed. 'Colonialism corrupts, and we are still colonized. I doubt the infection will ever clear.'

'I knew Krobo wasn't up to the job,' Palmer said, 'but I didn't realize how bad things were.' Another thought struck him. 'Does Odansey know about this?'

'I doubt it. But then he has bigger fish to fry.' Koranteng began to cough, a convulsive upheaval of his lungs, parched and abrasive. He fumbled for a handkerchief and held it to his lips. A long draught of beer cleared his throat, and he smacked his lips as though nothing untoward had occurred. 'There is a lorry in town,' he said. 'On its side is written THEY HAVE JESUS FACES BUT STANDARD INTENTION. You must have seen it?'

'It makes me feel guilty every time I do.'

Koranteng laughed. 'Me too. But he's a wise man, that driver. I'm afraid the more one has of freedom the more of a problem it becomes. I found that out to my cost in the UK as a mere boy – practically squandered the cupboard bare. No doubt by now you have heard the rumours of my misspent youth. They are true – all of them. But our new masters . . . My dear, one feels an absolute beginner.'

But Palmer's mind was darkened by Koranteng's levity. And troubled too at the thought of his friend's life here at the Palace, circumscribed as it was by a round of obsolete ritual, the daily roster of unrightable wrongs, interminable palavers. It must spell captivity to a man who had tasted life beyond the tedium of the forest and learned to look upon himself as a hopeless anachronism.

'In the meantime,' Koranteng was saying, 'we must watch and wait. And one mustn't cry in one's beer. I had my chance in the UK and I took it. Of course, the sons of oil-sheikhs and rajahs could afford to stay the course. But it was fun while it lasted. You must remember that next time you see me decked out like a stegosaurus in my regalia. But what about you?' His face was suddenly more serious. 'Kay is long gone, I hear.'

Palmer nodded.

'Sad. Pitifully sad. You should have come to me sooner . . . Not that I could have helped. This place is no good for the women, you know. Particularly those with a bit of spark in them. I've seen it before. In colonial days – a DC's wife. Poor thing cut her wrists. They saved her, of course. Hushed it up. Shipped her back. Tropical neurasthenia, I think they called it – you see, even the name leaked out. Nothing is secret here. This town is as preoccupied with its own events as a dog with its fleas . . . Such a cold name, I thought, for such a wretched condition. I rather liked her. Kay too . . . I always regret not seeing her give Odansey a flea in his ear about the Preventive Detention Act.' But he looked up and saw his friend's discomfort. 'You decided not to go back yourself then?'

'There was no point. It was finished. We'd hurt one another too much.'

'I see.' Koranteng shook his head. 'This bloody hole! Snakes, soldier-ants, tsetse, bilharzia, blackwater fever, kwashiorkor . . . only the shit prospers here. You should have gone, my friend. Kay may have been right . . . This place soon won't be worth living in.'

'I don't feel that way,' Palmer said quietly.

Koranteng looked across at him, shrewd, a little critical perhaps. 'You have taken a place in town, I believe?'

'Henry Jalbout offered it to me. It seemed like a good idea.'

'Rent-free too. A small miracle that. And there is a girl?'

Palmer held the African's gaze. 'Yes.'

Koranteng tapped his lip with a ringed index finger. In the square outside a pye-dog yapped. They heard the thud of a vulture alighting on the iron roof above them.

'You know her father,' Palmer said. 'That *is* why you asked me to come, isn't it?'

'Not entirely. Not entirely. I do enjoy your company, you know. But yes . . . I thought a word to the wise might not go amiss. We are friends?'

'Verily, O King. But you are not my Dutch uncle.'

Koranteng laughed, and his laugh became a cough, a further violent convulsion of his body. He did not quite conceal the blood-fleck on his handkerchief. When he had recovered he said, with exaggerated sombreness, 'You do realize that my forebears would have regarded that as a grave insult?'

'Not so grave as your insults to your heath,' Palmer ventured with real concern, for during the coughing fit Koranteng's skin had faded to an elephant-grey. 'Have you been to a specialist yet?'

'It would serve no purpose.'

'Don't be a damned fool.'

'We Africans do not greatly care for that word, Austin.'

'What about care for yourself? Perhaps you're right about this place – for you, that is. This climate can't help. You should go somewhere you can convalesce, recoup your strength.'

'Switzerland perhaps? Only the Mr Christians of this world can afford such luxuries these days.'

'Surely money could be raised. I could . . .'

But Koranteng forestalled him. 'I'm touched by your concern, but that's not quite the point. However foolish the notion may be, I like to think that I am needed here.'

'You're needed here alive and well. If you carry on like this you'll be no use to anyone.'

Koranteng raised the ringed finger. 'Be careful, Austin.' But then he relaxed, smiled again. 'Here is an African riddle for you: *There is a medicine we all must take – yet when it is drunk it must not touch the mouth, it must not touch the teeth, it must not touch the tongue. What is it?*'

'It's not the medicine you need. Not for a long time yet.'

'Now who is being the Dutch uncle? We have a proverb

also: *The long-awaited arrives late; Death will come, but it chooses its own time.*'

'Fatalism.'

'Or wisdom?' Koranteng gave a comical grimace. 'Anyway I may have a trick or two up my sleeve before I go.' He pulled at his beer, looked across at the corner where Bonsu sat rocking his head as though disturbed by the vibrations of this encounter. The old man inserted the peremptory croak of his voice into the silence. There was an exchange between him and Koranteng, then the King nodded and turned back to the Englishman. 'Bonsu thinks that another of our proverbs might help you. He says when the palm tree tilts it is because of what the earth has told it.' He smiled at Palmer's wry shaking of the head. 'Bonsu also reminds me that this is not the point of our conversation. I'm going to turn the tables on you. The girl?'

Palmer waited.

'As you say, I know her father. Komla Odum is one of my retainers. I am accountable to him.'

'Not for me, I hope?'

'For the welfare of his family. He would like to know . . . I'm not quite sure how to put this . . . what your intentions are towards his daughter?'

Palmer savoured his friend's embarrassment for a time.

'You see,' Koranteng added, 'people have begun to talk.'

'The Sunday Whiteman who likes to taste palm-wine?'

'You have heard, then?'

'Appaea has a tongue of her own.'

'What African woman does not, my friend?' Koranteng sighed from the depths of his experience. 'However, she does not only speak for herself. There is the honour of her family to consider. Have you thought about that?'

For an instant an image of the labyrinth of dusty passages between himself and the outside world filled Palmer's mind, but he quickly dispelled it.

'I feel dreadful about this,' Koranteng conceded uncomfortably, 'but I'm afraid it's a case of *noblesse oblige* – never my favourite tipple.' He cleared his throat. 'You could always leave her alone. There *are* others. Equally attractive. If you like, I . . .'

'It's not like that.'

'I see,' Koranteng said, and frowned.

'The fact of the matter is, I half expected Appaea's father to be here this afternoon.'

'He is waiting downstairs. I thought it best : . . The girl is here too. In the women's compound.'

Palmer nodded and looked down at his sandalled feet. 'I don't know if you will understand this,' he said, 'but I need her. I need her very much.'

Koranteng raised his brow. 'The girl has a certain way with her . . .'

'It's more than that. I think she may have saved my sanity.'

The room was quickly darkening. Bonsu got up and put a match to a kerosine lantern and placed it on the table beside the head of the crocodile, which grinned up at Palmer – who looked down into those mantrap jaws for a moment, then back to study the effect of his last remark on Koranteng.

The African's frown was troubled and uncertain. 'Were things that bad?'

'I hadn't realized myself until . . .' Gratefully Palmer reached to take the proffered cigarette and light. 'You really shouldn't smoke these, you know.'

'I know. Go on.'

'I was frozen, inside . . . after Kay had gone. Sounds strange, doesn't it? In this heat, I mean. But I was. Half out of my mind really. I think I may have been that way for a long time. No good to anyone. To Kay. Myself . . .And, Appaea – she's very special . . . She matters to me. She makes me feel alive again.'

He looked up in the light of the lantern.

'Then what is to be done, my friend?' Koranteng's face was so solemn as to be almost comical. His eyes widened and narrowed again. He was, for all the world, like a contemplative bullfrog.

Palmer found himself smiling.

'The honourable thing?' he suggested.

Koranteng cleared his throat, drew on his cigarette, examined it with distaste. 'You are not expected to marry the girl, of course. Not legally, that is . . . But if this thing is to continue she must be a little more than . . .' He hesitated. 'Oh dear . . . You take my point, I think?'

'I want her with me.'

'But you should think about this, no?'

'I have. And I'd rather you didn't try to talk me out of it.'

Koranteng grunted deep in his throat. 'Austin, I have never thought of you as a casual man; but I wonder if . . .' He looked up and saw that no searching questions, however well-intentioned, would be welcome. 'And one has to think of the girl too,' he said.

'I do. All the time.'

Slowly, thoughtfully, the African answered Palmer's smile. 'What a romantic you are! You will take her to live with you then? As your wife? African-style, I mean?'

Palmer smiled more broadly. 'I might even take better care of her than that.'

Koranteng shrugged, opened his hands. 'Then I suppose congratulations are in order. Welcome to my tribe, dear man. I shall expect a little more respect henceforth.'

'You've always had that.'

'And there will be a few formalities, of course. Gifts for her father, I mean. Bride-price, you know?'

'Of course. What do you suggest?'

'A crate of Schnapps would go down well for starters.' Koranteng hesitated, smiled, 'But the thing is, he'd rather like a TV set – if you could run to that?'

'Surely, but . . . electricity?'

'I know. I did point that out. But Odum is a patient man. He says he's prepared to wait for the cables to reach Old Town. No one else up here has one yet, you see.'

'You've discussed this with him already, then?'

'Of course, though no doubt he'll add to his shopping list when he hears the news. Also a goat or two will have to be sacrificed. I can supply the goats. However, you *will* have to slaughter them yourself.' He took in Palmer's dubious frown. 'You're quite sure that you want to go through with this?'

Palmer drew deeply on his cigarette. 'And her mother?' he asked. 'Wouldn't something be appropriate?'

'If you are feeling generous.'

'I am.'

'A bolt of cloth? Some expensive soap? That kind of thing.'

'I think I'm getting the best of the bargain.'

'Such innocence! You do realize that you are acquiring a whole family with your new wife? I promise you, that can prove expensive.'

'I earn far more than I need these days.'

'For now perhaps. But should you ever return to the UK?'

'I shan't do that.'

So certain was Palmer's reply that, for a moment, Koranteng thought he had heard not a promise but a prophecy. 'Austin,' he said quietly, 'after what you have been through . . . You said yourself you were . . .' He faltered, coughing a little, then looked up from his handkerchief. 'Marriage and palm-wine are not the same thing, you know.'

'So Mr Christian tells me.'

Koranteng saw from Palmer's smile and the studied lightness of his tone that further attempts to counsel would be fruitless and embarrassing. 'And he should certainly know!' he answered. 'Have you met his wife?' Koranteng rolled his eyes. 'A caramel dragon! Thank God she insists on staying in Badagry. The politicians I can just about endure, but their wives . . God shield us! Still, each man to his own cross, I suppose. Now you must excuse me while I break the good news to Bonsu. Then I think we will get drunk small, eh? Before you join your new-found family. It will help you to cope with the noise and libations and what-have-you downstairs. Not to mention the jokes. I don't usually enjoy this kind of thing, but . . .'

'As it's at my expense?'

'Not at all. Not at all. I'm delighted for you, dear fellow. Truly. I am.' Then the King turned away and spoke to his beaming Chief Minister in their own language – a language that one day, Palmer promised himself, he really must learn.

Afterwards the rites of that weekend were no more than a colourful blur in Palmer's mind. Almost from the first he had been very drunk – not from choice, but of necessity, for it was impossible to refuse the vast quantity of alcohol pressed upon him. Nor was he ungrateful, for he could conceive of no other condition in which he might cheerfully have drawn a blade across the throat of a tethered, bleating goat.

But he would never forget the first heart-stopping sight of Appaea in traditional dress, untypically silent, shy and demure among her sisters and her friends.

And he remembered the noise and the smell of sweat in the palace-compound, the music and the dance. He remembered the many libations poured into the dust, the invocations of the fetish-priest and priestesses, and the crackle of fat in the fire from which smoke rose, stinging his eyes and watering his mouth with the taste of night barbecued in spices. He remembered some of the faces and few of the names of Appaea's – of *his* – enormous family; her sisters, Adowa and Lovia, and her parents – the mother, plump, chuckling, a little bossy perhaps, particularly when unconvinced that some feature of the festal proceedings might not have been improved upon; the old man, proud and garrulous, boasting to all who would listen, and many who did not, of what his youngest daughter's incomparable beauty had achieved. And even more, perhaps, of the splendour of his TV set which had arrived, amazingly, by lorry, intact and on time – a splendour evidently undiminished by its silence and the sightless gape of its screen.

He remembered the bewildered but benevolent smile of the headmaster, observing his senior English teacher in this unanticipated context, and Mrs Quagrainie's freely-rolling tears as she clasped the groom to her bosom, then retired into the throng, content and shining, modest as the moon by day. Coastal people, the couple were foreigners, to the local language and customs, and had not stayed long, but Palmer was grateful for their blessing. Samuel and Efwa Opambo remained much longer, waltzing together when the music allowed, or thrusting their generous hips outrageously towards each other when a wilder rhythm was encouraged. They assured Palmer that his new wife's pelvic girdle promised large numbers of children who would all, no doubt, combine their father's intellectual capacity with their mother's sweetness of temper.

Less expectedly, he remembered the haughty presence of an old lady with the face of an empress, presiding as of right over the women's side of the celebrations. Through bleak, critical eyes she studied the bridegroom long and often. He asked in a whisper who she was, and Appaea – in an even more awestruck whisper – informed him that this was the Queen-Mother. Later, peeing under the stars with Koranteng, Palmer had congratulated the King on his impressive mother. After a moment's confusion Koranteng muttered in a gin-bleary, deferential hiss that this she-eagle of a woman was not *his* mother, but the Mother of the tribe, the present incarnation of the Triple Goddess, and – the hiss sank even lower – among the gods there was none greater. What did Austin think this whole elaborate commotion had been about if not to ask Her mercy on the bride and groom?

He remembered falling into the suddenly unstable silver bed to the accompaniment of a vigorous and bawdy clamour from the square outside; and waking very late the next day to a thunderous head and the sound of Appaea berating Mamadou in the kitchen-quarters below.

He remembered vaguely also that he had promised to visit Henry Jalbout that weekend, before he turned in the bed and surrendered to a profound and complicated sleep.

The rains were late that year and the land languished under a poultice of hot dust. Palmer found himself sipping at a furnace-mouth for air, sweat running like lice about his body, his shirt already soaked by the time he arrived out at the school.

Clouds, trees, the dogs around the compound, all were stuck fast in the ache of it. Everyone was fractious, for the long hours in the classroom turned on a slow spit. Staff-meetings were cursory and bad-tempered affairs. Even Mr Quagrainie's equanimity turned tinder in the heat. He carped at the laxity of the staff, complained that the dormitories were pigsties, the latrines an abomination, insisted on fastidious, military inspections.

Shortly after hearing that Palmer had taken a new wife, Sal Rodriguez fell mysteriously ill. Subrahmaniam, the little Sinhalese doctor from the town's small hospital, came out to see him briefly and left perplexed. 'He tells me I should drink less gin,' Rodriguez said wanly to Palmer, who sat beside the rumpled bed afterwards. 'I think that mongoose wants me to die so he can probe about at leisure inspecting my pipes. I shan't give him the satisfaction. And you, Austin? Is married life good for the health? Found any hairs in your food yet?'

'Hairs?'

'The pubic variety. I can't remember whether it was Opambo who told me . . . might have been Henry . . . Anyway, it's not unknown for the local ladies to shred some of their pubic hair into their husband's food. A charm! Keeps them faithful, they say.'

'There's no need for that.' Palmer deliberately left unclear whether he spoke of the love-potion or the Indian's droll comments on his marriage.

Sal's sickness meant that Palmer had to work all the harder, and that other staff-members lost free periods too. And if the staff were half-mutinous the students were more so. It was not merely the heat that bore down upon them. Prices were rising almost daily. More stringent economies were forced on the school. The quality of food in the dining-hall deteriorated, and there was less of it. When chemicals were exhausted in the labs they could not be replaced. The generator was switched off except at night.

In the run-up to the referendum the political climate also became more oppressive – it was now too hot to handle in conversation at the school. There were more arrests of lecturers and students at the University, and the fact that a couple of flagrantly corrupt Party officials in the far north were also detained did little to dispel the growing unease. On the political question Palmer was completely gravelled now.

Nor was home life quite as he had expected. Too often he found himself returning to quarrels between Appaea and Mamadou – though the servant's part in these affrays was little more than a resentful silence. For a man who had come with excellent references, it was hard now to take orders from a woman whom he regarded as less than his peer, particularly orders which relegated him to the most menial of tasks. These days he regarded his master with glum, reproachful eyes.

'I don't know for why you pay that Muslim man,' Appaea complained. 'Every day when you at the school he insult me.'

'What's he said?'

'He don't say, but he got evil eyes. I think is best we tell him pack and go, and get one small boy for do his work.'

However, Palmer would not concede on this. He was held to Mamadou by bonds of loyalty, and knew that Appaea was thinking more of money than of justice. Also a little familiar male companionship about the place did something to offset the frequent gatherings of Appaea's sisters and friends who preferred, understandably enough, to converse in their own tongue. Unless, of course, he agreed to take part in their long, squabbling games of Monopoly – a diversion which soon cloyed.

He asked Appaea to be more patient with Mamadou, a little more considerate of the man's feelings. Yet such disagreements threw a pall of silence over their life for an hour or two, and he hated that. Eventually he saw there was nothing to do but leave Appaea to make her own way back towards him. Sometimes it was disconcertingly perverse.

'I think you are too fond of that Comfort Okelo.'

'I beg your pardon.'

'You have heard what I say.'

He had been enthusing over this star-student's remarkable flair for poetry earlier that evening. He looked up from his tedious pile of marking now. 'I think you're being . . .' He was about to say 'silly', but remembered in time how deeply the epithet would have offended her.

'Yes, what do you think? Tell me.'

'. . . . over-sensitive.'

'What is that – over-sensitive?'

'I think you're jealous,' he said, smiling.

'Is not I who am jealous. Is you who are unfaithful.'

He sighed. 'You know that's not true.'

'You think I don't get eyes.'

'Beautiful eyes – but sometimes they glow green.'

She did not understand the inference, and disdained it.

'You don't think she is pretty?'

'Yes, she's pretty.'

'And smart?'

'That too.' He scowled to see that the sweat on his wrist had smudged the exercise book.

'So.'

'So what?'

'So I think you want to do the thing with her.'

'That's ridiculous.'

'You see – you think I am ridiculous.'

'Not you – what you're saying.'

'Ha, that's because I'm not smart, eh? Like Comfort Okelo.'

If he was not careful this might go on all night. He put down his pen, turned to face her. 'Appaea, I don't give a damn about Comfort Okelo except that she's a good student. You're the only woman in my life. Okay? Now if you'll just give me a chance to finish this marking . . .'

She returned to her sewing. He picked up the pen again, scribbled a gamma in the margin.

'You don't think that I too can write a poem if I get time to do that thing?'

'I'm sure you could.' He opened the next essay.

'Even I will try.'

'What will you write about?' he asked, abstractedly.

'I think I will write some poem about a Sunday Whiteman who come to the forest and take African woman for wife and then it get too hot and then . . .'

'What then?' He drew a red ring round a spelling error.

'Then he go to sleep.'

It took a moment for the remark to sink in. He looked up again.

'So the African woman she say to herself; even a husband who sleep all the time is no good at all. I think maybe we need some loud noise here.'

'So she interrupts him while he's trying to work by talking all the time, I suppose?'

'No, that is not in my poem. No, this African woman talk to herself, and she say; maybe this Sunday Whiteman don't go to sleep all the time and dream dreams about doing the thing with other woman if there were some baby in the house? That would make plenty noise, she think.'

He looked up from the essay, stunned.

'And maybe perhaps this baby is real smart baby because he get born with book all around him and because his mother like to tell him good proverb and stories like her mother have told her. So he grow up very fast and talk like book, and soon his father . . .'

'Appaea, are you pregnant?'

She looked back at him, as though in surprise. 'I?' She bit off the cotton with her teeth. 'I only writing some poem. Is interesting, eh?'

'But . . .'

She gazed at him unhelpfully.

'What are you telling me?'

Then she smiled. 'Ah – I think maybe the Sunday Whiteman have woke up, eh?'

For a moment the breath in his throat could shape no words. A hot flare was shooting through the sky inside him. He was utterly unprepared for this.

'Appaea, I didn't know . . .'

She held him for a long moment in those black, suddenly docile eyes, then solemnly shook her head. A hand reached out for him, and her face dissolved into a smile that became a laugh; a strong, full-throated laugh at his stupidity, his Englishness, the sudden transparency of the adult male become a child.

'White man,' she said, 'you don't know what you don't know.'

The time came for the senior class to take their mock-examinations in preparation for O Level. The headmaster had put Palmer in charge of the arrangements, and the day before the first paper he was to supervise the class as they moved their desks into the Assembly Hall. 'Okay, ladies and gentlemen,' he said as he entered the classroom. 'Judgment Day tomorrow. Let's prepare ourselves in an orderly manner, shall we? Front row, take up thy desks and walk.'

Nobody moved.

He was confronted by a room of silent, truculent, and one or two nervous, faces.

'Come on, you heard me.'

The room was a cube of heat in which nothing stirred.

'All right, what's going on?'

Charles Smart – perhaps the most intelligent student in the room, the one for whom Palmer had the highest ambitions – stood at his desk. 'Please, we have been deciding that these mock-examinations are a waste of time.'

Palmer studied the nodding heads before him. 'I think,' he said, 'that you would be wiser to trust our judgment about that. Now come on. Move.' His tone became more peremptory. But ineffective.

'Comfort?' he appealed to the girl in the front row, who blushed and looked away.

Seth Otoo, soccer-captain, house-prefect, rose to his feet. This class had received such poor teaching in the early days of the school, he complained, that they still felt unprepared. They did not want to lose valuable class-time, for which they paid high fees, by sitting mock-exams. They demanded more instruction for the real thing.

For all Palmer's efforts to reason with them they refused to move their desks through into the examination hall. It was only when the formidable senior housemaster heard what was happening and came to Palmer's assistance, crashing a cane down across a desk-top, that they complied. The desks were moved, but mutinously. All that afternoon the school was untypically sullen.

Palmer was on prep-duty that night and so stayed out on the compound. While waiting for the students to finish supper he was talking the matter over with Sal Rodriguez when the school-messenger came running across the compound summoning help.

As he stepped outside Sal's bungalow he heard the din from the dining-hall, the smash of crockery and the harsh clatter of knives and spoons against a pandemonium of screams and shouting. He had to push his way into the hall through a flock of girls squealing as they fled like panicked geese back to their dormitory. He recoiled at the stench of sweat and food – a stale, unsavoury gruel had been splashed around the room. The hall was in darkness, the bulbs smashed. In the moonlight seeping through the windows he could make out only the dim shapes of figures writhing in the gloom – some standing on tables, others pushing and cowering below, half swept-up in the frenzy, half terrified at the violence around them. Opambo, grim-faced, stepped past him with a kerosine lantern in one hand and a length of bamboo in the other. In the glow of the lantern Palmer saw Mr Quagrainie pushing boys towards the door, shouting threats and commands in a still-cultured, utterly irrelevant English.

He heard the swish of Opambo's bamboo and a startled yelp of pain. Then the sudden sting of a dry crust of bread on his eye sparked a vengeful fury inside him. He stepped into the confusion, feeling the crunch of glass beneath his feet, cuffing at ears and noses, roaring without thought for what he roared, and taking a horrid delight in the fear and panic in the faces wilting before him.

It took twenty minutes to clear the dining-hall and get the students back into the dormitories for roll-call. They were restless and truculent still, dazed by their own violence. Palmer stood, trembling and sick at heart, in the shambles of the refectory. With a frown of pained bewilderment, Mr Quagrainie picked up and displayed a twisted spoon. 'I have heard of this kind of thing elsewhere,' he said, '. . . but that it should happen here, in my school . . .'

Appaea listened in amazement to Palmer's account of the riot. 'I think is because is too hot and they study book too much,' she said.

'It's because they don't study books enough,' he retorted. 'They were like animals.' However his heat was, in large measure, shame at his own unexpected violence. It had possessed him from nowhere and left him a stranger to himself.

'Anyway,' Appaea said. 'I don't think they should have builded the school in that place.'

'Why not? What's that got to do with it?'

'Is not good place,' she said quietly. 'I glad we don't get house there.'

He looked at her in bewilderment. Sometimes she was incomprehensible to him. She saw the impatience in his eyes.

'Is bad spirits in that part of the forest,' she declared.

At any other time he might have laughed dismissively. Now he remembered how the girls out at the school had once believed themselves possessed by evil spirits. He recalled the malevolent devil-mask on the wall of Jalbout's house, and the glum conviction in Fuseini's face as he talked of juju. Of course sorcery was alive in Africa – Palmer had known it for a long time – and there was no reason why Appaea should be free from the superstitions of her tribe. He'd teased her about them often enough. Yet as he looked at her now he saw a stranger where his wife had been – a sullen-faced African woman remote inside her own locked mind.

The headmaster's outraged homily at assembly the next morning was an ineffectual attempt to inspire shame and remorse. The senior class did not appear in the hall for the first examination.

Mr Quagrainie stood, stone-faced, looking at the ranks of empty desks like the host of a poorly-attended party. A breeze stirred one of the papers and lifted it from desk to floor with a vapid crackle. The headmaster's eyes flickered uncertainly from Palmer to the senior housemaster. Then he clapped his hands together, as though at that signal the will he needed would spring like a genie to his feet. He frowned, turned on his heel and walked across the compound. Minutes later he returned alone.

'They are gathered in the classroom block,' he said. 'I have informed them that if they are not at their desks in ten minutes the entire class will be suspended from school.' The firmness in his voice dissolved into a sigh. 'I do not like to do this,' he added unhappily, 'but they leave me no choice. If I have to return across the compound I would be grateful for your assistance.'

'Perhaps if I were to talk to them?' Palmer suggested.

'I have already made the position clear.'

'We must regard this as part of their education,' the senior housemaster agreed.

And so they watched the clock's slow progress, the senior housemaster at the desk browsing through Palmer's English paper, Mr Quagrainie humming without tune or continuity, Palmer staring across the compound from the open door, wondering what had become of his beliefs.

When the three crossed the compound and entered the classroom a loud debate abruptly expired. In the hush the headmaster frowned at the delinquent students, selecting his words. 'I did not think you were so foolish. But you have made your choice. Very well. You will now pack your boxes and go. When you have cooled your heads and are ready to sit your examinations – shall we say, in two weeks' time? – we will send for you.'

One of the boys made as if to speak, clearly about to break solidarity.

'It is too late for that now,' the headmaster snapped, transported at last into genuine anger. 'Last night you were savages. Today you are fools. Go home. Your presence in my school offends me. Be gone, I say.'

After a moment's astonished hesitation the students filed from the room. When the last of them had left the sternness faded from Mr Quagrainie's features, and he began to shake his head.

'There was nothing else you could do,' said Palmer.

'This is as much our failure as theirs,' the headmaster answered. 'It should never have happened. I shall have to report to the Governors. The DC will not be happy about this. As you know, his nephew is in the group.' He stood in silence, surveying the ceiling as though looking for rain-damage. 'Still, he is a reasonable man,' he added without conviction. 'He will understand that they left me no choice.'

The rebel students left the compound quietly enough during the next hour on two lorries summoned from town. The rest of the school pursued its routine, tensely obedient. A number of fourth-formers were temporarily appointed prefects to supervise the now decapitated school houses.

Late in the afternoon the headmaster announced that there was to be an emergency staff-meeting that evening. Krobo Mansa had run up from the town demanding to know what was happening. Mr Quagrainie, the initiative lost, had decided to rally his staff around him for the confrontation to come. 'I shall expect you to remain on the compound this evening, Mr Palmer,' he said. 'You are a principal witness to this affair.'

The students had left the dining-hall and were drifting into prep when the staff gathered outside the headmaster's office. Unwilling to miss what he called 'the first bit of excitement in this damned hole since the girls were goosed by the Holy Ghost', Sal Rodriguez had abandoned his sick-bed for the occasion, and was looking remarkably spry. 'Where tact and diplomacy are concerned,' he said, 'the DC is a charging rhino. This really could be quite diverting.'

Opambo, who all afternoon had been muttering sombrely about the Rubicon, said, 'We shall see the quills of the Porcupine tonight. There's going to be big trouble. Mark my words.' He rolled his eyes and fell silent as the headmaster joined them, unsuccessfully trying to mask his apprehension. The staff entered his office and sat in their customary circle, unusually silent. They were up against the Party now.

Mr Quagrainie inspected his watch again. 'The DC seems to be exercising the politician's prerogative of unpunctuality,' he said, and ended his sentence with a poor imitation of a laugh.

'Perhaps he has thought better of it?' the senior housemaster offered dubiously. However at that moment they heard the sound of lorries pulling up the drive and a raucous din of shouting and singing. The students in prep scraped and banged their desks as they rushed to see what was happening and, suddenly, beyond the staff's ring of startled faces, there was uproar.

'What the devil is happening now?' Mr Quagrainie snapped, and led his staff outside. A lorry skidded to a halt in the gravel and students who had left the compound that morning leapt from the sides, chanting a slogan in their own tongue, like a rugby team returning from victory. The words ALONE WITH GOD IS MAJORITY were painted over the cab of the lorry. Another truck – KILL ME AND FLY – pulled up. More of the rebels piled out, shouting to the students who had rushed from prep to meet them, laughing, jeering, spoiling for trouble.

Opambo, his eyes aghast, turned to Palmer and said, 'They are shouting that they have now got themselves a lawyer and we shall soon see who is in the right.' His fat lips burst into a mime of spitting. 'A lawyer! Now do you see, Mr Palmer, why we say in this country that such men should be buried face-downwards.' He turned away to join the heated confabulation of the African staff. The dread they had felt earlier was displaced by rage as the students milled riotously about them. Palmer felt himself more and more distanced from the scene, a spectator to a farce who had somehow got mixed up with the action. He had not come to Africa for this.

Then a Mercedes flying the Party flag pulled up the drive, braked, and Krobo Mansa stepped out, burly and pugilistic, followed by three other men – two young Party activists in T-shirts and red golfing caps, and a small, bespectacled, rather bewildered man in a grey suit. The headmaster gave up his vain struggle to discipline the students and went to meet the DC, offering his hand. Krobo Mansa took and dropped it. 'What is your palaver here?' he demanded. 'I am a busy man. I don't get time to teach my teachers how to manage their school.'

Mr Quagrainie stiffened and looked away at the agog, excited faces round him. 'I think it would be better to discuss this matter in the privacy of my office,' he said firmly, and walked off in that direction. The staff followed him, and the DC muttered peremptorily to his own small legation to do the same.

There were a few moments of awkward fussiness while the staff settled themselves, and extra chairs were found for the

Party activists and the lawyer. The games master was posted to keep students away from the windows. Then, with an exaggerated air of protocol, Krobo Mansa introduced his comrades from the Party and the lawyer, Mr Hayford Banson, who offered a propitiatory smile to the unyielding faces around him, took off his glasses, and sat unhappily cleaning them. The DC informed the staff that, as a lawyer, Mr Banson was well-experienced in dealing with such troubles and would soon sort things out. When he had finished his speech he stood for a moment looking about him, like a stone-age man improbably thawed out of the ice and blinking in the alien light.

'Perhaps,' the headmaster said, 'it would be as well if I were to explain the position briefly.'

'We already know what has happened,' the DC snapped. 'What we have to do is decide what has to be done.'

Mr Quagrainie dithered. Then Hayford Banson spoke up, aware of the hostility to his presence. 'It will perhaps be easier to see our way when the picture is quite clear.' The corners of his mouth twitched in the glimmer of a smile. 'It is only just that both sides of the story be clearly heard.'

There was a murmur of approval from the staff. Glowering at his companion, the DC sat down again. 'Very well. But I am a busy man,' he reminded the assembly. 'I don't get all night for this palaver.'

'I promise I will be brief,' the headmaster said, and proceeded to break his promise.

Palmer watched the DC's eyes roving around the room, settling in turn on each African member of staff, yet skipping indifferently over himself and the pale, yellowish figure of Sal Rodriguez beside him.

Mr Quagrainie's account had long taken on the hollowness of one who knows himself ignored, when the DC got to his feet again. His smile lacked humour. His eyes drifted blearily towards the ceiling as he spoke. 'I understand your trouble,' he said, 'and now you must understand mine. My town is filled with troublesome students who cannot get lorries to their towns. So what am I to do? I have discussed this thing with my friend, Mr Hayford Banson. These are small boys who do not yet know well which side their breads are buttered. Sometime they do foolish things.' He paused as though he considered that train of thought complete, and his eyes fixed themselves on Mr Quagrainie's worried frown. 'You see, I have not come to order you to take these students back into your school, but to beg you.'

His words were met by an uncomfortable, exasperated silence. Traditionally, to beg was a last resort which was rarely refused. It had once been a valuable means of achieving reconciliation, and to reject such an appeal was still to incur guilt. But the DC was flagrantly abusing the tradition. As he had intended, his African audience was left at a loss.

Not so Palmer. He had listened to the DC and watched his silent menaces with mounting outrage. Was this the true face of the Party he had defended against criticism for so long – a man who would send his minions marauding among the outlying villages, whose very manner corrupted the meaning of the word 'Freedom' and turned it toxic on the tongue? A man whose pretence of good will was heavy with the promise of reprisal now?

He said, 'I think I understand your problem, DC. What I don't understand is why – if we are being begged rather than ordered – you have already brought the students back to the compound without consulting us first?'

The DC's response was rapid. The thick voice uncoiled, trembling to a shout that stilled the ripples of assent among the staff. 'Because this school is government property and is subject to government control. We do not need white men to tell us how to manage African affairs.'

Shocked as they were by the abrupt change of tone, the African teachers released a gasp of protest and demurral. The DC turned to Hayford Banson shouting heatedly in his own language, gesticulating towards Palmer, shaking his huge, prognathous head. The staff too were talking in their own tongue. Palmer looked away at Rodriguez who raised his eyebrows and whispered, '*Alice*? The trial scene, don't you think? Do watch out for your head.'

Equally excluded from the babble of the local language, the headmaster found control. 'If we are to get anywhere tonight,' he rapped, 'we must keep our heads cool. We ought to be capable of behaving with more maturity than the students whose fate we are debating.'

The DC was stopped in mid-sentence, astounded by this reproof from an unexpected quarter. 'Also,' the headmaster inserted into the silence he had created, 'I should prefer it if these proceedings were conducted in the official language of the nation.'

Which remark prolonged the baffled silence.

'As I'm not precisely white,' Sal Rodriguez piped up, 'perhaps I might be permitted a word?' He had sized things up and seen that only he and Palmer had much room for manoeuvre in this situation. 'Not that there's a whole lot to say, it seems to me. The DC came for an explanation. Mr Quagrainie has given him one. Nobody wanted to suspend those students. The decision was taken with real reluctance despite the extreme provocation. I mean, I was out of it at the time – not been too well, you know – but I don't really see what else could have been done.'

'That's right,' Palmer returned, still stinging from the DC's implication that he had no business here. 'The headmaster was left with no choice. The students made the choice themselves in fact. We were all sorry to see it happen.'

'And I am telling you,' Krobo Mansa exploded, 'that there were no palavers like this in the school before the foreign teachers came.' It was an attempt, apparently, to appeal over his opponents' heads to the African staff. 'They do not understand our customs,' he insisted, 'and still expect us to live by theirs.'

'Rubbish,' said Austin Palmer.

But whose language are we speaking, he thought? Wasn't the entire paraphernalia of the school absurdly, irrelevantly British – the house-system, the examination papers, suspensions, the now disaffected prefects – all the arse-end of a beggared British tradition from which he'd tried, so fruitlessly, to escape. It was the last insidious thrust of Empire – *if you want to be human, dear Africans, I'm afraid you're going to have to learn to talk like us, to think like us, to be our sort of tin soldier, friends.* And how much of what was going on here did he really understand? Already he was undermined by the way this grotesque confrontation was mimicking the country's larger dilemmas.

Unaware of these seditious reflections behind the Englishman's stare, Krobo Mansa had stiffened at the dismissive insult from a white man's lips. Nobody spoke to the District Commissioner so.

Mr Quagrainie hastened to intervene. 'I am more than satisfied with the work of all my staff. We must preserve a sense of proportion. This squabbling is undignified.'

'The students cannot stay in my town,' the DC thundered, changing his attack to surer ground. 'They cannot get lorries at this late hour, and there is nowhere for them to go. You are paid to control them here. The Party expects you to do your work.'

Opambo noticed that the DC had wilted a little under the Englishman's disdain. 'Like your nephew,' he dared, 'many of the students live in Adoubia. They can take their friends to their houses for the night.'

'If the others had gone home when they were sent,' the headmaster said, 'there would have been no such problem.'

'My nephew has nothing to do with this,' the DC bellowed. 'This is a matter of principle.'

'Precisely,' retorted Palmer – but what was happening to him? Something of Kay's impatient rage was in his voice, God help him. 'And the principle at stake is the entire discipline of the school. What do you think it will be like here if we're forced to take the students back this way? I can tell you – it'll be sheer bloody anarchy. Every matter of discipline will end up on your desk whether you like it or not.' He tried to calm himself, to appease. 'You must see we're trying to build a good school here. If we back down on this now it will ruin everything we've done.'

The DC ignored him and turned back to Mr Quagrainie. 'As headmaster these students are your responsibility. Am I to understand that you no longer accept that responsibility?'

'For God's sake,' Palmer said, 'that's totally unfair. He's a good headmaster and you're not making his job any easier by pressuring him like this.'

'I am not talking with you.' Krobo Mansa's fists were clenched, his face hot with the internal combustion of his rage.

'I want only what is best for the school,' the headmaster said.

'Then take the students back into it,' the DC commanded. 'You do not do any good by sending them away.'

'Perhaps,' Hayford Banson put in, 'if they agreed to sit their examination?'

'Hardly the point any more,' Sal Rodriguez said wearily.

'Once they know we've been forced to take them back,' Palmer said, 'what hope have we got of building a decent relationship with them again? And what about the rest of the school? Why should they take any notice of us? The staff would find conditions impossible.' *And perhaps they should, he was thinking, perhaps they should. This whole enterprise is absurd.* But he added aloud, 'You couldn't blame them for looking elsewhere for jobs.'

Around him the African teachers grunted their agreement. There were never enough teachers after all . . .

The lawyer removed his glasses once more. 'This is certainly a hard matter,' he hedged, aware of the DC standing over him expecting support. 'But I see the problem more clearly now. The students did not, of course, present things to us in quite this light . . .'

'What would you have done in my place?' Mr Quagrainie asked, encouraged.

'It's hardly my place . . .'

'We would value your opinion,' Rodriguez said drily.

Lips tightly gripped, the lawyer replaced his glasses on his nose, looked around, took them off again. 'I do not see what else you could have done,' he conceded eventually, his eyes averted from the stiffening of the DC's body beside him.

'And now?' Mr Quagrainie pressed, willing the man towards his conscience.

There was a momentary twitch of annoyance on the lawyer's face. The room strummed in its silence. Carefully Mr Hayford Banson selected his words. 'I think you must all understand the concern that brought the DC to the school tonight. This is a serious affair. Most serious. But, as has been pointed out, it is the students themselves who brought it about. I think perhaps they must learn to live with the consequences of their actions. For a short time, at least. It will, as you say, be best for the long-term interests of the school. Perhaps also for their education as good citizens. We must all learn to respect authority.'

Incredulously, the DC listened to the affirmative grunts that greeted this judgment, and then began to bark violently at the lawyer in their own tongue. Hayford Banson opened his palms, vainly attempting to justify his defection. Mr Quagrainie sighed back into his chair. In the babble of jubilant conversation the Party activists were on their feet, malevolent and angry.

One of them stalked across to Palmer. 'Is only because you threaten to break up the school that this thing happen,' he growled.

'Oh, come on,' Palmer began, 'let's be . . .' but stopped when he realized that the man was barely restraining himself from assault.

Krobo Mansa turned away from his own fierce row with the lawyer and said abruptly, 'We are now going.' The headmaster leapt rapidly to his feet, hoping to limit the damage done, but the DC had no interest in reconciliation. 'We shall see what the Minister has to say,' he said, and turned to go. For a moment he looked down on Palmer in bewilderment and fury. His nostrils flared, lips trembled, and then he pushed past him. 'This is not yet finished,' he threatened and went out followed by his comrades in their jaunty red caps.

The staff watched as the disbelieving students were ordered back into their lorries by the DC. His own Mercedes spat back gravel as it sped down the drive. The lorries followed in dumbstruck contrast to the din with which they had arrived. The other students hurried back quickly to their dorms.

'I would like to be in town now,' said Opambo, his face lambent with glee. 'I'd like to see Krobo Mansa drive back through the people.'

'He is a bush man,' the senior housemaster said. 'He has got his just deserts.'

'Good Lord,' Rodriguez said, 'so we do prefer the dangers

104

of freedom to the tranquillity of servitude after all!'

Palmer stood alone, grave and pensive.

Mr Quagrainie approached him. 'I wonder, Mr Palmer, whether I could ask you to give Mr Hayford Banson a lift back to town?'

'You have tell the DC that he speak rubbish?' Appaea exclaimed, half in awe of her man's courage, half aghast at his folly.

'Someone had to.' He was reluctant to speak about it, would not have done so at all that night had not the news of the DC's humiliation preceded him by bush-telegraph throughout the town.

Appaea shook her head.

'Don't worry,' he said. 'I talked to Hayford Banson about it on the way back. It'll blow over.'

'Good Lord, Austin,' Koranteng said, 'were you quite drunk? I mean, such temerity! Such impolitic adhesion to the simple truth! Have you packed your bags yet? A Deportation Order must be on its way.'

'The odd thing is,' Palmer disregarded his friend's levity, 'I felt sorry for him in a way . . . afterwards, I mean. He's holding down a job that's too big for him. I think he's afraid himself, really . . .'

'Now it's my turn to cry "Rubbish!" Liberal sentimentality and twaddle, dear man. With a touch of condescension, if I may say so. I can't believe you're still looking for excuses. Still infatuated with the Party's prettier rhetoric?'

'All right,' Palmer conceded, 'so Krobo's a crook – we all know that. But . . .'

'Let me guess: somewhere you still want to believe that the President is above all this, that it goes on behind his back, without his knowledge . . . That while he dreams of a united Africa the lesser men think only of their own interests, yes?'

'It's possible.'

'Then you *are* infatuated. Though whether with our Redeemer's dreams or your own I wouldn't care to say.' Koranteng shook his head. 'I do know that his dreams are dangerous, my friend. And all the more so because of their apparent idealism. We have a proverb here: *A man comes to play only a part in the drama of life, not the whole*. Must all Africa settle for our Redeemer's idea of unity, then? Are unity and cowed conformity the same?' He leaned forward to stroke the skull of the crocodile on the table between them. 'This fellow too was a great believer in unity in his day.'

'You begin to sound like Jalbout. We're not animals. It doesn't have to be like this. Nobody really wants it this way. Not even Krobo . . .'

Koranteng was smiling no longer as he studied his friend's troubled frown. 'Perhaps we are all in the grip of forces we do not understand . . . Inside as well as out. What I do know is that you should save your pity for those who deserve it. And do be careful – I think Krobo has lost too much face to leave it at that.'

'There's not a lot he can do,' Palmer suggested.

'Why do you think so? Because you are white? Because you carry a British passport? Thin protection these days, friend, particularly when you have an African family . . .' He took in Palmer's alarm. 'Don't worry – I still have a little authority. They are under my protection.' Koranteng began to cough, kept the handkerchief tightly crumpled at his mouth, then pushed it away into a pocket as he leaned to pour more beer. 'By the way, is it true . . .the rumour I hear in the women's compound?'

'I thought no one else knew . . .'

'My dear fellow, there are no secrets left in Africa. Dare I congratulate you? You are a live-wire these days! It seems that the Triple Goddess has seen fit to shine on you after all, praise be! Come, let's drink to a better future for your child.'

Two days later another staff-meeting was called. The Chairman of the Board was to be present, bringing with him all the power and authority of a government minister. There was some dread at the announcement.

From the start, however, Christian Odansey was affable in the extreme, deliberately postponing serious discussion while he spread the infection of his laughter among the staff. A crate of beer was carried in. A toast drunk to the welfare of the school.

Palmer thought it politic to seek a moment aside with Odansey. 'We were all a little keyed up the other night,' he said. 'I hope the DC didn't take my stand as a personal affront?'

'Oh, you know Krobo,' Odansey smiled, ' – sometimes the warmth of his heart overwhelms the cool of his head. Did you wish me to convey your apologies?'

Palmer saw that this was not an offer of help. 'I just wanted you to understand that . . .'

'Oh, I understand, Mr Palmer,' Odansey said, 'I understand very well,' and turned away.

When he calculated that the mood was right Odansey opened the meeting with the brisk confidence of a man with answers. 'You all know how proud I am of my school, so you will appreciate how distressed I was when the DC told me of your troubles. It is something of an object lesson in how a few rascals can cause commotion out of all proportion to their importance – even in the happiest of communities. We in government are not unfamiliar with the problem. The nation too has its trouble-makers. It's a situation that nobody likes but it cannot be shirked. We have to find answers, strong answers. In the interests of the majority. I think I see what we have to do here today. But first' – he held the staff in suspense for a moment as he surveyed the circle – 'I want you all to know that I have had words with the DC about his own part in the affair. While I understand that he was doing as he thought best in confusing circumstances, I have persuaded him that, in future, he will not intervene in the affairs of the school without prior consultation through the proper channels.'

A gratified sigh rose from the staff. Mr Quagrainie shifted a little in his seat, restraining in the interests of dignity his obvious relief. A great weight of apprehension had been lifted. The matter was in sensible hands now. Reason had prevailed.

Palmer began to relax.

'So,' Odansey continued, 'to business. As soon as I heard of the problem I phoned my good friend the Minister of Educaton and sought his advice. As I expected, his ministry has regulations to cover such contingencies. Ours is not the only school to have met this difficulty. What we must do is quite simple: expel the ringleaders from the school, call the others back and get on with the good work. Once we have made a few examples I doubt we shall have such problems again.' He sat back in his chair, nodding to the headmaster as if the proceedings could now be safely turned over to him.

Lulled by the beer, delighted by the public snub to the DC, the staff were generally pleased by the neatness and justice of the solution.

'I'm sure we're all grateful to the Chairman for his help in this matter,' the headmaster said, 'and I think we can now bring this unhappy business to a close. All that remains is to identify the ringleaders.' There was a general nodding of heads and Mr Quagrainie turned to his senior English master. 'Mr Palmer, you were in charge at the start of these events so you are best placed to help us.'

All eyes shifted to Palmer who looked up now, flushed.

'Are you asking me to name names?'

'I think it would help us to expedite matters,' Mr Quagrainie answered, uneasily. 'You were there at the start – you know who the spokesmen were in this business . . .'

'I don't think I can do that,' Palmer said quietly.

The tension in the room rose perceptibly.

'I don't think I quite understand,' said the headmaster.

Palmer was aware of the irritation gathering around him now. All he had to do was name a few names, among which that of the DC's nephew would certainly have been prominent, and they could all disperse, consciences clear, problem solved.

'In my opinion,' he said, 'they were all in it together – the whole class. Some may have been more articulate than others, but they were only representing the general view . . .'

'Nevertheless . . .' the headmaster began.

But Palmer spoke over him. 'If we single them out as "ringleaders" we'll be expelling some of the best students in the school. I can't believe that's the right thing to do.'

The headmaster sat nonplussed, aware of Odansey beside him. In the silence the Chairman's fingers began to tap a soft tattoo on the desk-top.

Mr Quagrainie cleared his throat. 'I see.'

'I don't mean to be difficult,' Palmer added unhappily.

Or did he, he wondered? He sensed his own left hand at work again, seditiously, behind his back.

The room was unreceptive.

'I understand,' said the headmaster, 'but I don't quite see what we are to do in the circumstances.'

'Come now,' Odansey interjected, 'there's no point making things more difficult for ourselves than they need be. I take Mr Palmer's point – though it is a fine one. But I think I see a way through. Surely there must be some known trouble-makers in the class, some good-for-nothings whom the school might be better off without? Why not expel them and recall the others?'

By now everyone else in the room was thinking of the DC's nephew but attention was drawn away by Palmer's outraged release of breath.

'But that would be even more unjust,' he said – it was as though Kay sat at his elbow egging him on. 'If they've caused trouble before they've been punished for it already. We can't just wreck their lives for our convenience.'

'Then what do you suggest?' Odansey came back immediately, openly impatient now. 'A process of decimation? The arbitrary expulsion of every tenth student on the register? That seems even more unfair, wouldn't you say?'

Austin Palmer's mind was elsewhere.

He was remembering the defiant faces of the banished students, and the familiar music of the names he had refused to speak – Bimpong, Birikorang, Okelo, Owusu, Otoo. He called the roll of exiles in his mind. What had he been teaching them all this time after all: to acquiesce?

Was that how he had become a party to this punishment, to this mess that became more disturbing the deeper he entered it? What had they done but refuse to play musical chairs across the compound, to eat food that no one would choose to eat, to sit the paper he had prepared for them because it was expected of him by nameless examiners elsewhere, with their hallowed, European, colonized assumptions of what it meant to be a civilized human being?

Had they not, in short, been fighting their own small independence struggle against a regime that had cheated them? And was it now too late to call them all back to teach their teachers something about the courage of resistance?

This silent self-interrogation could have taken only a few moments, for when he looked up he saw all the faces in the room gazing at him, awaiting his answer to Odansey's challenge.

Sal Rodriguez thought him floundering, and came – as he believed – to the rescue. 'I don't see why we can't leave things as they stand,' he said. 'The headmaster has already decided the best thing to do and we all supported him.'

'You are forgetting,' Odansey said, 'that Ministry regulations for these contingencies are quite specific. We have the Minister's own ruling on the matter.'

'I think,' said Palmer, 'we are all aware of the harm that can be done by inflexible regulations.'

All pretence of affability stiffened from Odansey's face at this unmistakable reference to the Preventive Detention Act. The ease that had entered the room with the beer was now banished beyond recall.

'God knows,' Palmer breached the silence, 'I don't like what's happened already, but to do anything more seems worse than to leave things as they stand.'

'Those are my feelings,' said Sal Rodriguez.

'Mine also,' Opambo spoke up, quietly, but bravely.

Odansey ignored them and stared balefully at the headmaster. 'Gentlemen,' he said eventually – apparently indifferent to the presence of the girls' housemistress and the domestic hygiene teacher, 'I have presented you with the Minister's ruling.' His tone was final. 'What do you intend to do?'

Mr Quagrainie sought to avoid the gaze. As he looked around his staff, the mesh of lines about his eyes disclosed an older man, and one even less certain of his right to exist, than

Palmer had realized. Cries of students out on the football pitch drifted in through the windows. The silence returned, demanding to be filled.

'I'm afraid,' Mr Quagrainie said at last, 'that I'm inclined to agree with Mr Palmer on this matter. I have no wish to be unjust, and I fear that strict adherence to Ministry procedure would lead to injustice in the circumstances.' He looked up, meek and grey, to measure the consequences of his decision in Odansey's eyes.

'Very well,' said the Chairman stiffly – he had permitted an unpleasant moment – 'I shall, of course, have to report back to the Minister.'

'Yes,' Mr Quagrainie said, 'I understand.'

'He may see things your way, of course. After all, you have a reasonable case to make, and it is to be hoped we can sort out our problems like reasonable men. It's a matter of indifference to me what is done provided the school settles down quickly and returns to work.' He stood up, pulling down his cuffs. 'We shall see what transpires. Now I have other, more important affairs to attend to. If you will excuse me . . .'

The staff shuffled to their feet for his departure. As he walked out, suavely erect, he passed Palmer, paused, and chuckled briefly. But the mirth, whatever its cause, was absent from his eyes.

Sal Rodriguez's cheerful prediction that the Minister of Education would think it more trouble than it was worth to pursue the matter proved quickly sound. The Indian was elated by this double-barrelled raspberry at the Party bosses, and congratulated Palmer on the way a white skin had been exploited on the angels' side for once. But he was perplexed, even a little exasperated, by the Englishman's subsequent agonizing over the suspended students.

Palmer came home from school on the Friday after the meeting with Odansey to find Appaea waiting for him, silent and sullen.

'What's the matter?'

For a time she would not answer. He put down his books,

sat beside her, took her hand. 'Come on now, tell me.'

'I have been insulted.'

He had heard something of the sort before. He prepared himself for a renewed assault on Mamadou.

'How have you been insulted?'

'Very bad. They say very bad things.'

'Who did?'

'Kojo Donkor and Osei de Graft.'

'Who the hell are they?' It was insufferably hot. He took the handkerchief from his pocket, wiped the sweat from his neck.

'The Party activists.'

So it had begun.

Knowing how much it would disturb her he had played down his encounter with Odansey, making the politician's acquiescence in the suspensions a matter of sweet reason, no more. But since his last talk with Koranteng he had been carrying a burden of dread.

'What happened?' he demanded.

'Today. At the Cold Store. They insult me.'

He remembered the arrogant young men in the red golfing caps, the menace of their faces.

'What did they say?'

'Very bad things.'

'Did they touch you?'

'They have push me small.'

'Did they hurt you?'

She shook her head. 'But they have shamed me before the people.'

He stood up, reached for the car keys he had thrown on the table.

'What you go do?'

'I'm going to the police.'

'No.' He had never heard her so urgent before, or so afraid.

'Look, I'm not going to have those brutes shoving you around. If they have a quarrel it's with me.'

But she had hold of his hand, restraining him. 'No, please. Is all right. Is just I have need to talk about it small.'

His anger was up now. The heat, the failure to make himself understood, his frustration with the whole stupid business were at work inside him. 'We can't let them get away with this. Sergeant Dwamina's a friend of mine. I'll . . .'

'No,' she cried again. 'Even it will make the thing worse.'

Was she right? Would it be better to leave it at that – a few insulting remarks? But it smacked of cowardice, of evasion. He had let Kay down that way too many times.

'Trust me,' he said. 'I know how to handle it.'

But she would not release his hand.

'Please,' she said. 'I beg you.'

And he was halted by the humiliation of her plea. She released her grip, beat the back of one hand against the palm of the other – the traditional gesture of abject supplication – like a student at the school seeking to avoid punishment. Then she was down on her knees at his feet, her face pressed against his thighs. 'I beg you. I beg you.'

He stood, astounded by behaviour he had never expected to see in her – as though *he* were the cause of her distress, the terrible master of the situation. He bent to pull her upright, but she would not move; just knelt – a dead weight at his feet – repeating the phrase over and over again. The heat of the afternoon pummelled at his head. How, in God's name, had they arrived at this? Why was it that, in this dreadful, fly-blown place, everything careered out of proportion? He wanted to be gone.

'Stop this, Appaea. Stop it. Please.'

His pregnant wife looked up at him, more afraid of him now than of the Party activists. The shock of her gaze softened him a little. He pulled her to her feet, held her. 'It's all right,' he said. 'It's all right.'

'But you must not go,' she insisted. 'You must promise me you must not go.'

He felt her breasts shuddering against him. The fear communicated itself.

'Appaea . . .'

'Please. You must not go.'

'But if it happens again?'

'It will not happen again. Is finish now. Is finish. Please.'

How had he allowed himself to become trammelled so? On all sides he was vulnerable again. He could feel his mind

113

withdrawing in a bitter nostalgia for its own solitude.

We have to go, Kay was pleading. *We're dying here, can't you see? Something inside me's dying every day. The life in me is going bad. Don't you feel it? There are energies burning inside me that need to be let out into something alive, and there's nothing for me here. Nothing. So they just burn away, hurting because they're trapped. And I'm frightened because sooner or later they'll break out, and probably in a way I don't want. I'll have a stupid affair, or kill myself. You've got to understand. I'm deadly serious, believe me.*

How she had begged him, like this, in agonies of humiliation, again and again, to let them go.

'I won't go,' he said. 'It's all right, Appaea. I won't go.'

Suddenly he was filled with loathing for the town.

Why should he have imagined that things would be any different here than out at the school? The forest remained all around, endlessly rotting and regenerating, proliferating its drab green tedium, as though the sheer hot welter of life could somehow atone for the absence of meaning.

The town was no more secure from its advances than the school-compound. You could see the vegetation creeping back among unfinished buildings everywhere. Time and again foundations had been laid – a doorway outlined, blind sockets left where windows were planned – and then work stopped, frustrated by a death, a quarrel, a shortage of money or materials. Soon the weeds took their first confident grip on the breeze-blocks. Adoubia was an ossuary of abandoned buildings. Even the Roman Catholic church on the hill was no more than a wind-blown shell. Where other continents had ruins this one had abortions.

He could not sleep that night, lay sweating on the silver bed, tossing and turning, the sheets damp and crumpled around him. At one point a firefly trapped inside the mosquito-net settled on his arm, motionless, gleaming, phosphorescent. But the touch of its feelers among the hairs was an irritation. Tricked by some freak of perspective in the gloom, his finger must have caught only the head and killed the firefly without damaging the rest of its body. So he had to lie there in the darkness, watching its small light fail.

And when he woke the next morning he knew that, for a time at least – if only for a few hours – he had to get away.

'Come on,' he said to Appaea – unusually he was awake before her. It was still dark outside, but the cocks were crowing raggedly across the town. She opened her eyes, confused, a little alarmed. 'Come on, get up,' he said. 'We're going to the sea.'

He drove the 200 miles of almost empty roads at speed, in silence. The trees crowded the road at either side, cobwebbed and mute, at first no more than smudges on the early morning mist. The road twisted in senseless detours from the possible straight line between inconsequential town and town. He remembered that the European contractors had insisted on being paid by the mile, and someone in the Transport Ministry had, for reasons of their own, agreed.

Once, long before the bulldozers crashed through the bush, the coffles of slaves had limped through this wilderness – Africans sold by Africans to the waiting European ships. Corruption spawning corruption. Indifference breeding indifference, as the trees bred trees. History and all that was exempt from history in sullen conspiracy.

But then they were out of the forest and on to the coastal plain. His mood began to lift. It was so long since he had been here that he had forgotten this spacious horizon beyond the forest's introverted stare. His sense of smell quickened to the bright salt air. The scrubland stretched away for miles around him. Here, in the clear spaces, the coastal tribesmen of Ntia-Amadi hunted for the great Deer Festival; and that shimmer of haze southwards was the open sea where fishermen pushed their skiffs across the barrage of Atlantic surf. He should have stuck to his first intuition, and taken a job at one of the well-established schools on the coast, rather than driving himself, with an excess of virtue, into the unprivileged shadows of an up-country town. Too late – wise always too late.

At the huge, anomalous roundabout with its beckoning presidential statue, he turned off the main Badagry road and struck south for Cape Jago and the sea.

Appaea slept beside him in the heat of the car.

The sea was not Appaea's element. She sat in the shade of a palm staring at it with suspicion, as though she expected some freak caprice of the tide to pluck her from the shore while Austin's back was turned. Nor would she swim in the concrete swimming-pool that the European club had built into the sea long before. She would not even remove her dress.

For a long time Palmer splashed about with the crowd of Europeans in the pool, but he was not happy there, and not only because of the company – coastal whites, British, Italian, Lebanese, a few Russians, all making too much noise. No, it went deeper that that. In his haste to be out of Adoubia, to head for the nearest sea, he had forgotten what Cape Jago meant to him. He was amazed at how deeply the memory must have been repressed – but it was waiting for him even as he parked the car among the dunes.

Kay and he had come there long before and had spent the whole of one Saturday swimming, recuperating from their wretchedness, strolling along the shore to watch the fishermen haul in their seine-nets to the tinkle of a gong, and the women squabbling around the silver catch. In the late afternoon when they got up to leave, Kay discovered that she had lost her wedding-ring. For hours, until dusk stole the light, they had combed the sands, retracing their steps. Eventually they stood in the dark, arguing – he flustered and miserable, resigned to the loss; Kay demanding that they return when the pool was emptied, for she was now sure that she had lost the ring there. An old steward clearing away the debris of the day told them that the pool would not be emptied till the following Monday – another whole day of people trampling its sandy floor. But Kay would not give up. Back at the school her arguments had driven him to ask the headmaster for relief from duty on Monday so that they might resume the search. Perplexed, but responding to his dejection, Mr Quagrainie gave him leave.

When they arrived back at the pool it had indeed been drained, but eighteen inches of cloudy water still lay over a bed of shingle and sand. Palmer had hardly dared to look at his wife where she stood, gazing into the pool, all the crazy certainty gone from her. So he stepped down into the water, crouched, and began to push his fingers through the sand. 'Let's do it methodically,' he'd said. 'You start at the other end and we'll meet in the middle and cover it in strips. Okay?' Dumbly, Kay did as she was bidden.

As he stood in the pool now, Palmer could see himself and Kay as they must have looked to the mystified Africans on the beach – resolute and English, working their way up and down the pool for hours. It had felt as hopeless as a fairy-tale task – counting grains of corn, or spinning a barn of flax between dusk and dawn. They had hardly dared to look at one another, bent servile to the mad commitment they had made. But having once begun neither could suggest that they stop. They ploughed on in silence, the stench of water against their faces, the sun wide-eyed at their stupidity. Shortly after noon he had straightened to see the tide crashing back across the seaward wall. The level of the pool was rising. Within an hour it would be full and they had barely covered half the ground.

Even now Palmer wondered what could have possessed him then. Throughout the morning's search he had been nagged by the suspicion that they had begun at the wrong side of the pool. Once started, rationality demanded that they stick to his plan, but suddenly, with the water rising round him, he recalled standing near the eastward wall when Kay had burst up from the depths to surprise him. He had lifted her from the water, laughing. Perhaps that had been the moment when the ring slipped from her finger? With the tide mocking their methodical progress it was worth a try. Saying nothing, he strode across the pool, the water high at his thighs now, to the place he had in mind. He bent, pushed his fingers through the sand and, after exploring only a few inches this way, lifted his hand to see the ring dangling from the tip of his little finger.

Back at the school he expected no one to believe this. But it was true. They had their ring back, he and Kay; and – he had even dared to hope – their joy.

117

That ring was still among his possessions somewhere. Kay had left it with him at the end.

Walking back to join Appaea now he thought what pathos there was in the human appetite for symbols. He might have done better to recall the story of Polycrates sooner. A wiser man, that: when the ring he cast into the sea to propitiate the gods was later found in the belly of a fish served up to him, he knew his number had been called.

Palmer said nothing of this to Appaea. She was left feeling his grim silence as the consequence of her own failure to be gay. They lay unspeaking under the clicking fronds of a palm. A small boy observed them from close by, amusing himself by inflating a tiny bladder-fish with his mouth and hurling it to the ground. Irritated, Palmer shooed him away, but the boy retreated only a few paces and continued inflating and deflating the dead fish.

After a time Appaea said, 'I don't like to stay in this place.'

'We've only just got here.'

'I don't like to stay.'

'Why not? What's wrong?'

'Those men. They talk about me.'

Palmer lifted himself to his elbows. The party of Russians drinking under a palm-thatched awning averted their eyes and laughed among themselves. Suddenly Palmer was aware that, apart from the stewards and a couple of women collecting driftwood down the beach, Appaea was the only African on the strand.

'Let them talk,' he said. 'They're Russians. Probably bored out of their minds.'

'I don't like their skin,' she said. 'Is like yam.'

He lay back on the sand.

'I think in Russia there is too much snow,' she said. 'Maybe the sun don't like to shine there.'

He said nothing, listening to the pounding of the surf.

'Maybe it don't like communists.'

'Look, they're over here trying to do some good. Forget about them, can't you?'

'They don't forget about me.' When he said nothing, she added, 'I think maybe I take off my clothing and show my breasts, eh? I think maybe that's what they want.'

He looked up, and she was laughing at him then. Her laughter lightened his mood. 'You do any such thing, and I'll beat you – like an African man.'

She threw sand at him, and was on her feet. 'First you have to catch me, white man,' and she ran off down the beach, giggling as he clumsily pulled on his trousers, picked up his shirt, and set off in pursuit.

They ran parallel to the great thudding combers of the Atlantic, until Appaea stopped to watch a crew of fishermen push their boat across the barrage. Rising and falling with the breakers, spume blowing from the crests like hair, the skiff breasted wave after wave until at last it was out into the calmer water beyond. The fishermen clambered aboard to dig their trident paddles quickly against the tide. Their song was carried ashore in snatches by the stiff, salt breeze. Far out on the horizon a freighter steamed westwards, rounding the bulge of Africa, heading for Freetown perhaps, then north, past the Canaries, for Liverpool.

The sea had made them solemn again. They walked on down the strand to where the old slaving-fort shone white on the bluff over a huddle of fishermen's shacks. As they approached the gate an old and, Palmer supposed, unofficial guide in a Coca Cola T-shirt and khaki shorts sidled up to them out of the shade. 'Master,' he said, 'I show you where the white men one time make fit go store the famous slaves?'

Palmer encouraged Appaea to take an interest. Uncertainly she consented, and the guide led them between tarred cannon and pyramids of stone shot, down through a bailey to a heavy iron-bound door. They stepped through at his beckoning, down a ramp into a cellar reeking of excrement. And then, with no word of warning, the guide closed the door behind them. There was no light at all, the only air an evil-smelling darkness that musted on the lungs. Somewhere, through the thickness of the walls, they heard the muffled boom of the Atlantic Ocean. It took no effort of imagination to feel that black pit crammed with terrified men and women.

Palmer heard the whimper of Appaea's breath, and reached out his hand, suddenly scared himself that the guide might have closed the door on them for good. He was about to shout when the door was opened again. The guide stood in ferocious daylight, grinning. 'Not good place at all, sah?' He pointed out a small hatch at the far end of the dungeon where the coffles of chained wretches had once passed, single file, out on to the waiting ships.

Appaea did not wait to examine it. She pushed her way past the old man and quickly out into the light. Palmer made to follow her but the guide caught his arm, grinning nefariously still. 'Master, you go dash me small?' Palmer stood in the gloom, fumbling in his pockets for change. The guide took what he offered, and gripped Palmer's arm again. 'One stick?' he suggested, miming the smoking of a cigarette. Hurriedly Palmer fished out his packet, gave him one, then rushed out to find Appaea.

The light blazing off white walls dazzled him. It was some time before he found her, outside the castle, hunched beneath a palm, cowering as though with cold.

She would say nothing of her feelings, insisted that he take her home. On the long drive across the coastal plain before she slept, her silence made him feel the burden of history as an atrocity for which he was personally responsible.

He approached Adoubia with increasing dread. It was dark before they arrived. He half expected to find the house ransacked, or news waiting for him of some injury to Appaea's family, but nothing had changed. Mamadou was waiting there in the kitchen-quarters, reading his Koran. The old men played dominoes in the square outside. The sounds of argument in the DONT MIND YOUR WIFE Chop Bar were loud.

Over the next few days there were no further developments and, at the end of the week, the suspended students were readmitted to the school. Nothing further had been heard from Odansey.

Palmer would have relaxed completely were it not for a certain remoteness in Appaea that he had not encountered before. She was more than usually bad-tempered with Mamadou, spent more time outside the house, visiting her family and friends. It was as if she had begun to miss the world she had exchanged for this role as the Sunday Whiteman's wife. Yet he was glad of the peace it gave him to catch up on his work with the senior class.

Appaea was at her brightest when members of her family came to call, and in particular when talking about the child she was carrying.

'He will have African day-name of course,' she said. 'Also his father's name – Austin, which I like too much. But I think also Emmanuel . . . Austin Emmanuel Odum-Palmer. It sound distinguished, I think.'

'Why are you so sure it will be a boy?' he asked.

She shrugged. 'I think.'

'But if it's a girl?'

'Then Austina – Austina Appaea Odum-Palmer.' She saw that he did not care for the name.

'I think is very nice. But will not be girl, so we don't argue, eh?'

When her mother and sisters had gone she retreated into a more subdued mood, uncertain of her responses, anxious to please him, but less immediately present than she had been. He put it down to the early stages of pregnancy.

With the dispelling of trouble at the school his own dark mood had waned. He got on with his life, sometimes delighted by the thought of the coming child, sometimes worried by the responsibility, mostly accepting the fact that the cells were now at work and there was no reversing the process. Occasionally he would go for a chat and a game of chess with Koranteng, and would come away concerned at his friend's deteriorating health. It was distressing and depressing, and the King seemed increasingly preoccupied with the frustrations of his life. One night Palmer drove over to the Palace only to be informed that Koranteng was not available. There was no explanation. He spent the evening in a bar, watching the comings and goings of a disgruntled whore. Most nights he read. He was becoming an Old Coaster, less the master of his destiny than its client, and more or less patient with his lot.

One day on his way back from school, and more out of obligation than desire, he called in at the house by the sawmill.

Jalbout was drinking with Jamil. Though their welcome was formally generous, Palmer knew they were miffed by his neglect. Neither of the Lebanese mentioned Appaea, nor did Jalbout seem greatly interested in Palmer's account of the school's stand against political pressure.

'Krobo is a fool,' he said. 'He should have the sense to stick to his women and the things he understands – dash, juju. As for Odansey, I imagine he was glad to get away from his problems at the Ministry. What a mess they are making there . . . Two, three years at the most, and this country will be in ruins. If you are wise, Austin, you will make your dispositions now. Get as much out as you can while the Bank of England still honours parity with the pound. They are talking of changing the currency soon – Africanization! It will be worthless . . . Jamil and I were just talking things over, wondering whether the game is worth the candle. When the referendum has been forced through, this damned place will be intolerable . . . If you've had no further trouble with the Party activists it's because they're too busy organizing that charade, I think. First things first . . . a rare practice in Africa, I know. But, as the Redeemer promised a long time ago, once you have the political kingdom sewn-up, everything follows . . . as long as the money lasts, that is. And, when that is gone, what a scramble for the door we shall see.'

When Palmer arrived home Mamadou was waiting for him, his box packed. 'Mr Austin, I sorry, sah, but I must now go. Missis she abuse me too much. She have tell me I no-good Muslim man. I think is too hard to please Missis. I have try, Mr Austin, sah, I have try too much. But Missis she don't like Mamadou at all. Even I am thinking long time now is better I don't be here.'

Appaea was not in the house. Palmer tried to find out what the last straw had been but Mamadou would give no further explanation. Nor did he respond to Palmer's efforts to cajole him into staying. His mind was made up – he had friends in Badagry who would help him to find work. A lorry would be leaving in the hour and he was determined to be on it.

When he saw that his servant was immovable, Palmer sighed, and pressed a month's pay on him in lieu of notice, promising excellent references when Mamadou should need them. The loss of this familiar, loyal figure was like a block of his life sliding into the sea. Yet when Mamadou had left he felt a measure of relief, for the endlessly recurring conflicts in the kitchen had chafed his nerves. He had lost his own temper with the servant at times and, in recent weeks, Mamadou had taken to slinking about the house like a beaten dog.

But he was angry with Appaea. Where the hell had she gone?

By the time she arrived with her sister, Adowa, an hour or so later, he was in a foul mood.

'So what happened with Mamadou?' he demanded.

'I don't know,' she answered innocently. 'What happen with him?'

'He's gone. Left. And I think you know why.'

'He pack and go?'

'Yes.'

'Good. Now we get small boy, I think, who don't cost too much. Is better so.'

'You may think so, but . . .' He saw her eyes flash quickly towards her sister – she would not discuss this in her presence, particularly if there was to be a shouting-match. Which was, of course, why she had brought her home with her.

He couldn't face the prospect of their senseless chatter while he fumed. Nor would he risk a worse row by telling Adowa to leave. He wanted to get out, go to a bar, have a drink.

'Where you go?' Appaea asked as he made for the door.

'Out.'

'But I can cook you some good meal.'

'I'm not hungry.'

He was out in the square before he remembered that he had emptied his wallet paying Mamadou. And so he had to go back in, watched by Appaea and her startled sister, upstairs to the cash-box where he had some money stashed away for emergencies. He took the box from his drawer and opened it. It was empty.

'Appaea.'

There was silence downstairs. He shouted again. She came up nervously to the bedroom.

'Have you taken this money?'

'I?'

'Yes, you.'

'Even I did not know that there was money there.'

He stared at her, then back at the empty box. 'There was a hundred pounds in here.'

Her eyes were appalled. She might not have believed there was so much money in the world. They stood in silence until she said, 'I think maybe that Muslim man . . .'

'He wouldn't do that. The money's been around for a long time and he's never touched it.'

'Even he has not left before,' she said. And then, in sudden anger, 'I think you are foolish too much to leave that money here. I think you should go quick and tell police. They catch that bad man quick before he take lorry and go.'

'It's too late,' he said. 'He's gone. To Badagry.'

'But police get telephone. They catch him quick when he come to lorry park in Badagry.'

'No,' he said dully. 'I don't want that. Let him go.'

He went out on to the balcony, stared down into the square. He felt the first irritation of the sandflies at his wrists, and would have gone back inside but his ears were caught by a strange sound travelling across the roof of the forest, heading towards the town. The sky had thickened to a smoky, slate-grey slab against which the trees glowed intensely green. Steam was sweltering from the distant vegetation. He watched, spellbound, as the glistening drape of rain drew closer; then it was driving down on to the floor of the balcony, splashing with an impact so violent it seemed to spring up through the concrete at his feet.

The day of the referendum had been declared a national holiday, and there were no lessons in the school.

By then Palmer had heard, and believed, many rumours of the lengths to which Krobo Mansa had gone to make sure that dissidents could be identified. The ballot booth was a marquee that offered privacy to the voter, but the YES votes were to be placed in a box just inside the entrance, the NO votes in a box at the far end of the tent. It would take a suspiciously long time and a great deal of courage for anyone to vote against the Party. *Watchdog* had warned that abstention was tantamount to sedition. A register of votes would be kept. *Let no one suppose*, the newspaper column had concluded, *that the so-called secrecy of the ballot box will shield those good-for-nothings who seek to destroy our hard-won solidarity from the righteous vengeance of a united Party and People.*

Palmer read this and remembered the jaws of the crocodile in Koranteng's Palace. He decided to stay away from the football field that day. He had no wish to witness the public humiliation.

What sickened him most was the thought that none of these menaces were necessary. Certainly the first glamour of Independence was long gone, but the majority of the population still had faith in the President and his vision. His personal charisma alone would have been enough to carry the day. Yet the Party must bully and threaten and fix. The intimidation was as crass as had been Krobo Mansa's ill-conceived invasion of the school; its logic as false.

What were they frightened of? Was Jalbout right? – did they know how close catastrophe was? How rotten the foundations of their own spendthrift regime? Or were they themselves in the grip of forces so impersonal, so indifferent to decent human aspirations, that they had become little more than agents of their own eventual destruction?

What they were after now was silence. The silencing of thought by rhetoric, of principle by power. Speech was the first freedom: when that was gone everyone was in preventive detention.

Of the effects of silence Palmer knew more than he would wish to know: he was a master practitioner. It was his silence that kept Appaea with him in the house that day. He knew that part of her ached to go to the football field – not out of eagerness to vote; simply to dance her way through the tensions with her family and friends. When she raised the matter he would not argue the case; merely left her to guess how severe his disapproval would be if she abandoned him. So she too had become expatriate, severed by his will from the

125

common destiny of her family, her tribe, the nation that was, however crudely, being forged anew that day. And there was no comfort in her company. Worse, during those vacant hours, as a threadbare fabric of ideals crumbled around him, he saw that nothing but Appaea, and the child she carried, tied him to this desolate place in the bush. It began to feel the frailest of bonds.

Late in the afternoon he stood on the balcony looking down into the empty square, listening to the distant commotion of the football field, while Appaea flipped restlessly through old magazines indoors. Again the world had veered on a course from which he was excluded. He felt, as he had felt long before in England, ill-equipped to live; that he and his humanist values were superfluous. He had not even had the sense to enjoy his life, like those of his contemporaries back home who waxed fat in the media-world by mocking the hands that fed them. All those opportunities thrown away . . .

He knew too well the depths on which such reflections opened, but could not drag his eyes away. He was mesmerized by his own futility.

A car – he recognized Sal's battered Opel – turned into the square. A vulture lurched away. Then Rodriguez and Opambo got out and looked up at him.

'Have you heard yet?' Rodriguez asked.

'Heard what?' Palmer answered. 'Come on up.'

'Koranteng,' the Indian said, ' – he's been arrested.'

Palmer had been rubbing his wrists where the sandflies were biting. He froze at the words, incredulous.

'Not long ago,' Rodriguez added. 'At the polling-station. As you hadn't shown up I thought I'd better . . .'

'Good Christ, why? What's he done? Come in.'

Rodriguez and Opambo looked at one another and made for the door. Palmer turned and saw Appaea behind him, leaning against the door-frame, the knuckles of her fist at her mouth.

'No one would dare do such a thing,' she said.

Palmer pushed past her to meet his colleagues at the head of the stairs. 'What happened, for God's sake?' he demanded.

'Do you mind if I sit down?' Rodriguez said, dabbing his brow with a handkerchief. 'I've been on my feet for hours . . .

And if, by any chance, a drink?'

'Appaea,' Palmer shouted, 'bring some beer.'

'He voted NO,' Rodriguez said, 'but in a rather conspicuous manner. It was amazing. He showed up at the polling-station in all his regalia but with none of his people. Drove himself there. I mean, just picture the scene – this long line of dismal people queuing up to vote, bands playing, loudspeakers bawling out Party songs, Krobo Mansa lording it over everyone like it was all his idea. And then this car draws up, right there on the pitch, and out steps Koranteng – bangles, pectoral, the whole state-paraphernalia jangling round him – and he walks up to the man at the register cool as a cucumber and says, "I am Emmanuel Adanse Koranteng III, Paramount Chief of the Ogun-Dogambey Traditional Area. I have come to cast my vote." ' Rodriguez looked up as Appaea came back into the room with a tray of bottles and glasses. 'Ah, thank God . . .' He filled his glass, drank, smacked his lips.

'Even he listed all his titles,' Opambo added as he too helped himself to beer.

Appaea retired to the back of the room holding the tray at her breast.

'You can imagine,' Rodriguez went on, ' – the chap at the desk was thunderstruck. Didn't know where to put himself. So Koranteng helps himself to a ballot-paper, nods to Krobo Mansa, and walks into the marquee . . . and he seems to be in there for ages and ages. All the Party boys are on tenterhooks. Tension rising in the crowd. The police looking very uncomfortable. Finally he comes out again and stands in the entrance so no one can pass him. Then he starts to make a speech.'

This kind of thing did not happen. On public occasions the King remained regally silent. His Spokesman spoke for him.

'What did he say?' Palmer demanded.

'Not in English, old man . . . I couldn't understand a word. But Krobo Mansa knew what he was saying all right . . . he starts to turn purple. I mean, really purple. Like a plum at bursting point.'

Opambo looked up from his beer, his normally bland face haggard and tragic. 'I can tell you what he said, Mr Palmer. I have it graven on my heart. He said, "I have done my duty as

127

father of my people and a free citizen of a free nation by saying NO to the abomination of a Single Party State." He said that he didn't expect his vote to make any difference to the outcome, and that he asked none of us to endanger ourselves by doing the same. But when the time comes – and he prayed it would not be long in coming – he knew that we would seize the opportunity to show our contempt and hatred for those who have subjected us to these indignities.' Opambo's scowl collapsed into a sigh. 'He would have said more, but then he began to cough . . .'

'You know how it is,' Rodriguez picked up on the break in Opambo's voice, 'when he has a bad fit, I mean . . . It was like a spell breaking. Up till that moment I don't think I'd ever seen him so dignified, but then his lungs let him down. It gave Krobo the chance to galvanize the police into action. They were totally bewildered. Krobo had to bellow at them to get them to move.'

'Didn't anybody try to stop them?'

'We were all stunned. Everybody. It happened so fast. He was bundled away in a car. We weren't even sure at first whether the police were attending to him or arresting him, he was coughing so badly . . . I tell you, it was quite extra-ordinary.'

Palmer sat, in shock, aware only of images of Koranteng displacing one another in his mind. He saw the King pacing the chambers of his Palace through that long day – and presumably for days, weeks even, before that. Struggling with his fear, detesting the chance for action that had presented itself at last, recoiling from it; yet returning, again and again, in fascination. Then finally, calmly even, making up his mind, committing himself with some morose joke at his own expense.

Opambo said, 'I fear he will not last long in Kende Castle.'

'Is that where they've taken him?'

'Where else?' Rodriguez said. 'That's where they take people who get vanished. They wouldn't risk holding him here. It's all too touchy. Koranteng didn't command much respect, but . . .'

'More than ever now,' Opambo interrupted fiercely. 'He is

our King. I feel this outrage, I tell you.' He slapped the fist of one hand into the palm of the other. 'That it should come to this.'

'What's the mood in town now?' Palmer asked, trying to still the turmoil within.

'Subdued. Apprehensive,' Rodriguez said. 'The police are out in force. We hung about till Sergeant Dwamina moved us on. He's expecting trouble. Afraid of it. Obviously unhappy at the whole damned business. Nothing was happening when we left.'

Appaea, who had stood in silence throughout the account, drew in her breath sharply, then slipped from the room. They heard the bedroom door close behind her.

Palmer looked up at Rodriguez, distressed. 'She was close to Koranteng. Her father . . .'

Rodriguez nodded. 'And you,' he said, 'I know how much . . . That's why I thought I should . . . Oh shit!'

Opambo stirred uncomfortably. 'I must return to my family. I sent Efwa back to the school when I thought there might be trouble. She will be worrying . . .' He shook his head, grim-lipped and baffled.

'Yes,' Rodriguez said. 'There's no point in hanging about . . . I'll get you back . . .'

'There's nothing we can do?' Palmer asked.

Rodriguez frowned up at him. 'It's their affair, Austin,' he warned.

'He's my friend,' Austin Palmer said. 'The man's my friend.'

Rodriguez shrugged. 'I know,' he said. 'I know he was.'

Appaea was lying on the bed chewing at her fist, her knees drawn up to her stomach. He lay down beside her, put an arm over her, unspeaking. The sky outside was bruised with more rain to come. A gust of wind flapped gloomily. A shutter swung on its hinge.

'He will die,' she said.

'Not necessarily,' he answered. 'They know he's ill. They may not keep him long.'

'He will die,' she said again.

And he had no more soft deceptions to ease their grief.

He was remembering Koranteng as he had first seen him years before, a lifetime ago, it seemed. Shortly after their arrival, he and Kay were taken into Adoubia to pay their respects to the King. Koranteng was in council in the largest of the Palace compounds, among the assembly of chiefs and headmen. There had been a formal ceremony of welcome and, with Opambo interpreting, Palmer had expressed his pleasure at being there, in Africa. Then he and Kay were paraded around the compound, shaking hands with all the chiefs – a hundred of them or more, ancient heads with veins beating visibly at the temples, younger faces starched with the pride of office, their rich cloths like molten-metal in the shade of the awning. Finally the visitors were brought before the ritually silent King. Koranteng reclined on his ceremonial stool, surrounded by attendants with horse-hair fly-whisks and ostrich-feather fans. A small boy with a chalk-whitened face crouched at his feet. Koranteng had smiled and offered a hand that bore a huge golden ring spiked like a sea-urchin. As Palmer took the surprisingly firm grasp, he'd thought: My God, this is Africa. The real thing. I'm really here at last.

How Koranteng had laughed afterwards at his naivety.

Palmer could lie there no longer now, impotent, prowling his mind. Though shock had not yet receded, it was giving way to a sort of sickened fury. He was filled with disgust for the whole damned country. *This bloody hole*, Koranteng himself had called it, *nothing but the shit prospers here*. The climate, its dismal history, the inertia, the corruption that took everything he valued and depraved it, turned it into something vile and contemptible – all the occasions of his own unease, anger and contempt closed in upon him now. He lurched up from the bed, scowling, stood for a moment as though on the verge of significant action, then banged his clenched fist against the wall. He was as much a prisoner here as Koranteng – more degradingly so, because in the end nobody gave a damn what he did. He was a prisoner in the most squalid oubliette of all – that of his own deluded fantasies. And self-sentenced. Self-confined. Again he banged the wall.

'What you go do?' Appaea said.

'I don't know,' he said. 'I don't know yet.'

'But you go do something?' It was a fear, rather than a recommendation, of action. 'Krobo Mansa – he is a dangerous man, I think.'

'He's a fool. A bully and a fool. I have to do something – don't you understand?'

She sat up on the bed then. 'Oh yes, I understand. Always I must understand.' And suddenly she was angry: it was the anger of her fear, her frustration, her own almost defeated hopes. 'You too are a fool. You are fools, all of you. You . . . men. You are in love with your own death, I think. That is all. It is the same with the King. You don't know how to live, so you make love with the death that is in you. I tell you – is an easy thing to die. But to get children, to watch them grow into men who will be fools, you think that is easy thing? To love them and to live, and to suffer the loving because that is how life is made – you think that is easy thing? You will be same. I see it now. You will be same damn fool.' And she turned away, her anger spent, and for the first time since he had known her, he heard her tears.

The next day the newspapers were exultant. Hardly had there been time to count the votes before they were on the streets, headlines proclaiming: THE PEOPLE SAY YES; FORWARD WITH THE PARTY. Nationwide, they claimed, a jubilant people danced in triumph, united in heart and mind. Ever afterwards, Unification Day would be celebrated as a public holiday.

Of Koranteng's arrest there was no mention. A passing reference to *the utter demolishment by the will of the people of all reactionaries who had tried to stop the train of History* was the only admission that there had been any resistance at all.

Palmer tuned in to the World Service of the BBC and in a small item long after the strains of Lillibullero had died on the air, he learned that there had been a number of arrests under the Preventive Detention Act after incidents at the polling-stations. No names were given.

That day he taught with a stone on his tongue.

'Please,' said Charles Smart, knowing full well why he asked, 'this sentence – what does it mean?' and he read from his well-thumbed text of Julius Caesar:

> Th' abuse of greatness is when it disjoins
> Remorse from power.

Sick at heart, Palmer paraphrased the passage for his class – the fiery idealists of the Youth Brigade, the turbulent heirs of the old tribal kingdoms, and those who occupied the bewil-dered middle ground. They were revising now. He encour-aged no discussion: it would have been like watching a desperate dumb-crambo of the truth.

Outside rain splashed from the gutters, flooded the ill-laid concrete quadrangle between the classrooms and the adminis-tration block. Steam rose from the forest beyond. Everything had been waiting for the rain a long time. Now that it had come it fell like nails.

He stared through the blur of the window, thinking of Koranteng. His friend had played himself like the joker in the deck, momentarily out-trumping circumstance. He had known that one way or another he must go down, so why not with a flourish, however quixotic, rather than in decay?

Somewhere, Palmer suspected, behind the fear and the despair as he coughed his life away in Kende Castle, Koran-teng delighted to watch the little men around him squirm.

Driving back into Adoubia he saw a spitting-cobra slither across the road ahead. He accelerated to intercept it; felt, in his imagination at least, the pressure of the wheels on flesh. Then he braked, shaking.

He knew that he could not simply go home.

Around four he pulled up, sweating and nervous, outside the DC's office in Independence Avenue. The Party banner sagged from its flagstaff in the rain. Two policemen in scarlet tarbooshes and khaki drill sheltered under the eaves. One of them accosted Palmer as he made to climb the steps.

'What business you get here today, sah?'

'I want to speak to the DC.'

'Today not good day, sah. DC busy too much. He say no appointment today, sah.'

'Is he in there?'

The policeman nodded dubiously. The DC's Mercedes stood in the drive.

'Then he'll see me.'

'For why you want speak with DC, sah?'

'That's none of your damned business. Now, if you'll excuse me . . .' He pushed past the embarrassed constable who shouted after him. A Party activist, still wearing his red cap, appeared blocking the doorway, and was joined a moment later by another. The same objections were raised with greater menace.

'Come back one time again,' he was told, 'the DC don't get time for your palaver now.'

He could not force his way past, nor was he prepared to turn tail. He said, 'Then I'll wait,' and sat down on the veranda.

He was told to get up and go, that he could not stay there like a beggar from the zongo. He chose not to speak, sat staring through the dense pall of rain across the valley at Old Town. There was fierce debate over his head, a collision of harsh African vowels and consonants. Then Sergeant Dwamina was summoned from the police station next door.

The old policeman lectured him, benevolently at first, then impatiently. Palmer insisted that he would speak only to Krobo Mansa. With difficulty Sergeant Dwamina restrained the Party activists from manhandling this intractable Englishman out into the rain. He went inside followed by the men in the red caps. The two constables, posted at the door, muttered together.

Muffled sounds of fury came out of the building and, after a time, a girl, straightening her uncurled hair and shouting something back over her shoulder. She had words for Palmer too as her skirt brushed past – an insult or a curse. A moment

133

or two later Sergeant Dwamina returned, mopping his brow with a white hanky. 'The DC says he will give you five minutes. But take my advice – go back to your school immediately. I beg you.'

The cell was small, windowless, with a Judas-hole in the door, and rank with the ammoniac reek of piss. The walls were scrawled with graffiti, some very old, harking back to colonial days. *I look to God*, one poor devil had scratched; another, *Their hate is my downfall*. A misspelt pencil scrawl finally yielded, *Is the bushmouse to be blamed for the millet in the stomach of the cobra?* Most were simply initials and dates; others obscene.

Had Koranteng been held here, however briefly, he wondered, before being 'vanished' to Kende Castle?

He thought and tried not to think.

Not that it could last. He was white, educated, British. Thin protection these days, Koranteng had said. But too many questions would be asked. Already Sergeant Dwamina had done what he could to make this embarrassing prisoner comfortable, had brought beer and cigarettes, tried even to chat, disconsolately. The words spent themselves against the cell walls.

No, it could not last; yet he had heard the sound of boots climbing back up the steps, a door clang shut, pistol-keys turn, and for some hours now he had been alone with the slop-can and the elemental powers. Both were entirely malignant.

For the first time in his life his cancellation was possible. Not a soul who cared knew where he was. It must be night by now and, despite the single unblinking electric bulb, he had seen more shades of darkness than he could name. He had seen fear in a simple blanket and a bench.

Late that night a glum constable came down, unlocked the cell, and pushed Palmer ahead of him up the stairs.

Christian Odansey was alone in Sergeant Dwamina's office, standing at the window with his back to the door. He turned, shaking his head, and ordered the constable to wait outside.

'This is a fine kettle of fish,' he said. 'I had thought you a more reasonable man.'

For a moment Palmer felt like a fourth-former summoned to the headmaster's office. The first relief he had felt on leaving the cell was dispelled as he met Odansey's eyes. All the affability was gone; in its place, impatience, disdain. Where there had been something almost comic in Krobo Mansa's neolithic rage, here was a colder power.

He said, 'I once had a higher opinion of you and your Party too.'

Odansey tapped his foot on the floor. How expensive those shoes were! Palmer remembered his mother saying that one could always tell a man by his shoes.

'I was hoping that the last few hours might have cooled your head a little.'

'They have. I'm seeing things very clearly now.'

Odansey shook his head brusquely. 'Sit down, for goodness' sake. Here, take one.' He offered his packet of Sobranies.

Palmer refused.

The politician shrugged, lit his own cigarette, perched on the corner of the desk tapping the leather with his lighter.

'So am I to understand you're my lawyer now?' Palmer said. 'As well as Chairman of the Board, my MP, Deputy-Minister of Finance, and presumably King of Adoubia now that Koranteng's out of the way?'

Odansey eyed him reproachfully. 'Such a manner does not help!'

'But I *am* on a charge, remember. Contempt of court, I think Krobo said. Or was it counter-revolutionary activity? Or loitering with intent to tell the truth? He couldn't quite make up his mind.'

'There are things you should understand,' Odansey answered slowly. 'Krobo was given a hard time himself – in the old days, under the British. He does not take kindly to abuse from Englishmen.'

'So I gather. But at least he doesn't pretend to be anything other than what he is – a bully and a thug. So what are you, Mr Christian?'

135

'I am a busy man . . . already with far too much on my plate. I do not have a great deal of time to get you out of this trouble you bring upon yourself. But I am determined to try – even if you see fit only to insult me.'

'Because I'm an embarrassment, presumably?'

'Yes, it is an embarrassment. I don't deny that. Stupidity always is. But, as Chairman of the Board, I am responsible for you . . . I see no reason why a single, ill-considered gesture should ruin your career. I have always been more than satisfied by your work for my school. Though you have tried my patience at times.'

Again the head-magisterial tone sought to diminish the Englishman to delinquent schoolboy. At least Krobo Mansa had taken him seriously. He was damned if he would be patronized now. 'That ill-considered gesture was an attempt to stand up for all sorts of decencies that your government seems too ready to forget. You can't really expect me to be impressed by your concern – merely because I'm white – while Koranteng and God knows how many others won't see the light of day till you and your like are gone. You're responsible for Krobo Mansa too, remember – directly responsible for his primitive brutality. I think it's time we faced facts.'

Odansey shrugged and said quietly, 'Racism takes many forms, I know . . . but I had not expected to meet with it in you, Mr Palmer.'

Palmer was momentarily thrown by the response. As he sought to shape an answer Odansey silenced him, angrily now.

'Very well, you wish to face facts. Let us do so. Fact one: you are a sentimentalist and a fool, my friend. Do you think a just society will come about simply because you ask nicely and whisper sweet reason in people's ears? If so, you may have a good heart but your politics are entirely inadequate. You tell me you are a socialist. Very well. Do you think the enemies of socialism will sit back and let you build Utopia in peace? I wish they would, I tell you. I wish they would. But have you any idea what it has cost in blood, sweat and tears to build the school in which you teach your high-minded idealism? Do you know how many of us went through beatings and prison for that?' Again he forestalled a retort. 'Fact two: it is always a mistake to underestimate one's enemy. No liberty for the enemies of liberty, eh? – it is a luxury we cannot yet afford. They will abuse our generosity, I promise you. We have a saying here: *Power is like an egg; hold it firm or it will fall and break.*'

'Koranteng was a dying man.'

Odansey held the accusation for a moment, then answered quietly. 'We have another saying: *If a cripple throws stones at you be sure he knows just how many stones he has.* Do you think I am without a heart? Do you imagine I enjoy incarcerating people? Have you forgotten that I am a Prison Graduate myself? I too have been held in Kende. I know what you were feeling down there, believe me. I know it multiplied a hundredfold. But how long do you think I and my comrades would stay out of gaol if we did not take steps to protect our revolution? The enemy is cunning, my friend. The real enemy, I mean. It makes tools of romantics such as yourself, of feeble reactionaries such as Koranteng. I respect its cunning and its strength, and I will forestall it by all means to hand. There is too much at stake. Politics is not a debate at the Cambridge Union. There are hard and painful choices to be made, and no one likes to choose. No one. Always something is sacrificed in the choice.'

'Or someone,' Palmer said.

'Yes. I accept that. I accept the responsibility for that, because there is a public good to be weighed against the individual suffering. One must choose. If there were only snails and tortoise in the forest who would need a gun, eh?' Odansey sighed then, from the depths of an almost passionate dilemma. 'I know Koranteng was your friend . . . Your association with him has not gone unmarked. I have been keeping my fingers crossed that it would not come to this, believe me, for I am sure you do not know the half of what the man was up to.'

'Like keeping track of corruption in the DC's office?'

'I was thinking of other things. For instance, did you know that . . .' But Odansey shrugged impatiently. 'I do not seek to justify myself, as he has done, by vilifying former friends. I suppose it will surprise you to know that he was once my

137

friend also? Oh, I can guess what he has said to you about me – just as now, if I chose, I could belabour you with his iniquities. But we were friends once . . .'

'And now he's in Kende Castle, while you no doubt are looking forward to your next trip to Zurich.'

Odansey tapped on the desk with his lighter. 'You have a fine intelligence, Mr Palmer – use it. Koranteng knew what he was doing. He knew the risks he ran, just as I knew the risks when I took up the cudgels against the British Empire. He knew that time was running out for him, and made his own choice. Please do not burden me with the guilt of his unwisdom.'

'Why not? It's yours, isn't it? You and your Party hold the guns.'

Again Odansey sighed. 'Listen, my friend. Learn something. Koranteng was representative of a power that was tyrannical long before the white man came. Have you heard of blood-sacrifice? Do you know how many people were ritually murdered at the death of his predecessor . . . not so many years ago? Do you know about the chiefs who waxed fat on the slave-trade? And when their power was broken by the British soldiers, how their heirs became the tools of imperialism, a client autocracy buffering the Empire against the threat of real freedom, against the legitimate aspirations of an entire people for their political liberty? Do you know how easily they could drag us back into the darkness, back into the old warring tribes, the old degradations?'

'That's not what Koranteng wants.'

'Do you think I don't know that? But it wants him. Koranteng himself is nothing. A cipher. It is the powers behind him, I fear – the powers that will proclaim him a martyr now because it suits their ends. I am talking of the power that resides on Wall Street, in the City, in Johannesburg. In the imperialist press, the State Department and the CIA, the British Foreign Office. And I am talking about other powers, older and darker than those. Oh yes, I am sure Koranteng thought he was acting as responsible King of his people. The sad truth is he is a puppet of forces that would dearly like to see this government fall. If our revolution fails here the whole of black Africa will be demoralized. This is still a provisional state of affairs. For the time being we are forced to choose between possible tyrannies.'

'I don't accept that.'

Odansey snorted. 'As a school teacher you have that privilege, I suppose. It is the indulgence of the liberal educator. Yet I would be most surprised if you have not detained students on fatigues in your time.'

'An hour's grass-cutting is hardly to be compared to imprisonment without trial.'

'And do I not recall you insisting in no uncertain terms that an entire class of students be suspended for the good of the school?'

'It's still not the same.'

'Really? Why so? Some small boy is making a nuisance in the back row. "Be silent," you say. He pays you no heed. The good order of the classroom is at stake. Do you submit the case to trial by his peers? I think not.' Odansey eyed Palmer with an ironical smile. 'More gravely still – a class of students refuses to sit an examination. "Suspend them," you say. The DC begs you to take them back. You refuse. "The discipline of the school must be maintained. The authority of the staff." And when I take the trouble to try to sort out the matter, you tell me the same. "Justice demands that all the students take the consequences." Wasn't that what you said? Well, Mr Palmer, I took your point. Now you must take mine. The lesson is the same lesson; only the scale is different. And, of course, for you the consequences were not so serious. Perhaps you have spent too long in the classroom after all, my friend. As Krobo has shown you – the world is a harsher place.' Odansey shook his head, sniffed. 'But come. I have no time to debate moral philosophy with you. We must clear up this mess you have made. The situation is rather simple now, I think.'

'Not from where I sit.'

Odansey smiled – a condescending smile, tinged with both sympathy and scorn. 'Rest assured,' he said, 'I have no intention of allowing you to remain in prison. This town has had a bellyful of martyrs. No, that nonsense is finished. Now it is time for you to make a hard choice, my friend.' He walked round the desk and sat in Sergeant Dwamina's swivel-chair, a ringed hand fondling his chin.

Under the barrage of the politician's logic some of the steam had gone out of Palmer. He was finding it difficult to think clearly. He needed Odansey now, and he loathed him. He felt the cogency of the African's argument – he had made the same case often enough himself. And yet he knew that somewhere an essential truth had been glossed over. But what was it? Where to lay hands on it? He was, God help him, profoundly implicated in the politics of power, and his head was muddled by it. And what sense did it make for him to rot in his own dubious self-righteousness, to no point, no advantage, while the unresolvable conflict between the claims of freedom and order was fought out by sleeker mouths across the world outside? Above all, what was going on now inside that shrewd African head opposite him?

'So what do you intend to do with me?' he said.

'No, my friend – it is for you to decide.'

'What choices do I have? I'm your prisoner, remember.'

'If you are wise you can walk out of here right now, a free man.'

'On what conditions?'

'Merely that nothing further is said of this – on either side.' Odansey's eyes swivelled away, then returned. 'After all, you would look a little ridiculous, I think, if you were to speak publicly of this – a pointless row with the DC, an hour or two spent in the cells only to return with your tail between your legs, nothing accomplished?'

'And these,' said Palmer, indicating the cuts and bruises about his eyes. 'I simply keep quiet about these too?'

Odansey shrugged, made a suggestion. 'You were drinking tonight perhaps – grief over Koranteng – you got carried away? Not so far from the truth, eh? You stumbled, fell, banged your head. People will understand . . . Believe me, it's the best way. I have no desire to cause you further humiliation. Simply keep silent yourself. I will see that the DC does as he is told. The entire farce will be forgotten.'

'I see. And if I choose to speak out?'

'Then I am afraid you will have abused my trust and taken the other course.'

'Which is?'

'Repatriation. Immediate and final, with no claim for compensation. If you have studied your contract you will have seen . . .'

'I can guess.'

'I understand this cannot be an easy moment for you. You would like some time alone? To make up your mind.'

Palmer looked up and saw his smile – patient as a predator is patient – and knew that the one significant act left open to him was to refrain from complicity. And to refrain in a manner that must cause as much embarrassment as possible. Not just to Odansey and to his government, but to the darkness that was spreading everywhere in silence.

'That won't be necessary,' he said. 'I think you'd better get your comrades to prepare a deportation order.'

Odansey drew calmly on his cigarette, less discountenanced than Palmer had expected. 'I think perhaps you are being over-hasty once more. I ask you to consider for a moment.'

But Palmer could not afford to deliberate. He shook his head.

'Then you are a more selfish fellow than I thought. High-minded, no doubt. But selfish. Think, Mr Palmer – an already handicapped class of students is preparing for examination. They have need of you. Do they count for nothing?'

'Sal Rodriguez will see them through.'

'His attention to duty is hardly of the same calibre. Your attitude disappoints me.'

'I don't really believe you give a damn about the students. It's the diplomatic stink you care about.'

'I think you have an inflated idea of your own importance, my friend. Nor am I so venal as you believe. My school matters to me. It has suffered disruption enough already. But if you insist on riding your high horse no matter who is under its hooves, so be it . . .' Odansey stubbed his cigarette and reached for the telephone. As he waited for the operator he said, 'Also you have a wife these days, I believe.'

The remark came as a casual aside, a matter of passing

interest, no more, but Palmer had been dreading it.

'She will come with me,' he said.

Odansey did not miss the quaver in his voice. He raised his eyebrows. 'She will need an exit permit.'

Palmer stared at him in silence.

'Such matters can sometimes be difficult. Ah, at last . . . excuse me a moment.' He began to speak down the phone. 'This is Christian Odansey. Put me through to Julius Kwansa at the Ministry of the Interior please.' His fingers drummed the desk-top. 'Can I be expected to know every number in Badagry, damn you?' he shouted into the receiver. 'Find it yourself.' He looked across at the white man. 'Still, she has her family, I suppose. Let us hope they did not expect a genuine commitment . . .'

Austin Palmer sat in silence and he knew. He had been offered a choice that was no choice at all, as the nation had been offered its referendum, and a freedom that was no freedom. Always one was robbed of more than one was given. Whether the manipulating power was an agent of international capital or socialist revolution, whether it presented itself as true believer or corrupt mountebank, the power remained the same, for all the world's weaponry was in its hands. It divested the individual of dignity, shred by shred. Smoothly oiled as an escalator, it would take one on the journey upwards to prestige and wealth, or downwards, in a gradual diminishment from name to number, to nothing of more account than a statistic for the future to bewail.

'Do you need my silence so badly?' he said.

Odansey ignored the question. 'The operator appears to be having difficulties. Shall I spare her the trouble?'

To refrain from complicity. To submit, yet still refrain. Somewhere there must be a place that remained untouchable.

Palmer looked within himself, and saw a swarm of aridities – stratagems of shame, evasion, fear. He saw an admirer of courage running scared. He saw a preacher of peace and reason who might gladly, at that moment, have silenced Odansey once and for all. And deeper, at a still place at the heart of this witches' kitchen, he saw the walls of the Hurricane Room. A tortoise dying in its shell.

Nothing was exempt.

Everywhere darkness was descending.

His eyes were closed.

'Hello, Julius? Julius, this is Christian Odansey. Can you hear me? Damn these lines. Hello. Hello.'

Palmer said, 'Put down the phone.'

Odansey nodded, raised a finger, then clasped the receiver between chin and shoulder as he lit another cigarette. 'Julius, just a quick call.' His voice broke into his own language. He spoke for a while, and in the rush of gutturals Palmer recognized Koranteng's name and Krobo Mansa's, but heard no mention of his own. Here was Africa speaking to itself in its own tongue. The Sunday Whiteman was irrelevant.

And then suddenly Odansey was speaking English again.'On Saturday, you say? At nine. That sounds like fun. I'll be there. Fine.' He put down the phone and smiled – as much at ease as on the night, long before, when he'd held out his arms in welcome to the English teacher newly arrived with his attractive wife at Badagry Airport.

'I'm sure it's for the best, my friend. My school has need of you. Now come, let us reach an understanding, as one comrade with another, man to man.'

Part Three

THE WITCH

Some weeks later, only a few days before the end of term and the start of the long vacation, Palmer fell ill. It was the day a rabid dog appeared on the school-compound. He had been drinking in Sal Rodriguez's bungalow when they heard the commotion outside – a dog fight; not the usual yells of a brief scuffle but screams of terror and a throaty snarl. They went out on to the veranda and saw one of Opambo's puppies running away on three legs, tail down, another lying on its back under a bougainvillaea snapping up at the damp muzzle of a yellow stranger.

Opambo came out of his house, hitching his robe, shouting. The yellow dog looked round and then loped off – not hurrying, but at a lithe and easy pace – between the houses and out into the bush. Efwa Opambo came out on to the stoop clutching a cloth to her breasts. 'A killer dog,' Opambo said. He approached the puppies, clucking his tongue, but they moved away, unwilling to be touched. Opambo looked up at Palmer and Rodriguez. 'Killer dog,' he said again.

'Is it rabid?' Palmer asked.

'Maybe hydrophobia, or so. Dangerous with children about. We must attend to it.' Opambo went back into his house and appeared a few minutes later dressed in khaki bushgear, carrying his gun.

Musa, one of the kitchen-staff, came round from the back of the house, pointing into the bush. 'Master, the dog be somewhere here.'

'Come and help us,' Opambo said to Palmer and Rodriguez. 'We need beaters for the hunt.'

Palmer and Rodriguez walked round the back of Opambo's house to where the clearing ended in a small plantation of cassava. Beyond the tall stems the trunks of the forest rose in glaucous shadow. A party of excited boys was already beating the scorched grass above the plantation. A vulture disturbed by their approach lurched on to a bough where it perched, squinting at the intruders. Stamping his feet, Musa walked to the place from which the bird had risen and picked something out of the grass. It was the remains of another of Opambo's puppies, entrails hanging mauve and gaudy.

'Dog he chop him,' Musa said, and let the carcass drop.

'Dog eat dog,' Opambo said, beaming, amused. He turned his head slowly, looking for signs of motion in the bush. 'Gone to ground,' he muttered.

A lizard scampered along a fallen log, stopped suddenly, entranced, then jutted out its orange head. A cock crowed.

Then Efwa Opambo shouted something from the house. She rushed out, clapping her hands, breasts tumbling from the cloth, and all turned to look behind them. The dog loped between two houses, passing between Opambo and Palmer, heading for the cover of the bush. Palmer stood, rigid, watching its passage, dreading that it would be driven his way. But it hurried towards the edge of the clearing, and he shifted his eyes to look at Opambo. The dog had passed within a yard of the armed African who must have been bemused by the suddenness of its appearance for he stood, transfixed, watching it cut smoothly for the bush.

Not holding a gun himself, it was easy for Sal Rodriguez to shout, 'Shoot, man, shoot.' Opambo acted immediately, as though he had been waiting for the command. With a wide sweep of his arm he motioned Musa out of his line of fire and rammed the stock of the gun to his padded shoulder.

The pellets caught up with the dog just as it was entering the bush and smashed into the back of its head. The detonation was followed instantaneously by a single, docked yelp, and the brute twisted and fell. The swallows pegged to the electricity cable rose at once, spinning from the heart of the explosion. There was the dull thud of the vulture's wings as it flapped to circle the scene. And on the ground, stillness, until the boys began to shout and dance.

Opambo lowered his gun and beamed again. 'So perish all enemies of the people,' he said, and chortled.

Feeling hot and giddy and sick, Palmer made for his car.

He fell hideously ill that evening. He moaned and thrashed on the bed, sweating, vomiting, then sank into delirium. He caught glimpses of Appaea's worried face, and that of her mother, fat as a cushion, tutting her lips. Dr Subrahmaniam must have been summoned from the hospital, for Palmer vaguely recognized his weary, olive frown. Dimly he was aware of the sounds of argument around him. But he was elsewhere, disembodied, in a phantasmagoria of dreams: a mad dog on the loose, vultures and prison-cells, a dying king in gaol. Kay was there, weeping over a crate of smashed crockery that had arrived, late and in ruins, having been shipped in error half-way round Africa and back. *Now there is nothing but you between me and utter emptiness*, she said, *and if I hurt there's nothing but you to hurt in return. Forgive me.* But, *No one has unlimited resources of sympathy*, he told her. *If someone else draws on them too heavily, they shouldn't be surprised when they run out.* Which should have settled the matter; but an old African woman, with severe and regal features, stared down on him saying, *More heat. More heat. We must feed this fire.*

He dreamed of lateritic earth – the parched dust of Africa. Beneath a curious monument like the ironstone altar outside the Palace something was moving, under the earth. A fissure appeared through which, fingers first, and then an entire hand, clawed. Gradually, painfully, a naked human body was striving to break out. Both arms were freed, and then the head – white features clotted with red earth. His own face. He wiped the dust from his eyes before pulling himself up to return to Adoubia where Appaea and the women of the court were waiting for him. But then Odansey and Krobo Mansa, and the Party activists in their red nebbed caps were standing over him, barring the way, demanding to see his exit permit.

Once, convinced he was awake, at night, he looked up and there was a face at the window staring in: it was Fuseini, Jalbout's steward, grinning through his terrible black embroidery of scars. He recoiled in terror, but the face entered anyway, hovered, had become the devil-mask on the wall of the house at the sawmill. He saw it, flame-lit, lurid, dancing to the sound of gongs and drums. He heard the harsh jabber of its speech out of the spirit-world. He was one among a number of human figures cowering under the goat-slots of its eyes.

Look, said Sal Rodriguéz, *they are making an African of you at last.*

He woke, alone in the bed, at dawn. He had no idea how long he had been lying there, but for the first time in years, it seemed, he was at one with his body. Things no longer swayed in the middle distance. A breeze blew unsullied air into the room. He heard the drone of a nearby lorry setting out for Badagry. But one sound drew his attention and held it.

It was a low-pitched, doleful wailing, tuneless, yet distinguishably a song, and the longer he listened the more hypnotic the sound became. At first he thought it might be Appaea, but no, it was carried on the breeze from outside. Weak as he still was it drew him from his bed to the window.

The square was swathed in damp mist. Already in a house over the way a woman was pounding cassava, and he could hear the clatter of water as someone bathed. In the square a family of sheep huddled over a patch of damp grass with three tawny goats. There were hens bathing in the dust and a piratical cock crowed to other birds across the town. Beads of rain-water shone along the skein of cobwebs in the wires to his house.

Among the boughs of the tamarind at the centre of the square a few flimsy straw mats had been arranged as a sort of rough tabernacle. They were bent under the weight of rain-water collected in them. An old woman squatted in their shelter with a thin Manchester cloth wrapped round her shoulders, chanting.

She was very old, her mouth quite toothless – a hole in the puckered skin of her jaw, like the mouth of a drawstring bag. The shape inside the cloth, hunched and angular, with that shrivelled mummy of a head protruding from it, was only remotely human. She crouched between the roots of the tree, almost a gnarled extension of them. Around her the mist seeped from craters and gullies where the night's rain stood, brown and still but for the interference of the flies.

Palmer shivered in the chill of the dawn. For a moment, listening to that wretched chant, he wondered whether he was in fact awake, but he heard a sound behind him. Appaea came through into the bedroom, yawning, then gave a small whimper of relief.

'You are well?' she whispered hoarsely, hardly daring to believe.

'I think so.' His own voice sounded strange to him.

'You should not be out of bed without clothing,' she said quickly. 'You will catch cold. Come. Come.'

Still a little shaky, he allowed her to lead him back to the bed. She lifted his naked legs, pulled a sheet over him. He was puzzled and dismayed, filled with an immense sadness, homesickness. 'That old woman . . .' he began, but lacked the energy to continue. He felt like a man deprived of coherent speech by a stroke. She fussed around him, plumping the pillows, feeling his brow, telling him how worried she had been. 'You want anything?' she asked. 'A little water?' He nodded, smiling vaguely, but by the time she returned he was asleep again.

He was a bad patient. Irritable. Resentful of his weakness. Appaea's solicitous chatter got on his nerves. When her mother and sisters came to see him he shouted through the open bedroom door that he wanted to be left alone. He listened to their hushed murmurs downstairs, heard them leave. The silver bed shone around him – a metallic, nauseating sheen.

Late in the afternoon he felt the change in the air that threatened rain. Appaea crept quietly into the room to close the windows and, as she did so, there came the sounds of fierce argument in the square outside. She stood at the window looking down. Though she had rapped the panes shut the noise still rose from below.

He listened, more out of annoyance than interest. Arguments were common there – women squabbling, passengers challenging the justice of a taxi-fare, the complaints of a cheated whore. But this row was particularly virulent, and over the raucous shouting of a number of people there rose a penetrating, injured howl.

'What's all that noise about?' he demanded.

'Is nothing,' she said dully.

The wailing stopped and a new voice joined the argument – cracked and bitter, guttural with fury at first, then almost chanting with hysteria. He lay, trying to pin down the associations it stirred, increasingly irritated.

'Tell them to shut up for God's sake.'

Appaea shot him a troubled glance, then turned away. In recent weeks she had learned to fear his fits of impatient rage. She was tired now, and drawn. Those days and nights of anxiety had told upon a nervous system already raw from his inexplicable, harsh indifference to her.

'It will soon stop,' she said.

But the wailing rose to a still-higher pitch. It entered his head and echoed there.

'If you won't do anything about it,' he growled, sliding out of bed, 'I will.' He pulled on his bath-robe, walked through into the sitting-room, and out on to the balcony. Down in the square the wind snapped at the thin cloths of a small crowd. The sky, greenish now, would darken soon, but the rain would come first, and the trees were alert. He saw an old woman hobbling away from the rest of the group, rocking as she walked, head lolling as her back bent and straightened again – a thorn bush in the wind. He remembered that desolate image from the dawn. No dream.

He was about to shout when the old woman opened her arms in a wide gesture of impotence and her voice screeched upwards out of some deep declivity of her stomach into a hideous wail.

He was aware of Appaea standing behind him.

'What the devil's going on?'

'She is begging her family to receive her back into the house.'

The old woman turned, beating the back of one hand against the palm of the other. Over and over again she strained out the familiar phrase of supplication to the family who stood outside their house, nervous and hostile. Other people stood, in silence now, observing. A baby strapped to the back of a child began to cry. A gust of wind shuddered among them.

'Why have they thrown her out?' he demanded.

Appaea said nothing. He turned to look at her. 'Well?'

She averted her eyes and, in a voice so low and impassive he could barely hear it, said, 'She is a witch.'

He felt the sandflies biting at his neck and wrists. Soon he would be able to think of nothing else. Her answer too, stupid in its dull conviction, was an annoyance.

Down in the square the man of the family hitched his robe around his shoulder and shouted something. The first shock of rain quivered the dust. He uttered a command to his family who turned back into the house. Not one of them looked at the old woman who stared, chanting, at the sky. The other people around the square dispersed as the rain fell more heavily. The blue fluorescent light in the DONT MIND YOUR WIFE Chop Bar flickered and survived. Inside the bar a radio brayed a sudden Highlife tune and the noise spilled out, drowning the old woman's moan. Rain pummelled the roofs and splashed down into the balcony. The old woman was making for the thin shelter of the tamarind as Appaea turned and walked back into the sitting-room. At a loss, Palmer followed her, tormented now by the bites at his neck and wrists.

'Appaea,' he said, 'bring some TCP.'

He sat down, uncomfortably conscious of the crone barely sheltered from the rain outside. She was ancient, neurotic, probably mad. The whole concept of witchcraft was monstrous to him, yet – given a superstitious cast of mind – he could see how she might well be taken for a witch. The old hag was perfect for the part in a world that chose to make sense of itself that way.

Appaea came back into the room bringing the bottle of TCP and a wad of cotton-wool. He held out his wrists where the lumps stood in blotches on his skin. She dabbed them with the cooling liquid. They were both trembling a little.

He said, 'Do you people throw out every old woman you think is a witch?'

'No.' Her voice was reticent and offended, shying from further question. Why must he hurt her so?

'Then what has this one done to deserve it?'

'Very bad things. You should not be from your bed. You are not yet strong.'

'What kind of bad things?'

'I don't like to talk about it.'

Something perverse born of his dissolution and the derangement of his recent sickness drove him to press her further. He saw that if he was to meet anything other than her silence he would have to probe more subtly.

'But I'm interested in your customs. I want to know.'

'You will not believe.'

'Try me.'

After a time – pleased perhaps that he was talking to her at all – Appaea overcame her reticence and he managed to build up a picture of what had happened.

Her voice was low and hoarse, as though it tempted fate to talk of such things at all. She told him that witches always celebrated their festivals in the thick forest. Leaving their bodies asleep in bed, their souls flew to a tree-top, and a tree blazing in the bush at night was a sure sign that witches were feasting there. At every meeting one of them must bring a soul to be eaten. Thus a family suffering an unexpected death might reasonably suspect there was a witch among them, for it was well-known that they had power only over their own blood-kindred. Apparently a young wife in the outcast's family had miscarried twice before the birth of her first child which had then died when it was eight weeks old. Another child in the family had since died after a sudden illness. A third had fallen sick. The old woman was being held to blame.

'But lots of children die,' he protested. 'Why are they blaming this woman?'

'She has done it,' Appaea said, the note of dull certainty back in her voice as she sensed his disbelief.

'But how do they know that?'

'She has confessed.'

He was taken aback. Both by the statement itself, and by the ferocity of Appaea's gaze. She had looked him in the eyes for the first time since the interrogation began, utterly sure of her ground.

They confronted one another. Two separate, irreconcilable

realities jarred in that stare. He felt a chasm opening between them so precipitous that it could never in a lifetime be bridged.

'What do you mean – she's confessed? How? You don't really believe any of this, do you?'

Appaea looked across the room. 'I said you would not believe.'

He could see that she was about to withdraw into offended silence. He was shaky still; shadowed by his own ill-dreams. Suddenly it felt urgent that he should not lose touch with her completely. This woman and the child she carried were all that he had now. It was as though the dark that had dropped on the square outside was seeping through into his life.

'What did she say? Tell me . . . I want to know . . .'

Appaea looked up at him again, mistrustfully.

'Please.'

She raised her nose slightly. He saw the rise and fall of her breasts. And on her face an expression that horrified him. It was that of a black confronting a white superior – as Fuseini had confronted Jalbout that night, long before – proud, reserved, concealing more than it gave away. But there was more to it than that. It was, agelessly and beyond all cultures, the face of woman confronting man – hurt and frustrated, impatient, yet grave with a resignation that was not defeat. The face of one who has access to the most obvious of realities, and will never comprehend how men can be so stupid as to miss so elementary and vital a point. It was an expression he'd seen often on the face of Kay. And – sure as he was of his own rational ground – he wilted before it a little now.

She sensed his uncertainty, decided to press home the advantage of her greater knowledge. Let him find an answer if he could.

Once charged with the family's suspicions, she told him, the old woman had broken down and admitted her guilt. She had taken the menfolk to a charred tree in the forest, the place to which she had flown with the soul of the dead child. 'Even,' Appaea added conclusively, 'she has boasted that she have flown there in a large American car.'

155

'A large American car?' He could not restrain the snort of amused disbelief.

Appaea nodded, deterred again. Once more he had to press her to continue.

The old woman had been taken three times to a witchcraft shrine to be purged of her guilt. Despite her abject confessions the gods had rejected the sacrifices she had made. All the beheaded cockerels flung into the air had landed breast downwards – the omen of rejection. The gods would not cleanse the woman of her guilt, and so her family had now abandoned her to die. There was nothing else to be done.

'So the old woman believes herself to be a witch?'

'Yes.'

'And she believes she has killed these children?'

'She has devoured their souls.'

'But, Appaea, it's ridiculous. Scores of children die from all kinds of diseases. Do you think they were all killed by witchcraft?'

Appaea was silent, impervious. She was not talking about scores of children. She would not waste her breath in further futile argument.

'Appaea,' he reasoned, 'cars don't fly. Not even American cars.'

She would not respond to his smile.

'If a tree burns in the forest it's been struck by lightning – you know that.'

She shrugged and turned way.

'The old woman's mad,' he said impatiently. 'She should be pitied and cared for.'

Her eyes wandered the walls.

'Do you really believe all this?'

She said nothing.

'My God, do you really believe that one person can devour the soul of another?'

'It is true,' Appaea said, and got up with dignity and left the room.

When he went out on to the balcony later it was night and the moon lay on its back in the sky. He could see the old woman huddled under the rough awning among the roots of the tamarind. In the bar the radio was playing still, and down the hill the Light Church of the Spirits of God was holding a service in its tin chapel. A service or a seance – he had never understood what presences were invoked amid that frenzy of song and drum and hand-clapping. A late lorry pulled up the hill, and he could see that same motto: THEY HAVE JESUS FACES BUT STANDARD INTENTION.

Unlikely as it seemed in the din of the evening the old woman was asleep, ignored by the men playing draughts in the yellow glare of a kerosine lamp across the square.

After only a short time he realized that, of all the people in the square or passing through, he was the only one even to look at her. For the others she had already ceased to exist.

He slept late the next day but was up and about by the time Subrahmaniam called to see him.

'I was thinking I had better look in on you,' the doctor said, 'just to make sure your name is still written in the Book of Life.' He checked Palmer's temperature and pulse, inspected his tongue, lifted the eyelids. 'If I had had my way you would have been in the hospital. But your cook seems very attached to you . . .'

'She's not my cook.'

'Ah, I see.' The doctor returned the thermometer to its case. 'Well, you will live. But take it easy for a day or two yet. No relapses, please. I go on leave at the end of the week and I have no more time for house-calls . . .'

'I feel fine,' Palmer said. 'There's someone outside who needs you more.'

'And who would that be?'

'An old woman. She's been thrown out by her family. If she stays there much longer she'll die.'

Subrahmaniam clicked his tongue, shook his head, went over to the window. 'Old,' he said. 'Very old. What has been happening?'

'They think she's a witch.'

The doctor showed no surprise. 'The twentieth century stops at this window,' he said. 'But it awaits me at the hospital.' He scribbled a prescription, said, 'Get your cook to take this to the dispensary. Take them after meals. They should help. Eat lightly for a while. Nothing too spicy. Now, I must be on my way.' He snapped his bag shut.

'You're not going to do anything?'

The doctor looked up, puzzled. 'What more would you like? Tender loving care? This is not Harley Street, you know.'

'About the old woman, I mean.'

The doctor shrugged. 'What can I do?'

'I thought perhaps . . . the hospital . . .?'

'My good man, do you know what it's like out there? Do you know how many people are waiting for me? It's like trying to clear an estuary. Each day I am labouring to clear the compound. Each day, from first light, it silts up again.' He shook his head impatiently. 'Some of these people I can save – if I get to them in time, and if the competition in the bush has not already damaged them beyond repair. But I have no time and no beds to waste on the hopeless. One must let nature takes its course.' He sighed, remorsefully. 'I need these months of leave, I can tell you. Don't worry, my friend, I doubt your witch will be about here for long. Good day to you now. Take care.'

'She's not my witch,' Palmer said to the departing back.

It was four days since he had fallen ill. In the meantime term had ended and the students had left the school-compound. He still had unfinished business there. Nothing that could not have waited, but he wanted to be out of the house, in the world again, away from the sight of the old woman under her tabernacle of mats. Despite Appaea's protests he drove out to the school that afternoon.

The deserted compound felt like an abandoned army in-stallation, the relics of some fantastic scheme in the bush. The gardener was at work, trying to chivvy life through ground stripped of topsoil by Baldinucci's bulldozer. Darko, the bursar, was snoozing in his office and Palmer had no desire to disturb him. He finished off his paper-work in the staffroom, spent an hour returning books to the library shelves, smoked five cigarettes. He had already discovered that Sal Rodriguez was not about – the Indian had talked of spending some time with friends in Badagry. Opambo was out hunting. Nothing to do.

He looked out of the window and saw Mr Quagrainie loading his car outside his house at the top of the hill. Perhaps he ought to have a word before leaving?

'Ah, Mr Palmer, I see you are on your feet again.'

Sweating from the climb, his legs uncertain still beneath him, Palmer said, 'I'm sorry I missed the staff-meeting. Anything important I should know about?'

'Routine, praise be, routine. We have had excitements enough this term, I think. I shall be glad to be away.' The headmaster bent to re-arrange some boxes in the boot of his Opel. He was humming as he worked.

'Taking a break?'

'Ah yes. I am taking my family to my town on the coast for a few days. It will be good to be among my own people again . . . Do you have any plans, Mr Palmer? A trip to Timbuctou perhaps?' He gave his nervous chortle . . . water in a blocked drain.

'No, I've nothing planned.'

'You should get away, I think. A change of air. Reinvigorate the spirit, eh?'

'I might do that. It's a bit dismal where I am these days . . .'

'Why so?' Mr Quagrainie asked, not greatly interested.

Embarrassed – though why he should be he could not imagine – it was not his responsibility after all – Palmer explained about the old woman in the square.

With no more reason the headmaster was embarrassed also. His eyes shifted warily. Why was it that wherever this earnest Englishman went discountenancing circumstances seemed to follow?

'You have some home-leave due, Mr Palmer,' he suggested.

'It is in your contract. I'm sure it's not too late to arrange a flight . . .'

Palmer shook his head. He had considered the matter before he fell ill, but the thought of Europe terrified him now – as, after a long sentence, criminals are terrified by the thought of freedom. 'No,' he said lightly, 'I'm more African than English these days.'

Mr Quagrainie was unconvinced, but not anxious to pursue the matter. He looked at his watch. 'What is my wife doing in there? It will be dark before we leave at this rate.'

'Will they really leave her to die?'

The headmaster averted his eyes. 'I do not understand these up-country people,' he said. 'On the coast we are more . . . Our customs are not the same.'

'I think something should be done about it.'

Mr Quagrainie nodded his agreement, attempted a further unnecessary re-arrangement of the boot.

'Who would be the responsible authority in such a case?'

Mr Quagrainie scratched his head. 'There is a social welfare officer in Adoubia. Mr Darko's brother, I believe.'

'Another relative of the DC?' Palmer said. *Another Snow-dunda*, he thought.

'Er . . . yes. So it would seem.'

'A sinecure?'

Mr Quagrainie cleared his throat. 'I should not concern yourself with this matter, Mr Palmer. Some things are better left alone. It will sort itself out.'

'DV?'

'Indeed, yes. We must always look to God.'

'Which one?'

'There is only one, Mr Palmer.'

'The fetish-priests don't seem to think so.'

The headmaster was openly impatient now. 'I am not answerable for those people, Mr Palmer. We do our best here. By our lights, we do our best. However, it takes time. Rome was not built in a day. I think perhaps you take too much upon yourself . . .' But then he seemed to regret his impatience. After all, he was talking to a man who had been recently ill, who was sweating and trembling a little now as he leaned against the car. 'It has been a long and difficult term,' he said. 'We all need our well-earned rest. Take my advice, Mr Palmer . . . A change of scene . . .'

He saw as he parked his car in the square that the old woman – he refused to think of her as the witch – was still there under the tamarind.

'Whiteman. Sunday Whiteman.' She was calling to him, trying to attract his attention. He slid out of the car and straight into the house. As he closed the door, sweating, he heard her shout something after him in her own tongue. A plea? A curse? In neither case did he want to know.

Appaea was not there. He stood with his back to the door for a moment, then went to pour himself a drink. The house was appallingly empty. He sat on the plush couch, drumming his fingers on the arm. And then, drawn by morbid fascination, went out on to the balcony. The old woman was looking up at him.

He pulled back. Hid.

For the first time since he had shoved them away months before he went to the cupboard where his journals were stacked. He took out the new exercise book he had bought at the Presbyterian Book Depot, sat at his desk. He read through what he had written on the first page, then tore it out, scrumpled it. The back leaf also came adrift from the staples. On the new first page he began to write.

Something has begun. I feel it. It presses in on me with a gloomy intensity out of all proportion to the circumstances. I am just beginning to accept the reality of the situation. Realities. Contradictory realities. So irreconcilable that I begin to wonder whether my mind

He stopped, paused, sucking his pen, read through what he had written. Then resumed, leaving the sentence incomplete. A fresh paragraph:

Even Appaea accepts the verdict of the shrine-gods – gods in whom, as a Christian, she professes no belief. I wonder what her pious Methodist minister would make of that. Most derangingly of all, even the old woman is persuaded of her own guilt.

No one wants to know about it. I seem to be alone in perceiving the monstrous absurdity of it all.

He drank the last of the whisky in the glass. *The illness perhaps*, he wrote. *The bad dreams. Every sodding thing that's happened.* He stared at the words for a time, was about to push the book away in disgust, and then began to write more quickly:

The entire situation is absurd. Appallingly so. But it won't be laughed out of existence. Unless someone does something the old woman will stay out there till she dies. I'm confronted by an alien mythology in action – not brutal, but certain, complete, and utterly rational in the terms of its own logic. There is a temptation to engage in moral posturing – why is no one doing anything about this abomination, etc., etc.? But they are. These people are immersed in the reality of the situation and they've reached a realistic conclusion. It's reprehensible only in terms of a different reality – one which 'understands' chronic abortion, bacterial disease, the neurosis of guilt, and the terrible dynamics of projection.

MY reality.

I feel uncoil inside myself an anxiety I've met before. It touched me in those hours in the cell, and again afterwards in the atrocious silences between me and Appaea. But I remember it best from those moments when Kay and I had worn our problems to the bone – the feeling of having broken through the skin of things to peer into a void. All meaning drains

He heard the sound of Appaea coming in through the front door, closed the exercise book, shoved it away into the desk drawer.

* * *

'You are now feeling well?' she said.

'I'm fine.'

'I have brought you some good food. To make you strong again.' Diffidently she crossed the room to kiss him and smelt the whisky on his breath. 'Eh . . . I think you should not be drinking this. Not yet.'

'I needed it.'

She looked down at him in mock disapproval. 'Anyway, I am too happy you are now well.'

'*Very*,' he said. 'It's *very* not *too*. *Too* makes it sound as though you regret it.'

She shrugged. 'Sorry. I don't regret. I'm *very* happy. Very. Very. Very. Now we be very happy again together one time, eh?'

'Anyone who is happy these days is either a crook or an imbecile.'

'What is that?'

'Never mind.'

She was injured by his rebuff, but renewed her efforts to be cheerful. 'Look what I have brought you. Is a gift from my mother.' She unwrapped an enormous pineapple from her cloth-parcel.

'That's very nice of her.'

'Yes, I think so.' She was encouraged by his smile. 'Also, now you are well again, my father he want to ax something from you.'

'*Ask.*'

'Yes.'

'What does he want?'

But she was having second thoughts. 'Is not important.'

'Then why did you mention it? What does he want?'

'He want . . .' but she faltered again.

'Well?'

'He want to watch at his TV.'

Palmer stared at her.

'He don't get electric at his house.'

'He knew that when I gave it to him.'

'Yes.'

'So he wants to bring it here, I suppose.'

This was not going the way she had hoped. 'He is thinking that now you are not fevered no more . . . maybe you like to watch at his TV with him? For amusement. Till you get strong again.'

'I don't think so,' he said.

'He want to share his TV with you too . . . very much.'

He pressed his fingers to the lids of his eyes, watched the patterns there. Without looking up he said. 'There's an old woman been left to die in the square out there, and your father wants to sit in here watching television?'

He heard the sound of her swallowing. 'I think I tell him you not yet well,' she said.

'Tell him the truth,' he answered. 'Tell him that even if I wanted the blasted telly in the house I wouldn't have the stomach to watch it while that's going on out there. Jesus Christ, I don't understand you people. What sort of world are you living in? Tell him if he wants some amusement he can come and sit on our balcony watching the old woman die. Or are we supposed to pretend that's not happening?'

'The old woman is not of our family.'

'And if she was?'

No answer came.

'If she was, Appaea – what then? Would it make any difference?'

'What I go do?' she cried. 'I try to make you well. I try to make you happy. What I go do? I don't understand. I don't understand at all.'

At that moment, but in what different ways, they were both thinking of the life shaping itself inside her.

He sat, feeling the silence close round him once again.

He slept badly, woke early, could not bear to lie in that ghastly silver bed. Furtively he went out on to the balcony, looked down.

The mats were still there in the tree but the patch beneath them was empty. For one sick moment of relief he thought the old woman had gone – wandered off in the night, or died and been transported from the face of the earth. And then he heard a sound in the corner of the square.

She was there, her thin Manchester cloth hitched over warped legs, straddling the open drain, pissing out a bright silver stream. Her eyes moved warily to cover her rear, like those of a dog doing its business on the end of a lead.

Every day when I go out I'll have to walk past her, get into the car, drive off, as though she wasn't there. Every day till she dies. But I can't shut myself away here in the house. I'll go crazy. Anyway, she's already infiltrated that seclusion. Is here. Inside my head.

It's as though this mad bush country has finally found the one, unstoppable chink in my defences. It feels like a calculated assault upon my residual moral sanity. Appaea is an agent slipped behind my lines.

Afterwards – perhaps even at the time – he saw how stupid, stupid beyond belief, was his attempt to reason with the old woman's family. If he could get nowhere with Appaea what did he expect from them?

Only one of the small boys had a smattering of English. Appaea had refused to come with him, so he was stuck in a humiliating farce of miscommunication. When finally they realized what he intended they stiffened, pretending to understand nothing. Polite but menacing, they implied that the white man should go back to his school – stick to the mysteries of book-learning. Tend to his own affairs.

He remembered a Dogambey proverb that Opambo had once quoted: *If you who are lying on your back complain of not seeing God, how can I see him who lie with my face to the ground?*

Whatever the incomprehensible gibberish she's muttering out there, it resolves into a single devastating syllable: HELP.

So do I take her in?

It's unthinkable. I can't speak to her even. Madness.

The whole town would cut me off. The crazy Sunday Whiteman fostering a witch. Appaea would leave. I'd be stuck, for years maybe, with a withered hag around my neck, terrified of me, trying to die, while I, stupidly, tried to keep her alive. For what?

I mean – sweet Jesus – can it really be so difficult to help somebody?

Dammit, if there is a God he has no right to hold himself aloof from this. He should be dragged out there in the square to witness the harvest of his misbegotten enterprise. He should be hung in chains and made to see.

He read through what he had just written and was struck by a sudden scary thought – in this situation he was God. There he hung in his chains, literally and metaphorically above it all. By his own definition he was possessed of superior understanding. The everyday human world was down there, in the square, below, while he sat in his upper room, on high. If anything was to be done to halt this horror it would only be through his intervention.

Deus ex machina if he acted.
Deus absconditus if he did not.
Either way, responsible.

Was this what God felt then, he wondered? Or was feeling a merely human affliction?

'Fuseini,' shouted Henry Jalbout, 'bring some beer.' He led the way out on to the sun-balcony and gestured towards a wicker chair. Palmer was glad to be outdoors, away from the gaze of the devil-mask. Perhaps Jalbout had noticed how often his eyes strayed towards it as they'd talked about the old woman. But the move had interrupted the uneasy course of the conversation, and now the two men sat in silence for a time, looking out across the river.

'But then perhaps we are all a little mad,' Jalbout said eventually, ' – we expatriates, I mean. Mad to come here. Mad to stay. And maybe a little in love with our madness, don't you think?' He smiled across at the Englishman, refusing to take him quite seriously. 'I have lived in this forest since before the war. It is my back garden and my farm. I owe my living to it. And I think I have come to hate it so crazily that I could not bear to leave. Do you understand me? I would be lost without it now.'

'But I thought . . .'

'That I was planning to get out?' Jalbout shrugged. 'We all have our despondent moments, but they do not last. I have decided that I can outstare this government. They will blink first. I will outlast it even. Just as you, my friend, you will outlast your disappointments here. In any case, have they not been an education? I think you have begun to learn from Africa, eh? Perhaps if you had trusted my judgment sooner . . .?'

Palmer laughed without mirth. 'I would have left a long time ago.'

'With Kay?'

'Perhaps.'

'You can still go. You have your life before you.'

'I have to see this through.'

'The government? Surely . . '

Palmer shook his head impatiently.

'Ah, the girl? Your new wife?'

'She's pregnant.'

A momentary wince quickly masked as a thoughtful frown was the only response to this admission.

'That's why,' said Palmer, 'I need to know what sort of man this father really is.' *And how very odd it still felt*, he was thinking, *to refer to himself this way*.

'I can tell you' – Jalbout's smile was sympathetic – 'he is a man who makes great mistakes. Out of a good heart, perhaps, but nevertheless mistakes . . . I think you take some things too seriously, my friend.'

'A child? Can one take that too seriously?'

Jalbout shrugged. This would not be the only fatherless, coffee-coloured piccin in West Africa, though it would be indelicate to say as much. But Palmer was no longer looking at him. He was staring down into the garden where the malevolent old monkey that Jalbout kept in an iron cage was fretting at its fleas. The air was damp to the touch, yet he could feel it crumbling around him into dust the colour of baked brick.

'I don't want it growing up to believe in witchcraft . . . sorcery . . .'

'Then you must take it from Africa, my friend. Everything here believes in sorcery.'

'Do you?'

'It is a fact. It surrounds us. Like the forest.'

'But do you believe in it? Really believe?'

'I believe that the Africans believe. Their belief is fact. My belief in their belief is fact. And I have seen strange things in my time here. They are not at all easily explained . . . Self-inflicted wounds that do not bleed, though the knife has gashed the flesh . . . People who have died from no clear cause . . . healthy people, young. Have you been inside the DC's bungalow ever? Have you seen his collection of medicines, fetishes? Do you know of the unorthodox people the President retains among his advisers?'

'Rumours.'

'Perhaps.'

'Koranteng . . .'

Jalbout shook his head. 'If Koranteng had died,' he said, 'no one would have left their houses at night. Nevertheless he would not have passed to the other side alone . . .'

'Blood-sacrifice?'

'Indeed.'

'But he wouldn't have wanted that. He wouldn't have chosen it . . .'

'In some matters Africa leaves no choice.'

'I have a choice,' Palmer insisted. 'Over this old woman I'm free to choose what to do.'

Jalbout raised his eyebrows, then left the Englishman alone with that statement for a time. Palmer stared down into the river.

'She's not a witch. She's a mad old woman.'

Jalbout sighed. 'I see no contradiction.' He watched the Englishman shake his head, studied the tight grip of his frown. 'But you, my friend . . .'

'What about me?'

'I am concerned. Are you quite sure you are not a little bewitched yourself?'

Palmer looked up, startled.

'I mean, to become too preoccupied with such things . . . Is not this to fall under a dark spell? There are some things one should not try to look between the eyes.'

'You do believe,' said Austin Palmer.

'I believe in taking care of oneself.'

'I think you do believe.'

Jalbout shrugged.

'But this business of people devouring one another's soul . . . surely you can't believe in that?'

Jalbout stared at him for a long moment, then said, 'That is the easiest thing of all to believe. That happens all the time.'

As he drove back towards the town an outrageous sunset unfolded around him, exultant and doomed, like the rough draft for the last act of an operatic tragedy.

He had left the house at the sawmill abruptly, without thanks or explanation. Mario Baldinucci had arrived and interrupted the increasingly desultory conversation. 'There is a good film tonight at The Star,' he'd encouraged them. '*Gunfight at OK Corral*. Western. Bang-bang. Plenty people die.'

Jalbout and the Italian stood perplexed as Palmer got up and walked out without a word.

He should never have gone there. Each time he left that lugubrious house he swore never to return. But he had needed to get away from the square.

Towards which – where else to go – he was speeding again. It seemed that his latitude for movement was so diminished now he could only lurch back and forth, from and to the house in the square, like a creature under compulsion.

And at this thought, somewhere on the road between the sawmill and the town, he put his foot on the brake. The car jarred to a halt among the muddy ruts. He lit a cigarette.

Ah, Sunday Whiteman . . . latest in a long line of pilgrims

to this dreary bush. Had all the others suffered this derangement in their day? The quirky Victorian missionaries brandishing the Bible like a torch, sweating salvation through each hairy pore, adding their inconsequential footnotes to the Acts of the Apostles. The lonely colonial administrators, strapped in their duty like a complicated item of surgical corsetry; dressing for dinner as though more than a photograph were there to receive the royal toast, and daily regretting the river-smell at Henley, snow across the downs, or some fairer posting in a more salubrious clime. At least they had brought with them a coherent world, to which they were accountable. Whereas he . . . He had brought the language but forgotten the world. He had come, poor fool, in eager quest of a new one, bartering the bright beads of the parts of speech for . . . What?

He was staring through the windscreen into the green frieze of the forest. How long since he had dared to step into those shades!

He got out of the car, stood for a moment, pondering, and then stepped off the road.

The ground was spongy and damp beneath his feet. Mud sucked at his shoes. The air was a green smell, tepid and rotten. And gloom lay in there, through which the tall grey trunks ascended, roots jutting high along their flanks like buttresses. Invisibly, birds chattered out their rights. He heard an agitated muttering of apes. Yes, there were tracks through these dense glades, farms even, scattered throughout the roadside margins of the bush, but how easily a man could be lost in here. You needn't go very far. You simply had to ponder on it long enough . . . allow it to lay its claims.

But the gnats and mosquitoes fretted him from this green trance. Also he should beware of snakes. The place must be alive with them. He blinked, shook his head, turned back to the road.

He drove past the residential area and the hospital, past the parched triangle of grass where a herd of bony cattle rested on their long journey from the northern savannah to the slaughter-houses of Badagry. He drove down Independence Avenue to the dead-end by the post office. He stopped the car there for a while until darkness dropped around him. He turned back, past the police station, the DC's office, the Presbyterian Book Depot. At the Texaco station, he took the road for Old Town. Smoke drifted across his vision from the dump. He drove the streets, hearing the repeated cry of 'Sunday Whiteman' like an insult in his wake. He stopped again in the square outside the Palace. The great carved door was locked and, should he knock, who was there to receive him now?

A black face appeared at the window of the car. 'You want jig-jig, master? Do the thing? I get nice girl. Number one nice girl.'

He reversed the car. The African leapt aside, shouting in his own tongue at first, and then, as Palmer turned to pass him again, 'I spit on you.' At the junction he almost collided with a lorry. The words ALONE WITH GOD IS MAJORITY flashed past him as he swerved. He braked only just in time to avoid the open drain.

He did not stop again until he reached the house. The square would have been deserted were it not for the solitary figure of the old woman squatting beneath her mats, rocking her head backwards and forwards. He got out of the car, stood looking at her, directly.

The old woman ceased her rocking, gazed back at him. He forced himself to hold her stare. There was almost nothing left alive in there – no accusation, no supplication even. Then she raised her hand. It floated upwards, slowly, like a waterlogged spar; not begging – perhaps she was past that now – but beckoning. An invitation. A summoning.

He broke his eyes away, turned briskly to the house. Behind him, a dry palpitation on the air aspired, vainly, to laughter.

The entries in his journal became more fragmentary.

I can settle to nothing now. She has inserted herself into my brain like a meningeal worm. I feel the fever of her everywhere. Even when she stops that mindless chanting. The silence is worse because it contains the possibil-

171

ity that she might be dead and gone. And to have done nothing.

I look at the sky and see the site of immense but cancelled schemes. She will never leave now. That shadow of Hiroshima burned into the stone.

The eyes of Appaea – beyond all argument. Have they found it out then – my Nothing?

The stag-beetle at my window – black and shiny, horned like a rhinoceros, and winged. When God rested did he have bad dreams, and is this one of them? I remember the students crunching them beneath their sandals. Does any of it matter? If any, then all. Exclude one and we are all desolated.

Fixed melancholy – the slaves' escape. They learned it, chained in coffles, on the long trek through the bush to stare in terror at the sea. It was rubbed home in the hellhole of the castles. They became it, packed tight as dominoes in the galley's black hold.

It is the courage of the damned.

He began to study Appaea's Bible. She watched him, troubled, hoping he might find some consolation there; for – whatever the deep cause of his wretchedness – he nursed it far beyond the reach of such comfort as she tried to give. She was afraid of him now.

He found and read the story of King Saul and the Witch of Endor. He reflected upon it. Having banished witches from his kingdom Saul, at the end, needs a witch. And yet it is to his old enemy, Samuel, that he speaks through her. What consolation there? To Samuel he was already a dead man. How if he had listened to the witch direct? What might have been learned from such a conversation?

He searched a long time for the parable of the Good Samaritan and found it finally in Luke's gospel. Again he studied it carefully, opened his journal to explore his thoughts, but wrote only: *Who is my neighbour? (Luke X, v. 29.)*

Much of the time he sat in glazed silence now, responding only mechanically to Appaea's questions and probes, or ignoring her altogether. There was a thought – a queer, paradoxical thought – struggling to shape itself in his mind. When finally it emerged into focus, it came as a further question: *Is it possible then to commit suicide by proxy?*

They were eating together. Convinced that somewhere he must still be in the grip of his sickness, Appaea had taken great pains with the soup. She awaited his response in vain.

'Meat is now very expensive at market,' she said.

'You have enough money?'

'Yes.'

They ate in silence for a time.

'Maybe we can go to Badagry soon?'

'What for?'

'Is better shops there. I can buy the things you like.'

'I don't need anything. You go, if you like.' Then he dropped the spoon, stared down at his bowl, wide-eyed.

'Is all right?' Appaea asked, concerned.

She looked where he pointed. 'I don't see.'

'You don't have to see. You know.' He glowered across at her bewildered frown.

'Is only what you like,' she said.

He pushed the bowl away in disgust, stood up, shaking his head as he looked at her in utter disbelief, as though she were an unsavoury stranger intruding on his privacy. He crossed the room, reached for his jacket, walked out of the house.

Perplexed, almost in tears, she picked up the bowl to examine it. She could see nothing more unacceptable than a single strand of hair that must have fallen from her as she cooked.

She sat in an agony of thought for a long time. Try as she might she could come up with only one dreadful explanation for her husband's behaviour in recent weeks. Nothing else could account for this estrangement.

She must seek advice.

* * *

For a long time he wandered the streets of Old Town, impervious to the calls around him, until he came at last to the Paradise Bar.

It was little more than a baked mud shack with a galvanized iron roof, and he would have walked straight past it but his eyes were caught by the mural painted on its outside wall. It depicted a beach scene under an outsize moon. A huge half-naked woman reclined on the sand, staring a brash sexual challenge between the eyes of anyone who cared to look. There was a synthetic depravity to the pose – the artist must have copied it from some film-star magazine, darkening the skin, superimposing negroid features on the face of an eternally anonymous starlet. A man in a sharp suit was painted disproportionately small beside her. One hand imperiously outstretched, he gazed at her enormous breasts with a disdainful smirk. In the purple shadows of the background more naked women rose mythologically from the sea. The mural offered an unbiblical, entirely masculine vision of Paradise. Palmer stared at it in glazed fascination.

Inside, the bar was lit by a cool blue lamp. He had not intended to enter until he saw a man in the street watching him stare at the mural. Distracted, fugitive, he went inside and found Sal Rodriguez in there, drinking alone. It was too late to withdraw.

'Austin, dear man,' Rodriguez called. 'How opportune! I was just reflecting that if a man is left on his own for long enough he forgets how to talk. I might have forgotten before next term. But here you are to rescue me. Come, join me in Paradise. What will you have? There is only beer. Unless you like palm-wine?'

'Beer,' said Palmer.

Rodriguez clicked his thumb. The beer was brought.

'So you're back in the land of the living? I did come in to see you, but you were in the spirit world at the time, and Appaea . . .' Rodriguez made a moue, opened the thin palms of his hands.

'How was Badagry?'

'Demoralizing. Nothing in the stores but tins and tins of Bulgarian jam. None of the spares I needed at the service centre. My car has died, you know? Unpardonable – it might have let me go first. I mean, the taxi fares these days! And one can't argue with them any more. I tried tonight. "You think I urinate petrol?" the driver demands, looking very ugly indeed. So one has to cough up.'

Palmer nodded, watching the barman who wound his old gramophone and danced for himself in the blue-lit rink of the bar.

'So how are things with you?' Rodriguez asked. 'Anything of interest happened while my back was turned?'

'Yes,' Palmer said deliberately, 'I think so.'

'Amazing! I thought that after that business with Koranteng the town had given up the ghost. Do tell.'

'An old woman has been left to die in the square outside my house.'

Rodriguez made an extravagant grimace of distaste. 'But that's depressing. The depressing is no longer interesting. It's merely par for the course.'

'The circumstances are interesting.' Palmer made one further effort to explain. Rodriguez listened in silence, swishing his beer around the glass.

'Well?' he said when his friend had fallen silent again.

'Well what?'

'Am I quite hideously drunk or did I detect a twinge of personal responsibility in your tone?'

Palmer sat in silence, regretting already.

'Oh dear,' Rodriguez sighed, 'that terrible moralist you carry about . . . I suppose he feels he ought to do something about it?'

'What can one do? Give her food and prolong the agony? Give her money? No one would take it from her. What would you do?'

'Put her out of my mind.'

'Not so easy.'

Rodriguez's face assumed the feckless glaze it wore when he was preparing some barbed sally or other.

'Austin,' he said at last. 'I used to admire your mind, you know. It was replete and tidy, civilized, with orderly flourishes of colour, like an English garden. What have you

175

been doing to yourself? I mean, if you're going to let the weeds in you should at least cultivate a small patch of Irony. It is purgative, tonic, analgesic. And it helps one to sleep at nights.'

Palmer looked away.

Rodriguez rapped with his knuckles on the table-top. 'Are you in there? This is Earth calling the Heaviside Layer. Are you receiving me? Dear man, do smile.'

'You haven't watched it,' Palmer said.

Rodriguez released a heavy sigh. 'All right. So – despite your own admirable logic – no point giving her food, money etc. – you still think something should be done?'

'Don't you?'

Rodriguez shook his head. 'We're not at all the same, you know. Of course, I've endured an English education – the sort that prepares one for everything except matters of life and death. But I'm an oriental still. It makes a world of difference. A world of difference,' he repeated blearily, and then stared up at the Englishman, almost angry. 'You can be quite insufferable, you know? I mean, be honest with yourself – do you really believe that the old woman's life has any value at all?'

'I think one has to.'

'Why? Where's the compulsion?'

'It's a human life, for God's sake.'

'For God's sake, eh? Which god? The Christian God? The one that condemned her? Her god? Do you believe in either?'

'I don't know what I believe in any more.'

'Good. An agnostic humanist. Your choice is clear. Her world has rejected her. She no longer has a world. So – either you become her world by taking her in, making her at home – not altogether an attractive prospect I would think – or you distance yourself from the whole vile business by recognizing it for what it is: a gruesome object-lesson in human stupidity.'

'And if it was you out there?'

'But it isn't, dear fellow. For the time being our survival isn't in question. Yours and mine, I mean. Our lives – such as they are – are still self-validating.' Rodriguez took in his friend's distracted wince. 'You find my logic heartless? I

176

prefer to think of it as unsentimental. I assure you that reaching this position was not a facile achievement. However, if you wish to play the Good Samaritan, pray don't let this landless Levite stand in your way.'

'I've looked at it – the parable, I mean. I don't trust it. What does the Samaritan do after all? – puts his hand in his pocket, pays for accommodation and medical expenses, and goes on his way. It's too easy. Any corrupt industrialist does as much when he writes a cheque for charity.'

'I can hear the priests of my childhood answer that he acted out of love – true charity – and did all that was necessary in the circumstances while others turned a blind eye.'

'That's just it. If it was a simple matter of financing the old woman's convalescence, don't you think I would have done it long ago? But if I lift a finger I'll never be rid of her. She'd be a millstone round my neck till she died.'

'So you have no problem.'

'She won't be argued out of the square.'

'Nor out of your head, it seems.'

Palmer sat in silence.

'Look,' Rodriguez resumed, quietly but with force, 'what do you want me to say? Do you want me to tell you that you do have a responsibility, that you ought to go out there and harangue the poor ignorant devils who threw her out, and when you get nowhere with them, take her into your own house and care for her till she dies, perhaps ten years from now? Appaea might have a thing or two to say about that! Is that what you want? I knew that house in town was a mistake. I knew you'd . . .' He broke off, shaking his head.

The barman stood in the shadows, watching the two men, mystified.

'This makes me a bit sick,' Rodriguez returned, untypically vehement now. 'All over the damned planet men and women and children are dying of misery and starvation – most of them with more life in them than that old hag – and you don't really give a fart about it – deep down, where it really hurts – until one of them crawls out of the darkness and starts to die on your doorstep. And even then you don't know what to do but

177

feel sorry for yourself. Isn't that what this breast-beating is really about?'

'At least I can't be cold-blooded and logical about it.'

Rodriguez smiled. 'That's better. Anger cleanses. Let's have some more. Listen: I'm not talking about logic or morality or whatever the western mind in its wisdom wants to call it. I'm talking about raw, crude existence. Your whole damn world of ideals and culture and moral sophistication is a mirage. Haven't you realized yet that this is a hostile planet? The realities here are hunger, desperation, disease, and whatever crimes we commit to avoid them. For all the platitudes you can mouth about the sanctity of human life, what is it when you get right down to the bone? I'll tell you – it's survival only at the expense of others. At this moment there are people dying in misery the world over, and when they're gone there'll still be too many of us. Even as they die a million or more babies are kicking and screaming their way on to the pile. Now – right now – this minute. And every one of them that survives – white, black, whatever shade you care to mention in between – every one of them devalues humanity just a little more. So what if your old woman dies? There are always more to take her place.'

Palmer was shaking his head as the Indian spoke, but there was no remission.

'Take another look at your witch,' Rodriguez pressed, 'a misshapen parcel of flesh with what inside? Ignorance, superstition, neurosis, pain. Sufficient guilt for wrongs felt and done for her to believe herself a witch. Take a good long look at her this time. Smell her, if you can stand it. And then come back and talk to me about the sanctity of human life.' He looked down into his glass and spoke more quietly, more bitterly. 'I sometimes think of existence – particularly human existence – as a sort of crust that has formed to cover a wound in the void. If a bit of it flakes off here and there, so what? It might be better if it were all gone – healed.'

'I can't believe that.'

At that moment Sal seemed to Palmer an even more pitiable figure than he was himself, even further out on the cold rim of existence.

'No more can I,' Rodriguez said. He opened his mouth to speak again, but Palmer anticipated him:

'I know,' he said, ' – life is a pig.'

Rodriguez smiled. 'We know one another too well. My friend, there is no answer. I don't know what you should do.'

'I think I should go.'

Rodriguez looked up, almost pleading for him not to leave. But Palmer needed to be out, in the night, alone. As he walked to the door of the bar he heard Sal call after him, 'Let the poor bitch die in peace. She'll be well out of it. You'll survive.'

The night sky was vertiginous, and oh, what pathos in the little lights of Adoubia! He walked back slowly through the streets of Old Town, breathing in the darkness. The night was hot and clammy but he felt himself possessed of a breath so cold it might put out the stars.

Round and round in his head went the words of the riddle Koranteng had put to him once: *This is the medicine we all must take; yet when it is drunk it must not touch the lips, it must not touch the teeth, it must not touch the tongue. What is it?*

He had met the answer on his very first visit to the house in the square. It had come in the shape of a handcart-hearse with a black man's head banging at the wood inside. He remembered the feeling that had come to him in the house that day – the certainty that something was waiting for him there. For a time – and what a pretty time that had been – he had thought it was Appaea. He knew differently now.

There was only ever, at the end of the search, one prize.

The witch lay under her rough tabernacle of mats, panting and stirring in her sleep. He walked across, stood within a yard of her, close enough to see the flies at her eyes and nose, and said to the unconscious body, 'What do you want from me?'

There was no answer, no sign that she had heard.

'Why are you doing this to me?'

He heard only the thin breath whirring through her.

'Why are doing this to me, Kay?' he said.

* * *

He entered the silent house, climbed the stairs, and opened the door into the sitting-room. It seemed full of Africans – Appaea sat on the couch between her mother and father. Two of her sisters were also there, one suckling a babe at her breast. They all stared at him in silence.

'What's going on?' he asked.

Appaea's hands were clenched in her lap. She looked down at them as she said, 'I think maybe it is time that we must speak.'

But why should this family gathering be required? Why were they here, crowding his room, when what he needed was stillness around him, a little time to think. He would have asked Appaea to send them all away, but Komla Odum, commander of the left wing of the King's army, got to his feet, unhitched his robe from his shoulder and began to speak.

He spoke in the only language that he knew, gesticulating often, nodding and rolling his head, beating the back of one hand against the palm of the other, repeating some phrases for emphasis many times. Once Appaea made to interrupt him, but he silenced her with a peremptory gesture, smiled at the Englishman, and resumed his long oration. He was convinced that such eloquent sincerity must communicate itself.

The noise rattled in Palmer's mind.

'I don't know what he's saying,' he appealed to Appaea, speaking over her father. 'Tell him I don't understand.'

'I have try,' said Appaea.

Komla Odum continued to speak, undeterred by this exchange, turning now and then to his wife, who nodded her support and encouragement. Palmer realized that Odum was drunk. There would be no silencing him. He reached for an empty chair, sat down, the tips of his fingers at his temples.

At last it was over. Odum re-hitched the cloth across his bare shoulder, stood to attention, gave a stiff, military salute, and returned to the couch. There was silence in the room.

How good it would have been to keep it that way, to nod some sort of gratitude for this incomprehensible sermon, and have them shuffle out. But it was expected that he speak.

'What was all that about?' he said.

Appaea looked down at her feet. 'My father have begged you to forgive me.'

'Why? Why should I do that?'

She misunderstood him. Already nervous, she was chilled by the tone of his voice, assumed that he could see no reason to act with such generosity of spirit, for all her father's pleas.

'Because,' she began without great hope, 'as my father have try to tell you there were reasons for why I have done those bad things.'

He stared at her in blank incomprehension. His mind was adrift. What was she saying? What did these Africans have to do with him? There was a strange swinging sensation in his head, like a shutter banging loose somewhere before the rain.

Appaea's eyes darted towards his face, saw only coldness there, and mistook its cause. Tears sprang to the corners of her eyes. The elder of the two sisters was saying something to her in her own language.

Then the mother was on her feet, the flesh of her brawny arms wobbling as she harangued Palmer, gesturing with both palms open towards him, then swinging her arms round to gesture similarly at Appaea. She began to speak rhythmically, then to chant – the same impenetrable phrase over and over again.

Clearly something was required of him. They were all deeply troubled. In some way that he did not understand he seemed to be the cause. The world was fragmenting around him. Now they were all speaking at once – a vehement commotion in the midst of which Appaea sat, head bowed, in silence but for the quick, faltering catches of her breath. The two sisters appeared to be arguing with one another, and the mother appealing to the father. The noise-level in the room was rising – a frightening jabber of alien sound that washed over him again and again. His heart was beating very loudly now, and his own breath stuck in his throat. The babe released its mouth from the nipple, peered with screwed eyes into the surrounding din, and began to cry.

'Stop this,' Palmer shouted. 'For God's sake, stop it. Please.'

Instantly the noise in the room shrivelled to the thin sound of the baby's wail. Its mother tried, vainly, to silence it with the nipple again.

'Appaea, tell them to go away. I can't stand this.' But so fierce was the urgency of his voice that again she heard only anger there. Her tears broke out. Her whole body was shuddering now. Her mother put an arm around her shoulder, began to mutter some sort of consolation.

The elder of the two sisters, Adowa, got to her feet. 'My sister have wish to say that if not for the money harm would come upon us all.' She looked to her family for encouragement, then back, valiantly, at Palmer.

'What money? I don't understand.'

'The money she have stole. Kojo Donkor have told her so. Also Osei de Graft.'

The baby continued to wail.

In the hot darkness of his mind a thin shaft of light fell on a picture of himself, long ago, staring at an empty cash-box. And widened to include his servant, Mamadou, saying, *I think is hard too hard to please Missis. I have try, Mr Austin sah, I have try too much* . . .

He looked up at Appaea. 'You took the money?'

Her own cowering, antelope eyes held his for a moment. Then she nodded, gulping for breath.

'It wasn't Mamadou?'

Surely he must know this? Why must he torment her so? Her voice was so thick with wretchedness that he could barely hear her say, 'They have tell me that if I don't get money then they will beat my father . . .'

He looked at her, then across at the old man who sat, stroking his bald head, lips trembling now in a proud, truculent grimace, like one of those old photographs in Koranteng's Palace, the vanished kings . . .

'But why didn't you tell me?'

'Because I am thinking you will get too angry and go to DC and then the trouble will get too bad. It will get very bad. And I am afraid for you and for what they will then do. They have tell me you already bring trouble on DC and if I tell you this thing then DC he get too much mad. Maybe more than beating then. Maybe they make arrest. Maybe it become Detention palaver then, and they can't help. But if I get money and say nothing then everything is all right . . .'

He stared at her as she spoke. This was all happening at a great distance. Somewhere, inside himself, he was listening to laughter – the laughter of a very old, demented woman, who was still out there in the square, still dying, as this fantastic scene unfolded in a virulently green room above her head. For what else could she do but laugh, as the well-intentioned pilgrim to emergent Africa sat in judgment now at the centre of a circle of abject, pleading negroes?

No, that was not how it was meant to be. Something was out of kilter somewhere. Something was wrong. It should be possible somehow to rewind the reel . . . like that ridiculous film they had seen, where everything came right in flashback and the adventure could proceed, because, after all, the hero was not dead. Something had come along to save him. Something very improbable, as he recalled.

But they were all so serious. And, look, that baby was determined to be included in the action, could not wait to add its senseless contribution to the farce. And, yes, another stirred inside Appaea as she wept – one more for Rodriguez's pile. A further irreversible devaluation of any possible meaning that human existence might have once sustained. But where? In Paradise? – that dingy, blue-lit, baked-mud shack where a blacked-up starlet sucked the whole world down her throat? No wonder she laughed. No wonder he aspired, vainly, to do the same.

'I sorry,' Appaea was saying. 'I too, too sorry.'

'It doesn't matter,' he heard himself say. 'None of it matters now.'

'Then I am forgiven?'

'There's nothing to forgive.' But he was not quite speaking to her – he was speaking to the Nothing inside himself, and to the greater Nothing on which his own nothingness reverberated with a curious hollow sound . . . Oh yes, he knew this place. He was coming back into his native land. So, so familiar! And how foolish ever to have imagined that by sharing with Appaea the secret of its existence in words, mere words, he could have made it vanish for ever. No, this inward place was his . . . rent-free, inalienable.

There was conversation about him, in a language he did not understand. There were sighs and grunts – of satisfaction, it seemed – as Appaea explained herself. Then her mother questioned her. Appaea shook her head. The father rasped his hand at his chin and barked out something. There was disagreement. Appaea sat in silence, listening, with a worried frown on her face as her sisters joined the argument. What was coming now? Why did they not go away and leave him alone with his sound? For that sickly flapping of the shutter in his head had gone, and there was only a low murmuring noise like bees humming a mantra from the dawn of time. It was, he thought, the true music of the spheres: the soft, undulant strumming of interstellar spaces consoling themselves for their own fathomless existence . . .

Appaea was speaking to him, falteringly, in English once again. He heard something about the DC which could not, he imagined, be of any further interest to him. Everyone was waiting, with arrested breath, for his reply.

'I'm sorry,' he said. 'What did you say?'

She said again, bravely, but in fear, 'Am I forgiven also for what I have done with DC?'

Now what could she have done with the DC? What could anyone do with the DC? The man was impossible. And what was that line of his? Oh yes, *I don't get time for this palaver now.* That was it. *I don't get time.*

He studied Appaea in vague bewilderment. How strange that he had taken this body to his bed; that a life of no possible consequence had been engendered between them there, and was, presumably, at this very point in time, busily arranging the genes into a further hopeless attempt at viability. Though he was not drunk he felt as though, just possibly, he might be so; for he had access to the drunkard's callous frankness, the drunkard's terrible lucidity. And, after all, why not? He was not just the Sunday Whiteman: he was the one who liked to taste palm-wine.

'Tell me' – he wagged an admonitory finger at her, smiling to counter the sick residue of feeling that had begun to slop

184

like bilge deep in the pit of his stomach – 'what have you been doing with the DC?'

She said warily, 'I think maybe you have been already told.'

He began to understand. So this was why the family was here. The money was less than the half of it. This was why they were all so eager to placate him, so terribly afraid.

How clever Mr Christian had been! How full the world of cunning men!

He was nodding his head. She took his nod for confirmation of her belief. So she had been right after all. Why had he not simply come to her like an African man with a stick long before? Why had she allowed her own fear to poison their life with silence so?

She looked away, to her mother, who muttered something to her.

Appaea held up her chin, eyes closed. 'I think at first I do right thing,' she said. 'But then I see it wrong. Is very wrong if I don't talk with you about it. And I want to talk with you about it. But you make me too afraid.'

Afraid of him? Who need be afraid of nothing, he wondered? Or perhaps there was, in the end, only Nothing to fear. Yes, perhaps she had been wise.

'Now I am not so afraid,' she said. 'The Bible say is the truth that makes us free, and now I want to be free.'

'Of course you do.' He was unaware now of the others in the room. His eyes were for her only, watching, fascinated, to see how she would find her way through this. Who would have dreamed that the simple desire to do good in the world – his coming to Africa, her attempt to shield her family – could prove so very complicated?

Time for truth-telling then. What was it Kay had said? *I'll tell you what I care for now – truth. That's all. I care for what feels real and true and alive. And so long as I can feel that, I don't care how much pain I feel as well. We've got to be true with one another now as we've never been true in our whole life together. Nothing else will see us through.*

'When you were in the prison,' Appaea began . . .

So she knew about that? All along while he had kept silent, kept his stupid word, she had known . . . Did they always know everything then, these women? Was nothing ever secret? *You should have told me this, Kay. Really you should. You could have saved us so much grief.*

'. . . the Party activists have come for me. Kojo Donkor and Osei de Graft.'

But I tried, my dear, I tried, Kay was saying. *But you wouldn't hear. And even after I had gone . . .*

'They tell me if I don't get more money then maybe something bad happen with you, maybe I don't see you again . . .'

Even after I had gone I tried to tell you, in the only way I could, the only way I thought you might hear . . .

'So I show them my money and they say even is not enough . . . and I tell them I don't get more money . . . I beg with them – I plead . . .'

. . . and I'm still with you now, out there . . .

'But they tell me I must come with them to DC and they leave me there alone with him . . .' She was holding her cloth, a tight knot, at her belly, and her face was twisted with the anguish of this speech. 'And DC he tell me what a bad man you have become and that bad things will happen with you. And that my father also is a bad man – even like the King – and even he too will be taken away and shut in Keŋde Castle . . . So I have begged with him too much. But he say is not enough to beg. He say one time he beg with you to take students back into the school but you don't listen to his begging . . .'

And whose language are we speaking now? he thinks. *I am the Sunday Whiteman and it seems I damage everything I touch.*

'So what I go do, I say. I say I try to get money, but he say he don't want money.'

And if I, who lie face upwards, cannot see God, what can I expect of you whose faces have been pressed into the ground?

'Then he say maybe if I do the thing with him, maybe this one time he let you go . . .'

'It's all right,' Palmer said. 'That's enough now.'

'I think maybe is right thing,' she said, 'I don't see what other thing to do . . .'

'That's right,' he said, 'we don't know what to do.'

She looks up at him at last, her face haggard in its appeal, awaiting judgment. Around him a ring of Africans watch. The baby sleeps again at its mother's breast. Outside an old woman is giving up the ghost. Inside himself it is now very, very still. If he had wanted to torment her, or to test, in cold experiment, whether or not he still retained the capacity to feel – well, all that was over now.

Enough of him remains to bring this matter to a timely end; but the rest, by far the major portion of his grieving consciousness, is already elsewhere.

ALONE WITH GOD IS MAJORITY, the lorry's legend said. *Ah, but without him, dear driver, what then? For it seems he leaves us with no choice these days.*

He considers: for too long he has loathed his own most secret absence of love. It is time for forgiveness. For exculpation.

An order of service, a secular litany for the occasion, seems to be shaping in his mind. He begins with Africa, the continent itself, shaped in crude likeness of the human heart: yes, forgiveness there. Politicians, chieftains, elders, fetishpriests, the people of the town, tribesmen, taxi-drivers, market-mammies, pimps, whores, thieves, beggars from the zongo: he assembles them all and asks them to accept his absolution. The crime is History's, not theirs.

Colleagues and students at the school, he thinks, *you too are included in this general amnesty, with gratitude for an unusual education – at last, I begin to understand.*

Jalbout, Baldinucci, Sal, dear Sal – my bitter comforters – sleep easy, pardoned now. Of course, none of this was your fault.

Kay, my dear, my poor crazed weeping Kay – the hurt you gave is all forgiven now and quite forgot.

Exhilarated by this new-found freedom, the embrace of his largesse expands. *World*, he calls out of the deeps of his silence, *from this obscure glade in the wilderness I address you in your entirety, and my message is Reprieve. I can condemn neither your ignorance nor your wholly comprehensible indifference. One stays sane as best one can, and none but fools dare count the cost too closely.*

And then he remembers God – for one must not abandon

Him, alone in the terrible isolation of his own majority. *Yes, you too, Lord, old Nobodaddy, I absolve you of every shred of blame. It was an interesting try . . .*

There is a thin smile at his lips now, of which he himself is unaware, but which puzzles and dismays the Africans around him.

After all, he is thinking, *we must forgive one another, we who know precisely what we do. Particularly when what we do is nothing.*

'I am forgiven then?' Appaea asks.

'Of course, my dear. Didn't I say? You most of all. We're all forgiven now.' He is smiling down at her from a very great distance.

She looks across at him, hardly daring to hope. 'And we shall be happy together again one time?'

Doesn't she see? He shakes his head in puzzlement.

'But I think we can . . .' she tries. 'I think maybe if . . .'

'No. Not now. Not any more. I think that would be asking too much.'

She stares at him, uncomprehending. The tears, held in abeyance by the willed courage of her confession, are gathering inside her now like rain. She looks to her bewildered family. Her father is muttering. Glum-countenanced, aware that something is going dreadfully wrong but uncertain what, her mother has begun to rock her head. Appaea looks back at this strange man whom she loves. She says, 'I think maybe when the child has come . . .'

Ah yes, the child. Austin Emmanuel Odum-Palmer; and would perhaps, like all white missionaries to Africa, his day-name be Sunday too? Somehow he doubted that he would ever know.

'I have to be alone now,' he said.

'But why . . . I don't understand.'

He must be patient just a little longer. 'Didn't I tell you once – I spoil everything I touch. We don't always mean to, you know, but we do . . . we do . . .'

What did he mean by this *we*, she wondered? She was very frightened now. Her hands were trembling.

He saw the quiver of her lips, the tear fall across the small sickle scar at her cheek. 'You mustn't be afraid,' he said. 'You must take the child into your family now . . . Yes, that's what you must do. He will be safer there.'

'But I want to be with you . . .'

He shook his head. 'The truth has made you free,' he said. 'As the Bible promised it would. You've told the truth and now you're free. I shan't hurt you any more.'

'But even you are hurting me,' she cries, her face a ruin of the one that had smiled impudently up at him so long before while dancing at The Star.

He takes her point. Yes, hurt must still be radiating outwards from him, like shock-waves crossing space from an imploded star. All the more reason to be gone. As best he can, the hurt must be limited. He is sure now that it would be wrong to relent on this.

'It's best this way, Appaea. Believe me, this is best.'

But she will not accept it. She stands, hands lifting to her braided head, begins to moan. There is confusion around her. The father, perplexed, apparently demands to know what is happening now; the mother, caught in the infection of her daughter's grief, is weeping too. The elder sister shouts, 'You cannot do this thing. You cannot do this thing,' while the younger one tries to comfort her baby in one arm and to gather Appaea in the other. Then Appaea breaks free from the hands reaching round her and throws herself down at Palmer's feet. 'I belong with you,' she cries. 'I and the child. We are for you. Our life belongs with you.'

He is very far away, considering how strange it is, how pitifully unwise, that she should love him so. 'No,' he hears a low voice saying, 'I belong to no clan. I carry my own coffin on my back.' And he leans, remotely, to stroke the weeping head that shudders at his knees, hurting itself by the refusal to accept the unrightable wrongness at the heart of things.

The family has become a rough, loud consort of grief around her, but something strange and terrible has happened to Appaea. She is looking down at the palm of her hand. A vessel in her nose has broken and her black skin is streaked with blood – a brilliant extrusion of the life within her, falling in thick splashed stars on her open hand. A dark stain spreads on the cloth of his trousers where it is stretched taught at his thigh. No one but he has yet seen, and something, surely, must be done about this. He stares, shocked, at her separate, injured existence in the world. He reaches, clumsily – it is so very far away – for the handkerchief that must lie somewhere in the depths of his pockets. But it is too late. The mother has seen what is happening, has drawn Appaea to her bosom, is pressing the gathered folds of her cloth to the wound.

An older sister is staring down at him, incredulously, in scorn – as though he were really there . . .

'Take her away,' he says. 'Take care of her. Please.'

At last the house was empty.

He was very tired.

He sat for a long time staring into the stillness that the Africans had left behind them. His mind was neither thinking nor at rest, but in some way-station sequestered between, where, of their own volition, images shimmered across its misty screen as mirages come and go on desert air. To none of them could he hold fast. Nor did any offer specific clues to his whereabouts. His mind, it seemed, had become a complicated instrument now. He was bungling its use as an amateur might misapply a sextant to the stars.

After a time he got up, and looked around the room. What had this place ever had to do with him? It was void of intimacy. Nothing here of home. He was attracted only by a furtive movement in the mirror.

Caught in the act, an interloper with no business there, his own reflection insolently offered itself for inspection.

Strange the way this face had disposed its variable expressions about the world with such conviction that everyone had taken it for him. But how little really they had to do with one another, this face and the person who examined it now, objectively, with some distaste. Except that it would lean towards him as he leaned, squint in impersonation of his frown, as a child will sometimes maddeningly echo everything one says, converting it to nonsense. Oh yes, there was a competent impostor here, who should certainly be exposed, although its malicious little smile defied him now to try.

There was something devilish there, about the eyes and mouth . . . particularly the way its wicked silence seemed to hint that all things were exterminable through a single, simple act . . .

He pulled himself away. For, no, revenge was not the thing he had in mind, and what that seditious smile was luring him towards would amount to no more than that.

He went through into the bedroom. That ghastly silver bed was swathed in its netting like a bride. Beside it, on the small table, he saw Appaea's Bible.

Had she consulted it that night – looking with the modern African's wistful yearning after wisdom to a book? How sad that these people had come to this when, from their own pricelessly unlettered lore, they'd taught him everything of value that he knew. How good it would have been to be one among them – long before all this – before the politicians and the imperialists, before the missionaries and the explorers, before the slaving-ships . . . in one of the old, golden kingdoms, a member of the dance.

His heart was filled with yearning. It echoed inside him, like a call that travelled across the parched and fly-blown squares of that sad town, out over the roof of the forest, to plunge steeply back into the Africa he had once dreamed of as a child. He saw it there, hot and magnetic, bathed in an auroral glow of sunlight, patched like a giraffe in black and gold. A long-relinquished region of the heart, to which, with a little patience, a little courage now, he might eventually return.

But how?

Perhaps, he thought, a little magic – a little white magic – might help. Wasn't there a way of using the Bible as a kind of oracle? Something to do with a Bible and a key.

He took the car-key from his pocket, opened the Bible at random, pointed the key at a verse.

I am become like a pelican in the wilderness, he read, *an owl that is in the waste places. I have watched and am even as the sparrow that sitteth alone upon the house-top.*

How true! How strangely true!

The words of a song from his days as a Cub-Scout drifted into his mind, 'Here we sit like birds in the wilderness, birds in the wilderness . . .' and he was grinning to himself.

Not a tortoise then, after all. Perhaps a bird.

A pelican.

A pelican in the wilderness.

How strangely things were altering.

He lay down upon the silver bed and waited.

Was he awake or did he sleep as the witch at last came in to him? Or was he wandering a curious twilight realm somewhere between? Stalking her among those unfamiliar rays and shadows even as, co-exile in this zongo of the mind, she laughingly sought him? It was perhaps a kind of hide-and-seek in which he knew he must eventually permit his capture.

But the terror of the ambush when it came was not entirely feigned, for her face at first was all things loathsome: the eyes; the toothless, wrinkled gap in her mouth; the demented grin. And the terror thickened as she began to unpeel this face, revealing another aged African beneath – but one less ravaged, sterner, imperiously stern, beneath whose gaze he knew himself in sin. Then the joy, the unutterable relief, when this second mask was also lifted away and he saw Appaea, laughing down on him. He reached. She pulled playfully away. *Now you must catch me, Sunday Whiteman*, she said, and ran away into the shades.

Such loss! And must the game really begin all over again?

It must, for Kay was a long way away by now . . . acre upon acre of torrid forest, the wide savannah of the northern territories, the far brown coils of the Niger, and then – dear God – the long shifting duneland wastes of the Sahara to cross, and still he would be barely half-way there.

Too far . . . Too far for one whose vital energy had long since spent itself in futile dreams.

Why do you take so long? the witch was calling to him still, and her face, drawn and shadowed by abject, unanswered pain, was palpitant with grief. *I have waited so long and now there is so little time . . .*

It was necessary to try, once more, to explain.
If only he were not so very tired.

Some time later he jerked suddenly upright, sweating, to the
sound of banging in the night – hammers, not drums – two of
them – beating hurriedly, without rhythm. The noise was
coming from outside the house. For a long time he listened.

He got up from the bed, went through into the dark
sitting-room, and out on to the balcony. The air was sweet with
night. He sensed that the whole square was awake to this noise
of banging, alert and silent. The whole vast night of Africa was
a single held breath.

The banging stopped and he looked down. By the light of a
kerosine lantern he saw two men carrying from the square a
crate no bigger than an orange-box. The tree was disrobed of
its mats. The space beneath it empty.

Part Four

THE PELICAN

Some days later – appropriately enough a Sunday – around noon, on the deserted school-compound. There was always a hush over the forest at this time – the sun at the meridian, the still day weeping heat, a few lizards scampering about among fallen logs.

On a weekday, in term-time, the students and staff would have been sweating in the classroom-block, waiting, though there was still a tedious hour to go, for the bell to free them. In the kitchen, the cooks would have been preparing the lunch-time meal, and a few women from the nearest village might have toiled along the road with their parcels of ground-nuts and bananas on their heads, hoping to earn some coppers from the ever hungry students. However, this was Sunday and out of term. There was nothing much to do and, in any case, Sal Rodriguez had accomplished a hard night's drinking at The Star the previous evening. He was in bed and dreaming still, this late into the day, of the vast combers he had once watched rolling in from the ocean off Cape Cormorin. There he stood in his dream, a kind of wandering sadhu once again, at the very vanishing-point of the great sub-continent, when he was woken, perplexingly, by an urgent knocking at his door.

Clutching his thin pyjama-bottoms at his waist, struggling with the inefficient lock, he was further puzzled to find the headmaster on his veranda; and then alarmed to recognize Sergeant Dwamina beside him. Peaked hat tucked under his arm, the policeman was dabbing his brow with a handkerchief; but something more than the heat must account for the expression of agitated displeasure on his face.

Nor was Mr Quagrainie quite himself. A funeral occasioned by the death of a distant relative had kept him longer than intended at his town on the coast. He and his family had arrived back at the compound only the night before, and very late. He too, though not so disgracefully as Rodriguez, had overslept. There was a more than usually pained expression on his face, emphasized by the sight of Sal's dishevelled condition. 'You must excuse this intrusion,' he said, 'but something

197

most disturbing has happened. It is to do with Mr Palmer. I wonder if we might enlist your help.'

For a moment Rodriguez was afraid that Austin had got himself into some sort of political trouble, and anxious fantasies of becoming embroiled flitted across his otherwise still-bleary mind. But Mr Quagrainie asked the police sergeant to explain, then stood, revolving his eyes heavenwards, and clicking his tongue as he listened.

'Actually,' Sergeant Dwamina said, 'I am very anxious for our friend. His troubles – the heat – who knows?' The hand with the handkerchief circled his temples as he spoke. 'Mr Palmer appears to have moved out of his house and is camping under a tree in the square. His wife has been begging him to return to the house but he will not move. He has said nothing . . . not a word. For most of the morning I have been trying to reason with him, but he makes no answer. Even he just sits there and smiles and will not move.'

Rodriguez stood in the doorway, winded by a sudden appalling certainty. Then, with his mind lurching like a runner through fog, he turned away, cast about in the mess of his room for cigarettes, found them at last. After all, there might be some misunderstanding, some mistake . . .?

'There is no mistake,' Sergeant Dwamina declared. 'He has been there throughout the night. The man will not move and the woman is making a great disturbance. It has become a matter of public nuisance, I'm afraid.' He shook his head unhappily. 'You will understand I am reluctant to use force . . . the indignity . . . It is all most unseemly. Mr Quagrainie has agreed to accompany me into town to talk with him again.'

The dismayed headmaster was humming now, wishing himself back on the coast, anywhere, in any other role than this. His eyes swivelled to plead with Rodriguez. 'I thought perhaps it might be helpful if you were to come along, Mr Rodriguez. You are his friend . . . It would make matters more comfortable, you understand. After all, Mr Palmer is a reasonable man. I am sure he will listen to you and I together?' His voice lacked conviction. It was clear from the way he kept rubbing his hair, as though to make sure it was still there, that by this time his faith in human reason was under serious assault.

Rodriguez wanted nothing more than to close the door on them and retreat to his bed, but he found himself nodding his dubious agreement, asked for a moment to dress, knocked back a swift drink, and then – so speedily did this calamity unfold – was being driven into Adoubia by the headmaster, following Dwamina's police-car along a road corrugated into cols and ridges by the passage of the recent rains.

His window shut against the red dust powdering from the car in front, Rodriguez slumped in the passenger-seat, hot, clammy, sick with almost neuralgic apprehension. The headmaster had switched on the radio, filling the car with hymn-song and the sound of a mawkish harmonium. Depressingly, it reminded Rodriguez of his childhood in Goa where he had been baptized into a Christian sect founded by an early apostolic mission before Europe saw the light. He'd long since rejected the idolatrous charade of faith, but it never really let you go. Even now his fingers itched to cross himself, as though it were the spectre of his own guilt that lay in wait for him beneath the tamarind.

He was haunted by the thought of that last unsatisfactory conversation in the Paradise Bar. Trying to recollect exactly what had been said, he wondered what damage he might have done in his ignorance. His memories, though remorseful, were vague. Also he lacked the dimmest idea of how he might begin to coax Palmer back into his house and talk things through more feelingly. Perhaps this wasn't really happening. Please God, let it all be a drunken dream.

As the car bumped over the railway lines and across the iron bridge beside Jalbout's house at the sawmill, he knew his prayer unanswered. He felt anxious and scared. A little resentful also: how often must he make himself vulnerable to this impossible Englishman? After Kay had left he had dared to entertain such hopes . . . But that was all water under the bridge. The thing now was to keep cool, make Austin laugh a little, show him a little tender care . . .

Rodriguez could not quite bring himself to contemplate the possibility that this last assault of circumstance might finally have unhinged Austin's mind. But one never knew. After all, the world was evidently mad, and life a pig – a sow, no less, that ate what it had farrowed.

What Rodriguez had failed to prepare himself for was that this was to be a public occasion.

All the streets approaching Old Town were unusually crowded, and had it not been for the siren on Dwamina's car they would not have got through into the square. Through the windscreen Rodriguez saw the sergeant shouting and gesticulating out of his window. The driver blared on his horn. The siren wailed full volume, scattering the throng of men, women, children, cripples even, who were hobbling towards the square, and food-and-drink vendors who were taking advantage of this unexpected Sunday gathering.

The scene in the square was, Rodriguez instantly perceived, phantasmagorical: the crowd packed deep on all sides, laughing, jeering, chattering in excitement, piccins howling at their mothers' backs, pye-dogs barking, the vultures peevishly surveying the turmoil from the roofs. Five or six constables in their flower-pot tarbooshes stood about looking dismal, or angrily trying to control the crowd with truncheons. Had there been bunting about it might have been a festival. A presidential visit even.

As the cars pulled up, the din in the square seemed to rise a decibel or two. Rodriguez and his headmaster got out of the car and stood blinking in the heat. Sergeant Dwamina walked across to them, fanning himself with his hat. 'Things go from bad to worse,' he said, and gestured towards the tree in the middle of the square.

There sat Palmer in the shade, like a dishevelled Buddha under the bo-tree, but not so poised: cross-legged, eyes closed leaning against the tamarind in a dusty shirt and trousers, white as a candle. Incredibly, he seemed impervious to the crowd around him. Had the circumstances not been fraught with madness, Rodriguez might have taken him for a tail-end batsman waiting his turn at the wicket, more interested in the sunlight and the sounds of summer than in the state of play.

'I understand the wife has been taken away by her people,' Sergeant Dwamina said. 'That should simplify the matter somewhat. But these crowds . . . You see my problem? We must put a stop to this nonsense at once. I can get nowhere with him. Perhaps you would care to try?'

The headmaster and Rodriguez looked queerly at one another, each hoping that the other would rise to the occasion. More out of duty than inspiration Mr Quagrainie led the way across the square, and a hush fell over the crowd.

Palmer's eyes were still closed as they approached. Both men stood at a loss, conscious of the hushed crowd around them. The headmaster cleared his throat noisily, but Palmer remained unaware of, or unresponsive to, their presence. He tried again, more loudly. 'Mr Palmer.'

Palmer opened his eyes and squinted in the sunlight. Then he recognized them – a little distantly perhaps – and smiled. It seemed the wan, shy smile of a man caught out at something questionable, but he said nothing.

'Mr Palmer,' the headmaster pushed on, stiffly aware that he was an educated and responsible man in an embarrassing predicament, 'this is not at all satisfactory. I understand that Sergeant Dwamina has asked you to move on and you have not felt able to comply. It is not the kind of behaviour I expect of my staff. Could we not perhaps discuss this matter less publicly – in your house perhaps? These circumstances are most undignified.'

Palmer looked up mildly. The language, it seemed, was incomprehensible, but that was no great matter. And he closed his eyes again – simply cancelled the headmaster and Rodriguez out, and withdrew into himself like a man intensely preoccupied with his own thoughts.

Mr Quagrainie flapped his hands against his thighs as though something might turn up in his pockets – a key, perhaps, to unlock the situation – and looked about him disconsolately. His eyes shifted upwards to the sky, and when it failed to open he looked to Rodriguez.

Who by now was in real distress. Perhaps alone among the hundreds of people in the square he had some inkling of what Palmer had gone through to bring him to this pass. He felt the

201

responsibility of that knowledge as a burden far heavier than his etiolated frame could bear. Scared and faint, he was unable to believe that things had come to this. Reality slid away in every glance of sunlight across the square. He was more sober than he had been for weeks, yet felt plunged into delirium. Memories, apprehensions, foregone hopes imploded in his skull as though all the long-insulted cells of his brain were rising in final, spectacular revolt.

'Mr Rodriguez,' the headmaster said, 'you must try.'

Rodriguez tried to shake his head clear, and crouched beside Palmer, looking for some semblance of intimacy in that impossible circus situation. He noted the bloodstains on Palmer's trousers, thought for a moment he was injured, but no, that was long dry.

'Listen, old man,' he began. 'Listen to me. It's Sal . . .'

He smiled as he saw Palmer open his eyes once more, but he faltered as he looked down into them. There was already a glassiness about them, but they were sharp too, sharp as glass. They seemed to pierce right through him, left him feeling shallow and transparent, as though he were about to mouth comforting lies to a patient who knew his condition terminal and would be offended by all pretence to the contrary. The sense of unreality swooped over him again. It was all mirage: the crowd, the heat, the stench from the drains, the nonplussed policemen. Everything was under a numbing sort of spell.

Then Palmer looked up at him once more, and there was a sudden, deranging reversal of energy: Austin was coaxing *him*. Those eyes were pulling him down, and through on to another plane where the laws of reality were inverted. It was like some improbable conjuring trick. The man had made no gesture, uttered not a word, yet all around him everything was sliding inside-out as smoothly as a silk-lined sleeve. The stare was fathomless. Rodriguez could feel it drawing him down. He shuddered back in recoil.

Immediately he sensed that Palmer had felt him pull away. When Rodriguez opened his own eyes again he saw Palmer smiling at him. No judgment there, and no reproach: simply this soft, comprehending smile that made a nonsense now of all Sal's thoughts of turning nurse and ministering to his sick friend's needs. It might have been a gesture of forgiveness. Then Palmer rested his head against the trunk of the tamarind, eyes closed again, like a man preferring sleep.

Rodriguez was sure that his own involuntary reflex of withdrawal had severed the last frail thread that tied Palmer to this waking world. He felt the man's mind float off, like a bird effortlessly unfolding the full span of its wings to a rising thermal, and drifting over the heads of the crowd, up over the hot roofs of the town, and out across the forest.

It was a pity perhaps that Sal Rodriguez fought his way through the crowd, out of the square, when he did, for had he found the strength to stay a little longer he too might have witnessed what Jamil – a late arrival on the scene – observed within the space of the next quarter of an hour. Later the event would make little sense to the small expatriate community of the town, but the fact was undeniable. Had Rodriguez seen it for himself he might have found it less perplexing; but only slightly so. Indeed, in some ways, it made the entire episode even more mysterious.

The news of the white man camped in the square had travelled quickly across the town that morning. The bush telegraph was alive with it, and soon people were coming in from the outlying villages to see the spectacle. There were whisperings even among the congregations of the Methodist and Presbyterian chapels, and an unseemly haste to vacate the benches. Thus there was unusual traffic for a Sunday morning in the main street of the commercial centre of New Town where Jamil was taking thoughtful stock of the diminishing wares in his General Trading Store. Eventually curiosity overwhelmed his business interests. He went to the door of his shop and stopped the first African who passed to ask what all the commotion was about.

'Na dis people say dat Sunday Whiteman go get bush in de head for juju, sah,' the African obliged. 'He make fit stay outside him house one time, like beggar from de zongo, eh? We all make fit go see him same. Is number one big deal dis day.'

There was only one Sunday Whiteman of whom the African could have been speaking. Jamil made haste to lock his store, clambered into his VW and made his way, with difficulty, towards Jalbout's house on the edge of Old Town. Such was the throng by now that he was forced to leave the vehicle, again carefully locked, and push his way through the crowd. His manner was sufficiently imperious to take him where many Africans were trying in vain to go.

He arrived in the square in time to witness the sudden, inexplicable change that came over the crowd. It was as if a new word passed swiftly among them from several directions at once. Gradually, what the exasperated policemen had been trying to achieve all morning began to happen of its own accord – the crowd dispersed itself. For no reason that Jamil could understand the townspeople seemed suddenly to be paying almost as little attention to Austin Palmer as they had done to the witch before him. It was almost as if Jamil's own arrival had broken the spell.

He turned to Sergeant Dwamina, who was scratching his head with the same hand that held his peaked hat, and demanded to know what was happening. But the old sergeant shook his head, shrugged, and would say nothing. He turned to look at the pale figure of Palmer again. The headmaster and Jamil did the same and all three noticed that the Englishman must have perceived the change around him, for his eyes were open and there was an extraordinary smile of relief and gratitude on his face. It was as though he had been expecting this moment for a long time, waiting for it.

Taking advantage of this renewed awareness, Sergeant Dwamina walked across to him, though looking somewhat uneasily about himself as he did so. 'Mr Palmer,' he said, 'it is my duty to ask you one more time to return to your home.' But Palmer turned away, smiling, and made himself more comfortable against the tree. 'I don't see what more we can do,' the policeman said to the headmaster. 'The disturbance seems to be at an end. As long as there is no commotion or public nuisance caused there is no law against a man sitting under a tree.'

Jamil could not quite put his finger on it but he had the

distinct impression that the ensuing, stilted conversation between the two Africans (who were of different tribes and shared only English as a common language) would have been of a quite different order had he himself not been there to listen.

In any case Mr Quagrainie was still troubled. He tried to cajole Palmer once more, talking about the dangers to his health and safety, reminding him of his personal duty and the good name of the school. He might as well have harangued a deaf-mute.

Sergeant Dwamina listened uneasily and impatiently. The word that had passed among the crowd had been spoken in his language, and he had heard. Having done his own duty, he wished only to convince the headmaster that his was also done, so they could both be on their way.

After all, he pressed, if Mr Palmer would not co-operate what could they do? If they forced him bodily from the square where would they take him? To his house, or to the school – what was to prevent him from returning? The hospital? He did not appear to be physically sick and there was no provision for mental health, and besides, the sergeant knew for a fact that Dr Subrahmaniam was away on leave. To the police-station? On what charge? And was the headmaster not concerned at the repercussions such a drastic act might have?

Jamil listened to them discussing the problem for some time. He was not convinced by the policeman's arguments – something important was clearly being left unspoken. Sergeant Dwamina appeared flustered and embarrassed by the headmaster's unwillingness to take a hint. At last the sergeant had had enough. 'Believe me, Mr Quagrainie,' he said, 'it is much better to leave well alone.'

'But this isn't well,' Mr Quagrainie protested, close to his own wits' end. 'It isn't well at all.'

Sergeant Dwamina shrugged. 'Sometimes,' he said, 'it is also better to leave ill alone too. Take my advice, my friend. Return to your school. *This matter is now in other hands than ours.*'

The whisper was low but Jamil was close enough to hear. He saw the perplexity on the headmaster's face resolve itself to uneasy understanding. Finally, with no more than curt nods to the bewildered Lebanese observer, the two Africans got into their cars and drove away, leaving a single constable posted in the square, unhappy but under orders.

So Jamil himself tried to talk to Palmer in his indifferent English. 'Is not good to stay here in the sun. You go get seek and bring plenty trouble for your frenz. And what we all go do but go get seek wiz worry same? Is better you go home, my fren, and take it easy for one time, not so? You leesen to your fren Jamil. He know this crazy country too good. For why you not come back to my place and we take some beers togezzer? Is better, Mr Palmer, is much better so.'

But he too got nowhere and finally gave up. He could think of nothing to do but drive out to the house at the sawmill and apprise Jalbout of this perplexing news.

Mr Quagrainie sat, in a state of some consternation, in his house at the school. Having taken his courage in both hands, he had just spoken to the DC on the phone and been told, in no uncertain terms, to mind his own damned business. But this *was* his business, he'd protested weakly. After all, Mr Palmer was on his staff, he was (though how dearly Mr Quagrainie wished he was not) the headmaster's responsibility. He felt it his duty to . . .

That no-good, white-faced, neo-colonialist agent of the international conspiracy against socialist Africa, he was told, had been nothing but a two-faced trouble-maker since the moment of his arrival, and this time he had gone too far. Did not the headmaster realize that the man had now invoked the powers of darkness on his side? If one was wise one did not meddle with such matters – except to take such precautions to protect oneself as one might. Which, the DC bellowed, this telephone call was preventing him from doing.

So even as the sound of the receiver banging down rang in Mr Quagrainie's ears, the headmaster at last began to understand. His first interpretation of Sergeant Dwamina's warning had been quite wrong then. He knew now why he had received so little assistance from the police sergeant, and why (though he had been grateful for it at the time) that most embarrassing crowd of people had dispersed. These forest tribes really were beyond his comprehension.

How complicated everything had now become. And the question remained: should he, or should he not, contact the Chairman of the Board at his private number in Badagry? On a Sunday afternoon? After everything that had already happened because of this difficult English teacher? To whom, however – it must be admitted – his school owed a great deal.

Perhaps it would be wise to talk things over further with his wife.

Henry Jalbout was not altogether surprised. He had been in West Africa for thirty years and heard stranger things. 'So is the young fool still trying to teach us all a lesson?' was his first dry comment.

But Jamil did not seem to feel that was explanation enough. And Jalbout recalled the rude and peculiar way Palmer had walked out on him the last time he visited. The old Lebanese had been offended by it – he and Mario Baldinucci had spent a lively half-hour vilifying the English assumption that their race was a cut above all others. Now Jalbout remembered certain untypical incoherencies in Palmer's manner – the way his eyes had shifted back and forth from the devil-mask, and that unhealthy preoccupation with witchcraft! When Henry had offered him the house in town he had never imagined for a moment that the man would go native.

Perhaps, after all, Palmer was still sick?

'Has no one contacted the hospital?' he asked. Jamil reminded him that Dr Subrahmaniam was on leave. And, he suspected, the African orderly, like all his tribe, would have nothing to do with the white man now. Which was – did Henry not agree? – a most peculiar thing. Could the politicos be behind it? Those rumours about the Englishman's palaver with the DC after Koranteng's arrest – perhaps there was something in them after all?

Jalbout briefly gave the matter thought, and doubted it. If the Party was behind this its hand would show. Krobo Mansa was not renowned for subtlety, and Odansey was busy with the financial mess in Badagry. No, they were dealing with some kind of juju here. After all, this followed hard upon the affair of the witch. Probably the fetish-priests at the shrines had put some sort of malediction out. Yes, for his money, that was it. And, by the way, had Jamil thought to check whether Palmer had locked the door of the house behind him? There were items of some value there.

To his shame, in the excitement of the hour, Jamil had overlooked that obvious precaution. He offered to drive back into town immediately and check the house. But Jalbout – intrigued, and thinking perhaps that here was an anecdote on which he might dine out in Badagry and Beirut – decided that he would inspect the situation for himself.

For a long time Sal Rodriguez had been a man capable of slipping in and out of alcoholic stupor like a creature shedding and resuming its protective colour. Later, when all these events were past, he would become much more so. And more silent too.

By the end of that first afternoon, already very drunk, he sat in the corner of a bar somewhere in the heart of Old Town talking things over with an uncomprehending African, whose sole contribution to the dialogue was an occasional encouragingly good-natured grunt.

'Had he been weaker, further gone,' Sal was saying, 'we would simply have picked him up and carried him off to the hospital. It must seem obvious to you, my friend. Perhaps we should have done that . . . there and then . . . But he's a big man, you see, barrel-chested, still physically strong . . . And the point is . . . to *touch* him, well, it would have been a kind of impertinence. He made you feel that; he always did, in a way. The man had rendered himself untouchable . . . He was asking simply to be left alone.'

His African listener was not greatly troubled by the slur in Sal's speech, or by the way his 'v's and 'w's seemed tangled in a conflict of identity. So much free beer, in any case, made all things acceptable. And it was amusing to watch the way this talkative Indian would move suddenly in an agitated manner – a seemingly radical re-arrangement of the bones that nevertheless left things in the same gangling disarray.

'I knew,' Sal insisted, 'that nothing I could say would make any difference. I knew it because – and this is the point, my friend, this is the hideous heart of the matter – *I had helped to bring him there* . . .

Rodriguez relapsed into a gloomy silence. Observing that his glass was empty, the African generously refilled it. But the action seemed to annoy the Indian for he was shouting something now. Uncertain quite what he had done wrong, the African apologized. He was not to know that Rodriguez had simply been emphasizing the fact that there was nothing he could do. Nothing. And the apology must have been acceptable, for when the Indian continued it was in a softer voice. 'I knew it when he looked up at me and smiled. The headmaster was muttering something to me but I didn't hear . . . I only knew I couldn't stay there . . . I turned away, you see . . .'

When they arrived in the square Jalbout and Jamil were dismayed to discover Palmer's African woman on her knees by the Englishman, weeping and wailing as though over a dead child. So deep was her distress that she ignored the car and the two men who stepped from it looking at one another in some embarrassment. Palmer was propped against the tree, arms limp at his side, his face averted from Appaea in an agonized frown. Jalbout saw that, whatever else could be done for Palmer, it was necessary to disencumber him of these attentions.

He signalled to Jamil but, when they approached, the woman turned on them like a tigress. She hissed something at them in her own tongue, twisting to place her body between them and Palmer. It was clear that her defence of her otherwise helpless man would be formidable.

As far as Jalbout could see, there was now more than one insane person in the square. It would be unwise to tangle physically with either. Again the woman shouted at them. Jamil backed away making calming gestures with his hands.

Jalbout stood his ground, staring at the glazed white face of Palmer. This was certainly a more serious matter than he had thought.

He turned to consult his companion and found himself alone. Worried by his earlier lapse, Jamil had retreated to check the door of Jalbout's house. To his horror he discovered it unlocked.

For a long time Mr Quagrainie mulled over this dreadful business, but the fact was inescapable: even though it was outside term-time, and the calamity had occurred off the compound, he was responsible for Austin Palmer. The coastal school in which the headmaster had been educated differed little in its code of values from an English public school. To his mind, that code must take precedence over such bush considerations as the DC had raised. Progress depended upon it. In any case, if the situation deteriorated further towards scandal and the Chairman of the Board had not been informed . . . No, there was no way round it. He must ring.

But the telephone was a fearful instrument these days.

Humming, he picked up the receiver, dialled the operator and asked to be put through to the Chairman's home-number in Badagry. A noise like drains in the rainy season came down the line. There was always a chance that it would prove impossible to get through, and he could not be held responsible for the telephone service. Nevertheless he felt obliged to keep up the long litany of 'Hello's that was the long-distance caller's only defence against premature disconnection.

Five more, he was thinking, should pay sufficient tribute to duty, when he heard in the receiver the briskly severe voice of the Chairman of the Board demanding, 'Yes?'

In the house of Komla Odum, field-commander of the left wing of the King's army, there was much disarray. Specific instructions had been given that Appaea was to be watched at all times. Even if she had looked sound asleep, dead to the world and all its troubles, her sister Lovia should not have left her. Was no one to be trusted any more? Did a man have to do everything himself?

He, Komla Odum, had known all along that only trouble could come from his daughter's infatuation with a white man. Not one of them was worth a gob of spittle. Hadn't he said so at the time? Were the young men of the tribe not good enough for her? He couldn't understand this modern generation . . . never had . . . never would. They had respect for nothing.

But his wife had no patience with his bad-tempered ramblings. Rather than beating the slack skin of his drum, she said, he would do better to rally those idle menfolk drinking palm-wine out there in the compound, and bring Appaea back before some further evil fell on her innocent head. Or was the woman's side supposed to take care of that as well as everything else? Odum was a commander, was he not? Very well, he should stir his stumps and command, before the entire family fell into shame and disrepute. As for that irresponsible daughter who had left Appaea unwatched, she would handle that herself.

There were bloodstains on the floor and furniture. Had Palmer then turned African enough to beat his wife? A little surprising that – Jalbout would not have thought the fellow had it in him. And, in the bedroom, someone – Palmer in his madness presumably – had scrawled upon the wall. *Who is my neighbour* was written there, correctly spelled, but without a question mark. Curious!

And even more so the single word in capital letters – HELL – for a loop had been added to the upright of the final letter so that it might equally well be read as HELP!

The fellow was in a bad way indeed.

Otherwise Jamil's agitated inventory had discovered no serious loss or damage. The prohibition put out by the fetish-priests must have been remarkably powerful to forestall such easy pickings. There were aspects of Africa's darkness for which one must still be thankful.

Jalbout saw that Jamil was troubled by the mess about the place and the smoke-stains from an unsuccessful attempt to burn a collection of exercise books in a metal litter-bin. A nuisance yes, but one should be grateful that a larger fire had not resulted.

Jalbout picked a charred book out of the bin and opened it at random. *You can withhold yourself from the sufferings of the world*, he read, *you are free to do so, and it accords with your nature. But perhaps this very holding back is the one suffering you might avoid. (Kafka).* It seemed that Palmer had a neurotic taste in literature. With a wife such as his – the real wife, he meant, the English one – perhaps that was not surprising.

He flipped the pages of the book with growing interest, and came across a piece of blue paper neatly folded – a note, simply addressed: *Austin.* He opened it, and read what was written there in a florid hand:

> My sleeping keeper dreams while I
> Watch out the nights incessantly –
> Rain, heat, the timid tree-bear's cry.
>
> I am no African to wait
> Six yards behind her man, a freight
> Of faggots balanced heavy at
>
> Her head, a baby at her back.
> No walking proverb I: I lack
> That resignation, cannot make
>
> Necessity a virtue. Come,
> Quickly, sleeper, wake, and bring me home.
> The faggots at my head are all in flame.

Good Lord – had Kay written that? Jalbout was no judge of English verse, but there was, it must be admitted, a certain unexpected pathos there.

Perhaps, if things turned out badly, these papers should be saved. There might be much of human interest to be perused among them.

The Chairman of the Board, busy lawyer, Member of Parliament for the Ogun-Dogambey Division in the National Assembly, and hard-pressed Deputy Minister of Finance was not pleased to be disturbed in the rare freedom of a Sunday afternoon by the pool, when his wife was already in an ill-temper (he just having declined the pleasure of her company on his forthcoming flight to Zurich); and – most particularly – when it transpired that this interruption was attributable, yet again, to that infuriating Englishman at the school.

'God damn you, Quagrainie,' he bellowed, 'must I attend to every minor crisis up there? Are you incapable of taking a sensible decision on your own? By all means have the man dragged off to hospital.'

'But it appears that Dr Subrahmaniam is on leave . . . Also I have reason to believe that the deputies there will be unwilling to receive Mr Palmer . . .'

Christian Odansey had no patience to investigate those reasons. 'Then have Krobo lock the man up for the night. That should clear his head fast enough. We can decide what to do about him later. He must go, Quagrainie – you do realize that? I've had enough. More than enough. And you – you'd better pull your socks up pretty damn quick. If you can't keep control of your staff there are others who can.'

'Yes, Mr Chairman, of course, I understand . . .' the headmaster answered, though privately he was beginning to think that another job, in another region, under less oppressive supervision, might not, after all, be such a bad idea. 'But about the DC?' he ventured. 'I think perhaps . . . if you were to . . .'

'Call him myself? As I must do everything, God damn it.' The Chairman of the Board slammed down the phone.

But Mr Quagrainie knew that the call would be made. Trembling a little, somewhat gleeful too at the thought of what awaited Odansey on his next call, the headmaster sat back and sighed. The matter was out of his hands.

As for poor Mr Palmer – he was in God's hands now.

However distantly, it was a relief when those people had come and taken Appaea away once more. For he had known she was

213

there, had heard her supplications and her grief, had felt the anguished tenderness of her hands at his brow. And, oh, what temptation there had been in those moments to try to return in answer to that call – to break this hard-won solidarity of the damned, and allow himself to be taken back inside the frail human fold in which he knew he no longer had a rightful place.

He had forced his mind, though it responded so sluggishly now, to concentrate upon that strange anvil of cloud that had swollen up in the eastern sky – strange not in its shape, but because it was burnished by the last rays of the dying sun, and the westward sky was darkly green, so that it seemed as if the day was setting in the east. But then, why not? Nothing now was as it once had seemed. Even the light, the lovely evanescent landscapes of the sky, were no more than the shot-silk lining of a vast dark cape that wrapped him round. Strange only that he had never seen it so before.

Nor had he ever perceived the true nature of the dark itself, though in those last few terrible days he thought he had entered upon it as deeply as a man could go. What a darkness had been there, brimming around him in thick flood. A darkness he had scried like a reluctant prophet. Darkness inside him and around. For it was not merely the coffin-shell of his own primitive failure *to be* – either for the witch in her extremity, or Kay, or Appaea . . . or anything beyond his own loveless self-absorption. He had also seen the coming darkness of the times – a mire of errors, follies, atrocities, of which his own delinquent heart was no more than a petty harbinger.

Alone, for he was self-elected into solitude, he had tried to support the bleakness of his vision, and his mind had snapped beneath the weight of it. And then Koranteng had come, stepping out of the shadows, bangled and diademed in gold, to comfort him. *No, we can't condone such darkness*, the black king of his waking dream had said, *but we can't disown it either. All one can do is push on into the darkness and try to make something human there.*

Yes; but how – when silence ruled, and all his own poor dreams of former days had proved corrupt? Ranging the empty rooms of his locked house, there had been, it had

214

seemed, no way. No way at all. Until at last the nature of the darkness crowding round him altered.

He smiled now to remember what a simpleton of light he'd been – he who had never dared to gaze into the shining dark that *they*, the women in his life inhabited . . . Though perhaps there had been moments, here and there, brief intimations of the lucid silver of things where light and darkness merged and married.

Had he not seen it, heard it ringing even, in those times, those very few and precious times, when his and Appaea's haste to meet one another had been like the rush of surf along a falling wave . . . His white, her black, mated, naked, making a soft exchange of spirit in the night? Oh, such a fool he'd been to fail to find a way to breathe the quickness of their meeting spirits back into the waking day . . . to bring it home, here, where it belonged inside his ever-fissive heart . . .

And she was gone now. Appaea was gone. Kay was gone. They were all gone now, but for himself and this strange rejected neighbour whom none but he could see and answer to. And it was dark around him. Cool. And there were stars. Such stars! And the Lady Moon was drifting quietly among the clouds while he waited patiently below in her long service . . .

Let others long for gold, his sad heart thought for him – he would settle for this silver now.

Try as he might on the telephone, Christian Odansey could find no one willing to lay hands on Austin Palmer.

Krobo Mansa was unavailable, both at his office and at his house in the residential area. The only person Odansey could get hold of was the DC's houseboy, and it took some time to get a straight answer as to his master's whereabouts. According to the houseboy he was out of town, up-country, at a native shrine where he had gone to buy medicine from a fetish-priest. The DC was now certain that powerful medicine was being used against him and it was necessary to protect himself. When Odansey asked who was using this medicine he was not greatly surprised by the answer.

The Deputy-Minister put down the phone, cursing. Once again Krobo had let him down. It would not be difficult to find grounds for his dismissal.

Odansey met with no better luck at the police station. When he tried to order Sergeant Dwamina to manhandle Palmer from the square the policeman stoutly insisted that the Englishman was breaking no law. Once bluster had failed, Odansey the lawyer was at a loss to answer him. Nor was he interested in making an untimely trip up-country. He had more important matters on his mind than a crazy Englishman. He decided to wash his hands of the affair and turn it over to the British High Commission.

For what happened then it is perhaps best to eavesdrop once more on Sal Rodriguez's account, for this was the only part of the story he could ever tell with anything approaching relish.

'It was a youngish chap they eventually sent up,' he would sigh. 'Pleydell, his name was – very British. Very public school. He came out to the compound to get some background, and the headmaster called me in to help again. Pleydell seemed most put out that Austin had never bothered to register his presence in the country as a British subject. I suppose he did his best to understand . . . I think he must have done some amateurish reading in psychology, and spent a long time telling us how they dealt with this sort of thing in England . . . the Welfare State would have moved in *tout ' suite*, an ambulance would have had Austin in a mental hospital under a Section Order in two shakes, anti-depressants would have been administered, a quick jolt or two of ECT to jolly his brain out of its relapsed condition. Oh yes, the UK was prepared for such eventualities – I suppose they have to be over there – and it never occurred to him to ask what possible answer *that* sort of witchcraft would have provided.

'In any case, he was pretty sure he had things summed up by the time he suggested we accompany him into town. So we drove in with him and stood in agony while he tried to get through to Austin.'

At this point Sal's Goan accent would slip into a passable

imitation of – what shall we say? – a Wykehamist. '*Now look here, old man, I gather you've had a rotten time of it, but this isn't the way, you know.* I suppose,' Rodriguez concedes, 'in his hopelessly polite way he was doing his best by a British subject in very peculiar circumstances, but to Austin he must have seemed like a man from the moon . . . *Look, I've got my car here – why don't you hop in and we'll have you down to Badagry in two shakes? Get a decent night's sleep, bit of TLC from a medic, and we'll have you back home in no time at all. And then you can forget about this whole rotten business. What do you say?*

'Of course, Austin said nothing. Didn't even smile – just gazed vacantly about the square, looking through Pleydell as though he wasn't there. *Don't think I'm getting through*, Pleydell pipes up. *Poor chap's a bit far gone. Do you know where I will find a phone?* He drove off to the post office, to ring his superiors, I suppose – but you know what the phones are like. He had no more luck getting through to Badagry than he had getting through to Austin, so he took his own decision. *Would you chaps mind giving me a hand to get him into the car?* he says, and immediately Austin stiffens and starts shaking his head. It was amazing really – no one had got this much of a response out of him in days – and we tried. Believe me – Henry, Mario, me, we all tried. The thing is, he was pretty weak by this time – he hadn't eaten for days and there must have been a whole hive of bugs sapping away inside him. It wouldn't have been too difficult for the three of us to bundle him in the car and off to safety and – if he was lucky – back to sanity again. But the man sat there, tense and stiff, holding us at bay. He made me think of a dog guarding its master's body. None of us relished the prospect of manhandling him. It felt as though it would be a violation – a sacrilege almost – upon his person.'

At this point in his narrative Rodriguez would become gloomy again. 'You won't understand, you weren't there, you didn't see him,' he insists. 'It must seem obvious to you that he needed carrying off into care. Well, all right, but have you ever contemplated moving a man against his will – someone who isn't drunk or totally incapable? Someone whose will is still burning away in there like an electric element? There was an extraordinary power radiating from him. Pleydell must

217

have felt it less than I did – or felt the burden of his duty more – I don't know. Anyway, he bent to lift Austin by the armpits, and no sooner had his hands touched him than Austin let out a ghastly injured howl. It went on and on, and Pleydell jumped back as if he had unintentionally touched an open wound.

'That cry was horrid. If I said *animalic* it could mean anything, and it was more than that, and worse than that. It was a human cry. Drawn from the bottom of the man's bowels, and it broke my heart. Austin knew he hadn't the strength to stop Pleydell. There was nothing he could do to resist except release this terrible howl – like a tree-bear. The power of the weak. It was all that was left to him. And it worked.' This statement always seemed to bring a glint of pride back to Sal's eyes, as though, in some small way, he had shared in this last, pathetic triumph, and found there a redeeming shred of meaning.

'And then,' he would add after a calculated pause, 'we were suddenly aware of the people who had gathered round us in the square. They must have been watching for some time without interfering. But now, at this terrible cry from Austin, almost as at a signal, they began to close in. Silent, but menacing. Two or three men leaned against the doors of Pleydell's car, and an old man came out of the crowd and began to harangue us.

'Pleydell asked the headmaster what he was saying but old Quagrainie was as much at a loss as he was – he couldn't understand the language either. Then one of the younger men by the car stepped forward. He was wearing a monkey-skin hat, and glowered at us from under it for a moment, then said, *This man is Owusu Bonsu, Spokesman of the Paramount Chief.* The headmaster and I looked at one another, bewildered – Koranteng was in Kende Castle, for God's sake – what was going on? But the young man spoke again. *The Spokesman say is in vain for the tsetse fly to trouble the tortoise. The tortoise belong to no clan.* Well, none of us could make much sense of that, and this young, rather handsome African . . . well, it was obvious that he disapproved of our limited intelligence. He decided to make things plain. *The Spokesman say that you must respect the dignity of the Sunday Whiteman and leave him in peace. He say that*

*you make yourselves undignified by troubling him this way. You
must leave now and not return.*

'You can imagine – we were all dumbstruck at this turn of
events. Pleydell stood scratching his head and shifting from
foot to foot. I suppose he was dreading being responsible for
what diplomats so blandly call an incident – the kind of thing
that might make him sweat in the night, and blot his copybook
back in Whitehall. I felt sorry for the man. I mean, he was
only trying to do a messy job the best way he could. He was
stupid perhaps – yes, I don't think that puts too fine a point
upon it – but decent enough, and he didn't want to insult or
offend anybody. He had no idea that his entire manner had
been offensive to us all from the start . . . And now, here he
was, surrounded by what must have looked like a bunch of
truculent savages threatening trouble if he laid another finger
on Austin. I see, he says, though clearly he saw nothing. He
hung around for a while trying, I suppose, to work out what to
do next . . . looking at me now and then – the closest thing to
another sane white face around . . . looking for help and
finding none. Eventually he turns to Austin again and says,
*Now listen to me, old chum – I think you're a bit more clued in
than you're letting on, and you can see I'm in a bit of a spot. If you
won't come with me of your own accord I certainly can't force you
. . . But think about it. You can't last a whole lot longer like this.
If you've any sense you'll come along with me now, while you have
the chance.*

'But Austin simply turned away, and I knew then how
wrong I'd been, drunk as I was, to trouble him with my own
feelings . . . The man had chosen. Finally and irrevocably
chosen. If it was madness it was lucid madness. Extraordi-
narily directed and certain of itself. It commanded its own
peculiar obedience. I heard myself – almost to my own
surprise – saying to Pleydell, *I think the old man's right. We
should leave him alone. It's over.*

'Pleydell seemed more stunned than ever – as though the
whole town had gone barmy around him. And perhaps it had.
Perhaps it had. It must have been a moment of total bewilderment for him, having driven up from his quiet posting in
Badagry to this dreary bush-town where the entire expatriate

community seemed to have gone off its head with tedium, or the sun, or God-knows-what mumbo-jumbo out of the forest. And what was he supposed to do now – single-handed and sensible – and worried about what would happen if he did nothing?

'So he sizes up the mood of the crowd again . . . it's getting very ugly by now . . . and mutters something about having done his best and not being held responsible. And then – I suspect with some relief – he got back into his car and drove away.'

Rodriguez is shaking his head as he speaks. You half expect him to murmur that Life is a pig as he drains his glass once more; but no, he's looking up at you, and there's a fierce defiant spark daring you to demur as he adds, 'I looked down again at Austin who sat, grinning, beneath the tree. Wan and drained, but yes, *grinning*, and – I swear – though it may just have been a trick of the fading light, there was a shimmer of radiance dancing off his hair.'

Towards the end of Palmer's story there was another mystery, and one for which Sal Rodriguez had no explanation. After the fiasco with the man from the High Commission nobody from the school or Ogun-Adoubia's small expatriate community ever saw the Englishman again.

Had he died in the night, they wondered, and his body been rapidly removed like that of the witch before him? Presumably so, though it must have happened very quickly, for no one who had seen his resistance on that last encounter would have thought him close to death.

In any case, there was no investigation, no inquest. No body to be found. The diplomats in Badagry were jolted into a flurry of activity at this time by the first military coup. The President was out of the country, preaching the need for African unity, when he received the news – his army had risen and he was now king of nowhere. In the ensuing confusion Palmer was forgotten. Only his friends were left puzzling, to no avail, over his vanishing.

And it was impossible for them to understand because they

were not there in the dusty Palace compound when the Queen-Mother of the Ogun-Dogambey people sent out the third of her commands.

It was not to the heralds of the court this time – those men in hats of black monkey-skin who had so efficiently dispersed the crowd. Nor was it to Owusu Bonsu, Spokesman and Chief Minister of State who had dismissed the man from the High Commission at her command. For Bonsu had deferred to this powerful old woman, as Koranteng, his absent but still-living lord, would certainly have done in such a case as this. Was she not, after all, the present incarnation of the Triple Goddess, whom all wise men revered and feared, and whom even the gods themselves recognized as the greatest among their number?

It was the time of the women now.

Impelled by certainties of her own, Appaea Odum had argued her way out of her father's house, through the locked gate of the Palace, past the elders and the Spokesman, until finally she was given leave to crave the audience she sought.

In awe, fearful, but with all the resolution of a spirit acting out of love, Appaea had spoken for a long time. And the Queen-Mother listened.

Eventually, impressed by the coincidence between Appaea's plea and her own most recently disturbing dreams, the Queen-Mother summoned the women of her retinue. Three fowl were slaughtered and their fall observed. The signs were clear. It was time the Sunday Whiteman was brought home.

So it was that, in the moonlit shadows of the square, Austin Palmer looked up with such small light as remained in his bewildered eyes and saw the women coming to fetch him, like dark sisters.

And this time he did not resist.

All Pan books are available at your local bookshop or newsagent, or can be ordered direct from the publisher. Indicate the number of copies required and fill in the form below.

Send to: Pan C. S. Dept
              Macmillan Distribution Ltd
              Houndmills Basingstoke RG21 2XS
or phone: 0256 29242, quoting title, author and Credit Card number.

Please enclose a remittance* to the value of the cover price plus: £1.00 for the first book plus 50p per copy for each additional book ordered.

*Payment may be made in sterling by UK personal cheque, postal order, sterling draft or international money order, made payable to Pan Books Ltd.

Alternatively by Barclaycard/Access/Amex/Diners

Card No.   ☐☐☐☐☐☐☐☐☐☐☐☐☐☐☐☐☐☐

Expiry Date   ☐☐☐☐☐☐

Signature:

Applicable only in the UK and BFPO addresses

While every effort is made to keep prices low, it is sometimes necessary to increase prices at short notice. Pan Books reserve the right to show on covers and charge new retail prices which may differ from those advertised in the text or elsewhere.

NAME AND ADDRESS IN BLOCK LETTERS PLEASE:

....

Name _____

Address _____

_____

_____

_____

6/92